Early Pr

J. Marshall Gordon's *A Sardonic Death* is a twisting mystery full of surprises, heart, and intriguing characters, just as it should be, but the bonus is that it crackles with wit and genuinely interesting knowledge. Don't miss this one!

--- *Jamie Mason*, author, *The Hidden Things*

In Penny Summers, Gordon has created a smart, endearing sleuth whose personality blossoms forth on every page.

--- *Mark deCastrique*, author of the Sam Blackman series

Penny's voice is amusing, and her preoccupations help to round out her character. Whether she's sleuthing, designing a garden, or coming up with a marketing scheme, she consistently shows creativity and attention to detail ... Readers should hope that this winning mystery series starring a gardener/detective will be fruitful and multiply.

--- *Kirkus Reviews*

From ornamental pond exotica to revolutionary advances in the prosthetics industry, *A Sardonic Death* marries the natural world with the technical to create its bitter-but-delicious brew. Our guide is Penny Summers, formerly of the U.S. Navy, now a horticulturist, a self-referenced "Curious Georgette," and a prime possessor of a Faulknerian heart: the kind in conflict with itself. Gordon's engaging heroine leads us through the gardens and waterways of the Chesapeake in the wake of deaths and troubled relationships that, in her own sage words, make an "earthquake-sized rent in the pavement of our lives."

--- *Elizabeth Lutyens*, Editor-in-Chief, *The Great Smokies Review*

A Sardonic Death

by

J. Marshall Gordon

A Sardonic Death - © 2019 John M. Gordon

ISBN: 978-1-950613-02-1

All rights reserved. No part of this book may be reproduced or transmitted in any form or by any means, electronic or mechanical, including photocopying, recording or by any information storage and retrieval system, without permission in writing from the author or publisher. This book was printed in the United States of America.

Cover design and layout by: WhiteRabbitgraphix.com

This is a work of fiction. Any characters, names, and incidents appearing in this work are entirely fictitious. Any resemblance to real persons, living or dead, is purely coincidental.

Taylor and Seale Publishing, LLC
3408 S. Atlantic Avenue – Unit 139
Daytona Beach Shores, FL 32118

For my wife, Jenny Lauren Jones-Gordon

A SARDONIC DEATH

Chapter 1

A Chopin mazurka sparkled from my phone. "Penny for your thoughts," I answered, knowing I sounded like a smart aleck.

A chuckle. "This is Ophelia Reid."

It took a nanosecond for the gears in my cranial computer to hum in counterpoint to the whine of my rental car's tires on the interstate. It was my landscape design client's wife. I'd missed my promised meeting date with Aidan Reid two weeks ago. And although I'd left him an apologetic message when I realized I couldn't get back to Annapolis when I'd hoped, he'd obviously asked his wife to rebuke me.

In the exit lane to the airport, holding the phone to my ear: "Yes, Ms. Reid. I'm terribly sorry about the delay. As your husband may have told you, I've been out of town—"

"That's not why I'm calling, Miss Summers."

I held my breath.

"Aidan died last week."

Oh. My. God.

"I am so sorry," I said, feigning sorrow with the best of

A Sardonic Death

intentions.

It was a serious blow. My first important garden design commission had crash-dived into a pile of manure. I had so looked forward to gorgeous photos of the new Ravenscroft entry in my sales portfolio.

Easy come, easy go, whispered my late lamented Grandpa Jack, who occasionally sends me astute observations from beyond the grave.

No! my brain answered.

"Aidan wanted so much to work with you." This was awkward. I had never met this woman.

"Ummm . . . is there anything I can do?"

"Nothing, I'm afraid, except I'd like to discuss your preliminary design when you get back."

My panic level subsided at the same time that I mentally kicked myself for selfishly thinking only of my own career.

"I'll be in Annapolis tomorrow," I said. "I can give you a call and we could find a time to meet."

"I'll look forward to hearing from you, Penelope."

That was weird. I'd told Aidan my name was Penny and my business card didn't show my full name. Just Penny.

Penny has always been short for Penelope, Grandpa Jack whispered.

"Likewise, Ms. Reid." I was ready to tap my phone off.

"Penny-lope?"

Penny-lope? I swerved to the shoulder, stomped the brake, and scrunched to a stop.

I shouted into the phone: "*What* did you say?"

"Don't you remember?"

Of course, I remembered. Penny-lope. I had pronounced it that way to my kindergarten teacher and the boy next to me never let me forget. "She's an *antelope*. Penny-lope Antelope."

When Mom tried to make me feel better, she said it was a sweet name, and it became her secret term of endearment. Sudden tears burned my eyes.

"Nobody knows that except . . ." I couldn't choke out the rest of the words.

"Except your *mother*," she finished.

"Mom?"

"I *used* to be Joan Summers," she said and disconnected before I could say anything more.

It took me a minute to wipe my eyes before continuing on to the rental return.

I couldn't believe Ophelia Reid was the same woman who abandoned us twenty-three years ago.

I snagged the Delta steward as he checked my seatbelt and ordered two airline-sized bottles of chardonnay. In the air, as soon as the seat belt sign was switched off, the steward slipped me my prizes, a plastic cup, and paper napkin. I chugged one and set the other on my tray.

Joan Summers, aka Mom, had left our family in the nineties for what my brother Spencer and I assumed was a flower-in-your-hair escape from the realities of motherhood. In my heart, though, I knew the catalyst for her getaway was my little brother Josh's drowning death. Which I'd tortured myself ever since knowing it was my fault.

At the ripe young age of ten, my life had been ruptured. There were ten with-Mom years which were increasingly difficult to recall. Then all the post-Mom years. Twenty-three of them now. Dad raised us as well as he knew how.

My older brother Spencer and I assumed Mom had joined a commune somewhere, growing organic veggies. Or had become part of a group to protest research on animals.

A Sardonic Death

Whatever. As my life stretched into high school, four years at the Naval Academy, six years in uniform, and now four years back in Annapolis, I had long since accepted that we would never see her again. As a ten-year-old, I'd concocted several punishments for her if she ever reappeared. One involved adding dog kibble to her granola. Another was to dye her undies with Montblanc pen ink. A third was to ask my friend Sheree to use her makeup kit to give me a bruise and black eye that I could tell the school nurse I had received from Mom. It might not have worked, but I was angry. As the years passed, though, I finally decided that I'd have to get by without a mother. I could "tough it out" as we used to say but even now, I'm still trying to understand her abandoning us.

I poured the second little bottle of chardonnay into the cup and wondered how I would handle meeting this woman who had cheated me out of my childhood. The real question was how my life might have been different if she hadn't left. And that, I concluded, was a kind of Zen riddle: one for which there is no answer. Did that mean my anger was focused on the unknowable? And did that mean I was truly angry, or did I only think I *ought* to feel angry?

Ultimately, I *would* tough it out because my hope for this commission was much bigger than my need to dredge up the past. Photographs of the new Ravenscroft entry could help sell my design services to future clients. It could be huge for my budding career.

The call also brought up the question of how Aiden Reid had died. When I'd left the preliminary concept with him, he seemed to be in perfect health. Ebullient, only slightly overweight, his sandy hair in a ponytail, and anxious to contribute to the design process.

With another swallow of chardonnay, I wondered whether

he might have realized I was Ophelia's daughter. I doubted it. Although when we first met, there was something about him that seemed vaguely familiar. What on earth could have caused his death in the three short weeks I was in North Carolina?

Let it go, Grandpa Jack whispered. *People die. Get over it.*

Chapter 2

Mid-morning Tuesday, a moment after I announced my presence into the little microphone on the post, Ravenscroft's ornate iron and bronze gates glided apart. Not quite a year before, I'd come here as a favor to my pond-guru friend Jason to add so-called "marginal" plants at the edges of their huge pond. That was when Aidan inquired about my landscape design service, explaining that his "honey-do" list included getting the entry area of the big house professionally redesigned and replanted.

In spite of my reservations about meeting the mom I'd given up on, I'd assured her on the phone this morning that I would like to continue working on the landscape plan that I'd begun for Aidan before going to North Carolina. I'd given him a preliminary concept and suggested he jot notes on it—what he liked and what he thought should be reconsidered.

I also hoped I could maintain my composure long enough to at least discuss that concept with her.

The entry area was as I remembered it: unkempt, in need of the makeover Aidan had requested.

What would I say to this stranger? *Mom? It's been so long . . . how've you been? You want to know what I wore to my senior prom?* Nope!

I snatched my satchel from the passenger seat and started for the door. My heart resisted. I stopped. Trepidatious. If I were an actress, how would I play this scene? I turned around and started back to my van. Then, remembering my military training, I did a slovenly about-face back toward the door.

Maybe I should just leave. Could I really go through with this? I stopped again. If I survived, this was going to be one of those moments like twenty-three years ago when she abandoned us. My life would be split again. There'd be the time before and then the time after.

I must have walked in front of her security camera before lifting the knocker because her Westminster door chimes only played the first four tones before the door eased open.

Show time!

It took me a beat to recognize the woman who was once my mother. It was like in a high school play where, between the second and the third acts, the mother has become a grandmother and welcomes her prodigal daughter home.

I probably said something inane, maybe *Hi!* Then, "Should I call you Mom or Joan, or Ophelia?" When I was young, children never called their mothers by their first names.

Her dark auburn hair that used to look ready for a slow-motion shampoo swirl was now a loose perm on a woman who could pose for a golf course estate ad: a wealthy retiree with graying streaks framing a face with gracious smile lines.

"Mom's fine," she said. "Come in. Come in." *Mom? Seriously? Just like that?*

The only things that hadn't changed about this stranger who used to be my mother were her devilishly red lipstick and matching scarlet flower in her hair. Today it was a roaring red zinnia.

Then I burbled another inanity, probably *What's new?* or some variant.

She ushered me from the front hall directly into a glass-roofed conservatory where the June sun sparkled through Birds of Paradise, tropical greenery, a pair of Ficus trees, passionflower vines in several hues, and an orange tree. A

A Sardonic Death

welcoming room with a blend of floral perfumes, as the architect had undoubtedly explained, would bring the outdoors indoors. There was a potting bench on the left and, on the right, a full bar.

After she left us all those years ago, I'd found her macramé necklace with five little cowrie shells and her father's (my Grandpa Jack's) Montblanc fountain pen, an heirloom of sorts, since it was a gift from his dad when he'd come north to matriculate in the new Great Books program at St. John's College. When I was a kid, I was fascinated by that old pen, learning to fill its reservoir from a bottle of ink and using it to create elaborate cursive letters. I've sometimes wondered if it had anything to do with Mom's nickname for me: Pen. It was a lot simpler than the four syllables of Penelope or the three syllables of Penny-lope.

"Mom" looked so different from what I thought I remembered that my brain jumped back and forth between the images, unable to reconcile the recollected with the real. There was a new look in her eyes. She couldn't directly face me. Seemed weird because years ago, we used to share smiles with our eyes. Now, she was focused on something over my shoulder or out the window, perhaps beyond understanding.

"I'm going to have a pineapple martini," she said as we passed the bar. "What can I get you?"

Way too early, but what the hell. "D'you have chardonnay?"

She mentioned a French name I didn't recognize—probably because I could neither pronounce it or afford it.

"Sure."

In the center of the natural stone floor was a glass-topped coffee table, empty except for a *Wall Street Journal*. Tropical greenery was not in my horticultural vocabulary but the various shapes and shades of green in the pots and containers made the conservatory a pleasant place to get reacquainted, which I thought should be easier with that chardonnay in hand.

Clearly, Mom and Aidan were somewhere in one of those top percentages of affluence. Were. Maybe she still was. I half expected to see a money tree with hundred-dollar blossoms lurking in a corner of the bright space. As she brought the drinks I wondered where their wealth had come from. Certainly not from her father, my beloved Grandpa Jack. Another mystery.

"Cheers." She sat beside me, placing her martini and my softball sized wine goblet on the coffee table.

I nearly choked on my first swallow when I noticed a huge jade ring on her wedding-ring finger. A circle of tiny diamonds surrounded the bright green stone.

"Is that," I asked, "what it looks like?" I felt like a fool as soon as I'd spoken.

A smile spread across her face as she blushed. "I've met the most wonderful man."

I couldn't keep from stating the obvious. "Aren't you supposed to be in widow's weeds for six months or something?"

"Penelope. That is so nineteenth century."

"Well, when *did* you meet this wonderful man?"

"Actually, I've known him for months."

"And when did Aidan die?"

"A week ago. His funeral was Friday."

"So, you were seeing him before Aidan died," I blurted. *Why,* I thought, was I sounding like this? I had never been my mother's keeper and I certainly didn't intend to begin now.

"Aidan had essentially stopped caring. Since our vacation last year, his love machine just went poof. I figured his

A Sardonic Death

business partner had become his mistress."

More than I needed to know. At least for the moment. "Have you set a date?" I said, trying not to sound judgmental.

"We're thinking August."

In romance novels, there's "love at first sight." But not, I thought, in real life. Someone, obviously, had done the proverbial sweeping her off her feet. She polished the jade on her velvet slacks and looked up, all smiles. After a beat, she returned to the present. "You just got back. From where again?"

I'd keep it simple. "My landscape design professor and I were in North Carolina." No need to dwell on the tragedies. "We visited a big garden we'd studied last semester. The last design by the landscape architect who designed Central Park in New York."

Mom wore a lascivious grin. "I hope you and he had a good time."

"*She.* Madison Lerrimore. She's married with a kid."

"I suppose the garden was important?" Crazy kid, she probably thought, hopping here and there around the country. As if *she* hadn't.

"Visiting the Brantleigh Manor gardens was an education in classical design. But I had to stay longer than I'd planned. Madison was wounded at a Civil War reenactment."

I was having a helluva time trying to stay in professional mode while staring at the woman I'd both missed and resented for twenty-three years.

Mom sipped her martini, giving me a moment to savor the oaky wine. "We stayed at Great-Aunt Zelma's place at Flat Rock."

"Good heavens," Mom said. "How is she?"

"Did you know she talks with dead people?" Although it

was true, I smiled at the thought. Great-Aunt Zelma is my late Grandfather Jack's ninety-three-year-old younger sister and until last month I hadn't seen her face to face for twenty-three years and hadn't known that she uses crystals and minerals to assist in seeing auras and communicating with the departed. Although I've learned to accept Grandfather Jack's occasional whispered advice, Mom's apparent acceptance of her aunt's abilities surprised the shenanigans out of me.

Mom lifted her eyebrows, confused. "So, what's wrong with talking to dead people?"

"You too?"

"I hear Aidan's lovely voice from time to time," she said. "I'm sure he means well, but it's a bit frightening."

Frightening wouldn't be the word I'd've used if *I'd* heard him. I'd have run, not walked, to the nearest shrink.

"But you haven't actually seen him?"

"Just the once."

What was going on? Back when she was my mom, she never seemed strange in any way. But a lot can happen in twenty-three years. I took another infusion of chardonnay.

"You *saw* Aidan?"

"It was Saturday morning, the day after the funeral. I walked down toward the pond. When I came through the trees, he was standing on the pier. He'd gone through the pavilion and was on the pier like he was getting ready to take his canoe out for a paddle. He beckoned to me. At first, I was terrified but then I started to run toward him. I went through the pavilion but when I got to the pier, the canoe was just like it'd been, and he wasn't there."

"Had you had martinis for breakfast?"

"Just one. But after that, I had, I think, two more. To settle my mind, you know."

A Sardonic Death

We sat and sipped our drinks quietly while I wondered when Mom had begun hallucinating.

"Tell me about the garden you visited," she finally asked.

I abandoned my curiosity into Mom's strange mental meanderings and decided to tell the whole story. "It turned out Madison's estranged step-father was a docent at Brantleigh Manor. The day we toured, we found him dead. Long story short, someone wanted Madison dead too. She had a couple of close calls including the accident that wasn't an accident at a Civil War reenactment. And then she nearly died from anaphylactic shock."

"Ana . . . what?"

"Anaphylaxis. It can kill. Like if you're allergic to shellfish or peanuts, and eat some without realizing it, you can stop breathing. Period. Fortunately, we got her to the hospital in time. But it was close."

"My Aidan wasn't that lucky. We had no idea the flu could kill him. Never got to the hospital."

"We?"

"Well, Dr. Brennan. Aidan had seen him twice and then he came to the house. Maybe the only doctor around here who makes house calls. And—"

"Aidan was on a prescription?" Mom sometimes would call me Curious Georgette and I've been something of a snoop ever since.

"Something anti-viral, and pain-killers." She flipped a hand past her head as if shooing a fly. "Did you figure out how Madison's step-father died?"

"Long story. But yes. Madison and her partner and their adopted daughter will probably fly back from North Carolina later this week."

As interesting as it was to get reacquainted, it was time to get on with the real reason for my visit. "Could we take a look at the preliminary concept I left with Aidan?"

"Be right back." The woman I was supposed to call Mom picked up her empty martini glass, went into the house and returned with the plan. She unrolled it and showed me their notations. Several would be easy to incorporate. None would require any major change.

"When Aidan showed me this plan with your name on it," she said, "I was so surprised. What a coincidence. I had no idea you'd become a landscape architect."

"Designer, Mom. Not architect. Someday, though, I plan to study landscape architecture at College Park."

"I had no idea you'd found a vocation after the Navy. I'd never have known how to reach you."

I had no idea she'd ever wanted to.

"From what I've seen, you're a talented . . . whatever you call yourself."

"When you phoned, I assumed you'd found another designer."

"No, no, no. Like I said, we want you to work on that plan. *I* want you to go ahead with it. I just hope it can all be finished before my Fourth of July midsummer swim party. You could bring your young man."

I raised my eyebrows. "What makes you think there's a young man?" She didn't need to know about my week-old semi-engagement to Aaron Hunt, who had helped me sleuth a couple of murders and a Civil War flag scam in North Carolina. We planned to exchange rings at a Summer Solstice party.

"You're *not* engaged? What are you doing with that rock on your finger?"

It had been more than a year since I'd explained that ring to

A Sardonic Death

Aaron. "It was my ex's. We were engaged the day I was commissioned. My ship was visiting Barcelona when it ended. I almost tossed it overboard but ultimately left it on to ward off being hit on by the pilots on my carrier. I wasn't in the mood for distractions."

"I knew, of course, from the paper, that you'd gotten an appointment to the Naval Academy. That was what? Ten years ago? I had no idea you'd been engaged."

"More like fourteen. Left the Navy four years ago."

"So, there are twenty years to catch each other up on." Her maddeningly charming Mom smile. *More like twenty-three.*

"What have *you* been up to?" I asked, playing the Curious Georgette card, "besides seeing this new man." I wondered what life was like for someone who didn't work at a paying job.

"In this town, my dear, this time of year one either sails, rents a place in New England, or travels."

"Which category are you in?"

"Staying put this year. Aidan and I did Italy last year."

"Where'd you go?"

"Venice, Florence, Rome. Then we flew to Corsica for a few days, then Sicily and Sardinia. I fell in love again over there."

I took a chance and snarked, "With the man who gave you that gorgeous jade ring?"

She laughed. "Oh dear, don't get me wrong. It wasn't a man, Pen, it was *mirto*. Aidan came back with *limoncello* and I brought a case of *mirto*. You want a sip?"

Might as well break a rule twice. My head was swimming anyway. "Yes please." She'd finished her martini. I sipped the last of my wine while she went to the bar and returned with a chilled bottle half full of dark liquid and a pair of small glasses.

She poured us each two fingers. I took a sip and found that I enjoyed the strangely sweet nectar.

"Wow!" I held up the glass. "Mom, liqueur importer extraordinaire."

Chapter 3

In addition to the circular drive at the entrance to Ravenscroft, the re-design I had planned included a new stone walk under the porte cochère to the front door, new plantings in the curvilinear beds across the front of the house, doing something "daring" (as Aidan had suggested) with the sad little pond in the center of the circle and, flanking the front door, containers with seasonal color. One of the instructions Aidan had given me (obviously from his better half) was the inclusion of bright red flowers for each season.

She led me out from under the porte cochère and into the circle, too polite to comment on my old Chevy van behind her angry-faced Ferrari. "How's your father?" she asked.

Dad, now retired from teaching engineering at the Naval Academy, raised me and my older brother Spencer after she left. "I have no idea. We don't talk much."

What is it with people who walk away from a marriage and twenty-three years later want to know about their former spouse? Morbid curiosity? The hope that they're dead or dying? Now she pretends to want to know how he's doing.

"All I know is that he's retired from teaching and sequestered himself on Arundel Island. He golfs with my boss at Lewis and Gregory."

"Lewis and who?"

"It's a public relations firm on State Circle. I've worked there almost four years—since I took off the uniform."

"I'd assumed you were still in the Navy."

"Dad insists I should have made it a career, so that's why he and I don't spend much time together."

Our path led us past a cutting garden, the swimming pool where a maintenance guy was cleaning the filters, the tennis court, and through a broad stand of mixed hardwoods and native evergreens thoughtfully retained by the original landscape architect. Ahead was the huge pond where I'd first met Aidan. My retired detective friend Jason who'd taken up water garden maintenance had asked for my help to install pond plants. It had been a one-day gig for newly-certified Master Gardener Penelope Summers of Summers Breeze Gardens, LLC.

"Mom, did you know that Jason hired me to put in those plants last year?"

"I think he told Aidan he was busy on a case, and that an assistant would do the planting. Aidan said he'd met the assistant who was a designer and that he'd asked her to help with a design, but if he ever connected you with the daughter I had, he didn't mention it. He did, though, say something about how beautiful you were." She chuckled at the memory. "I figured he was on his way to another girlfriend."

Looking back with twenty-twenty hindsight, Aidan might have guessed I was somehow related. After all, I had the same last name as the woman who had left her marriage for him. "I realized today he was probably the same guy who rode a motorcycle up and down our street all those years ago— probably hoping for a glimpse of you."

She laughed. "This is such a small town I'm surprised we haven't run into each other."

"I wasn't *in* town. I was either inside the Naval Academy, at Public Affairs Officer school, or on the *USS Enterprise* during Iraqi Freedom."

"Well, that explains a lot."

"We had no idea *where* you'd gone," I said. "You never

A Sardonic Death

wrote. It was as if you didn't want anything to do with Dad or Spence or me."

That was as close to a reprimand as she would get. But there I was again, judgmental about something that was none of my business. On second thought, it damned well was my business. My anger and disappointment hadn't faded completely. Probably never would.

"After a few years in California," Mom said, "Aidan and I worked our way back to Maryland."

"Were you at Grandpa Jack's funeral?"

She shook her head. "I didn't want to take a chance on seeing Matthew."

I couldn't believe she hadn't attended her own father's funeral. Even his sister, my Great-Aunt Zelma, had come up from North Carolina. Dad had undoubtedly been there. Curiously, he and Grandpa Jack remained friends for more than forty years after Dad asked his permission to marry Mom.

I couldn't attend Grandpa Jack's funeral because I was half a world away on an aircraft carrier. Not that a public affairs officer on an aircraft carrier was really in the war. More like watching from the sidelines. But I was truly sorry I couldn't get back for his funeral. He'd been the only grandpa I'd known, took me to movies and concerts and plays, and offered his counsel on everything from the best restaurants for me to steer my high school dates, to what college to attend (naturally St. John's College, here in Annapolis, as they say, since 1696, where he'd taught and later been dean). He finally made peace with the idea that I'd go to the Naval Academy. And I've finally admitted that the gene for the *second sight* had been passed on to me, which was why I hear his advice from time to time, as when he was alive. Although I never mention it except to my journal.

"The day I put in those plants," I said, "Aidan came down and asked if I was a designer. I didn't actually say I was a landscape designer. But he'd asked if I was a designer and of course I'd been one for a couple of years at Lewis and Gregory."

"I'd been on his case to get the front garden looking better."

"So, I'm afraid I may have led him on a bit by telling him I was very busy and that I'd get in touch when my schedule opened up."

"All I can say is that when Aidan showed me your concept, we both loved it."

My design professor Madison had reviewed my concept just before she and I went to North Carolina and pointed out a pair of problems that I could fix when I drew a revised plan. With a bit of luck, Mom might never know just how much of a newbie I was.

We walked into the pavilion that was built out over her huge pond. A trio of belt-driven ceiling fans to mitigate Maryland's summer heat were unmoving above. Midsummer around here can resemble the proverbial Hades. Another double door led onto the pier that extended another fifty feet into the big pond, where Mom had *seen* Aidan.

For a man-made water feature, it appeared very natural. "If Aidan came back from the dead to use that canoe," I said, "he left it just as it was."

Mom wore a frown but said nothing.

The pond was stunning. A flurry of waterlilies reminded me of Monet's paintings. Cattails and Horsetails had colonized the edges. The clumps of marginals I planted last year had thrived, now appearing to have spread naturally. Then I glimpsed a cluster of plants I didn't recognize.

A Sardonic Death

"Mom, those flowers over there that look like, well, a little like Queen Anne's Lace. They're new?"

"Oh my, that funny little thing has grown like topsy. I brought back a root from our trip. They called it Water Celery at a botanic garden in Sardinia."

"Never heard of it."

"An old gentleman came up to me after I bought it." She attempted to mimic his accent: "He said 'Itsa call the Devil's Parsnip.' Anyway, I snuck it through customs. Quite nice, don't you think?"

"It's not so little anymore." But the myriad tufts of tiny white flowers did complement the darker-leaved Arrowhead and Arrow Arum I had planted.

"The man explained why it's called the Devil's Parsnip. It's actually quite poisonous. Ancient Sardinians used it to make soup for their elderly and sick to help them die happy. At least they looked happy. It causes what they called a sardonic smile on the deceased."

"I can't believe you wanted to bring it home."

"It was so beautiful. And don't get all righteous about its being poisonous. Lots of garden plants aren't fit for eating."

"It seems to like it here."

"I just poked it in the gravel. Jason didn't think it would survive."

She was right that there are lots of plants with poisonous parts, but it simply wasn't rational to purposely put something like that in a garden. Had my mother's brain slipped a cog? I had a distinct feeling that I was missing something.

We went back through the pavilion and took the path through the trees. Overhead, an invisible woodpecker machine-gunned a dead branch.

"That Water Celery sounds too dangerous to have in your

pond," I said, probably beating a dead horse.

Under the circumstances, a bad cliché, Grandpa Jack whispered.

"You just have to enjoy its beauty," she said. "And don't put its roots in your stew." She laughed.

We continued around the pool and tennis court where she bent to pluck out an errant dandelion from a bed of bright orange and red daylilies. Summers Breeze Gardens could stay busy, I thought, maintaining gardens like these. But I couldn't work for my own mother. It would be horticultural incest.

I had to ask the question that had quivered in my cranium since her mention of the Devil's Parsnip. "Mom . . . what really caused Aidan's death?"

"I have no idea what Dr. Brennan called it. Aidan's gone. Why ever would you want to know about that?"

I can think of several reasons, Grandpa Jack whispered.

"It seems strange," I said, "after being perfectly healthy when I brought him the preliminary concept."

"He'd been in bed with a nasty flu and one morning he had a seizure and was gone."

"Did his doctor say what caused it?"

"He wasn't sure. He thought the flu could have morphed into pneumonia. His body just shut down."

"I'm sorry."

We continued back to the entry circle and under the porte cochère. I stared at her front door and envisioned large blue pots with red-flowering plants on each side.

"If you'll get me the marked-up plan," I said, "I'll get back to my drawing board."

She brought it out. I rolled it, snapped a rubber band around each end and, in spite of myself, hugged her. Must have been the mirto.

A Sardonic Death

"Sorry I sounded like a detective. One with a barbed tongue, at that."

She gave me a genuine smile. She wasn't offended. "It's amazing that we've met again after so long."

"We've got so much to catch up on," I said, muffling my inner cynic.

"Maybe after my Fourth of July party we'll have dinner together."

She didn't know how many irons I already had in the proverbial fire.

"Mom, I'm studying Feng Shui garden design. So in case you have any friends who might be interested, I'm adding it to my design practice."

"I don't have any idea what that fung thing is." A hint of a frown played on her face. "But will it keep you from finishing my design?"

"No worries. I'll see you in a couple of days with the revisions."

As I waited for the magnificent Ravenscroft gates to glide apart to make my getaway, I made a mental note to self: Follow up on the niggling concern that the poisonous Water Celery and Aidan's death might be related.

Chapter 4

Before returning to my drawing board, I had two more errands. The first was to register for the fall semester at Annapolis Community College. Madison had mentioned that the Horticulture and Landscape Design department had added a computer-aided design course. CAD was not only a digital method of creating designs but a super-fast way to make revisions. The instructor for the course, she said, would be Randall Dickert, one of the graphics professors in the landscape architecture department at the University of Maryland where she had earned her degree. Since I was hopeful of eventually following in her footsteps there, knowing CAD would be like already being able to read when starting first grade. Best of all, I could take Madison's second-level design course at the same time.

A parking spot in front of Kirn Hall opened as I arrived. My Great-Aunt Zelma would say it's my energy field that controls my surroundings, like opening a parking spot when I need one. I once explained to her that I don't believe in anything I can't see, but I've reconsidered since I started hearing from Grandpa Jack.

There are more things in heaven and earth . . . he reminded me. Sometimes I wonder if Grandpa Jack's whisperings come from a deep grotto in my own brain that rarely sees the light of rational thought. I was an English major at the Naval Academy, but I'll never know Mr. Shakespeare's plays as well as Grandpa Jack did.

It took only a couple of minutes in the registrar's office to learn that I had come just in time. The school's computer

A Sardonic Death

studio had only twenty stations and there were places for only two more students. After leaving a check for both courses with the finance office, I visited the library on the second floor of the student union and snagged two books on Feng Shui. The librarian coached me in the correct pronunciation: fung shway.

The second errand was to pick up Cookie, my flop-eared Dobergirl from Brock Moore. I had adopted Cookie last summer when her cocaine-smuggling owner was assigned to an institution that didn't permit pets. Then, before Madison and I left for North Carolina, her partner Cheyenne and their adopted daughter Kalea offered to give Cookie a home away from home. While I was away, I'd learned that my sweet Dobergirl had expressed her appreciation of their hospitality by festooning their living room with couch cushion stuffing. When Madison was wounded, Cheyenne and Kalea persuaded Brock to care for her when they headed south. I shuddered at the thought that she might have pulled a similar stunt at Mr. Moore's house.

Cookie bounced around the corner, her eyes bright, her Dobie stub vibrating.

"Thanks for taking over while Kalea and her moms were in North Carolina."

"She's no problem."

"No ruined cushions?"

Brock laughed and said he'd happily dog-sit Cookie for me any time. He was even considering contacting a Doberman rescue outfit and finding one to adopt.

With her uncropped ears akimbo, Cookie's expression was, "What are we going to do for fun today? Hunh? Hunh?" She sat facing me in the passenger seat on the way to the Cathouse Vacation Village where I picked up Thaïs, my Norwegian Forest feline, before heading back to Eastport.

Glancing up from my drawing board, I can look out across the mouth of the Severn River and watch white sails and power boats cavorting toward Chesapeake Bay. Grandpa Jack and I had probably watched some of these same boats on our weekend walks back when Moses was a mess boy. (That's how Navy folks refer to "way back when.") I'm only thirty-three but it seems like a long time ago.

On my drawing board, I taped down see-through drawing paper directly over the concept plan, collected my pencils in one mug, pens in another, and Prismacolor pencils in a third. A small square of flexible clear plastic, slotted to form a lettering guide, waited at the side for the labeling phase.

I began with a "snake," a flexible drawing edge that I bent to match the S-curve of the Reid's driveway, faintly visible through the drawing paper. When I picked up my pen, ready to ink the driveway's edges, a nudge from Grandpa Jack sent me to my MacBook to learn about the Devil's Parsnip. After five minutes I knew more than I needed to know about the Hemlock Water Dropwort aka Water Celery in Mom's pond. The wine-smell of its crushed flowers gave it its genus name and its full horticultural name is *Oenanthe crocata*, which I don't pretend to know how to pronounce. All parts are deadly, but the poison is concentrated in its roots that look like small white carrots (the Devil's Parsnips). It grows wild in ponds and waterways in Europe, but as Mom mentioned, it's infamous in Sardinia for causing its victims' mouths to distend in a rictus of a smile when they die. There are even pictures from a Sardinian museum of Phoenician death masks from 400 BCE. If you'll pardon the twisted maxim, *that's* a plant I can live without! Truth be told, I'm not at all keen on garden ponds so when I meet a client who wants a pond in their garden, I call on my

A Sardonic Death

friend Jason.

Detective Jason Keller is our town's maestro of garden ponds. We'd become friends when he taught the Master Gardeners' pond-keeping class after which I'd done the planting for him in the Reid's pond. He was recalled to work the murder and drug case last year that I had sleuthed as well. From an entirely different angle, I assure you. Let's just say that he never did learn who killed the St. John's sophomore I found in Lionel's pond.

Which prompted another nudge. Unless Mom had rung him, Jason might not know that Aidan Reid had died. Since Jason maintains her monster pond, I should at least bring him up to date on how the Devil's Parsnip was thriving. I called and was surprised to hear that he was back on the force full time, promoted to Detective First Class, and presently working a series of breaking and entering cases. Jason was willing to take a breather and meet me at our usual rendezvous, the St. John's College boathouse pier.

His uniform was spotless and his gold detective shield glimmered in the sunlight that slanted through the trees that bordered the walk from the parking area to the boathouse. Last year I thought of Jason as an old dude but now I realized he was also a handsome one.

"You were in North Carolina longer than you intended," he said.

"It was just my luck to find a corpse in the garden."

"Nothing new there." He chuckled. My reputation of finding dead people was growing, at least in Jason's mind.

The tide was out so we sat on the warm weathered planks dangling our legs toward the creek without the risk of soaked shoes. The odor of pine shavings blended with the scent of the brackish water in College Creek—quickly explained by the whine of an electric plane in the boathouse, signaling that some enterprising St. Johnnie was constructing or repairing a wooden boat between readings in the Great Books.

"I met Mrs. Reid this morning," I said.

"Not Mister?"

"No. I wondered if you'd heard. Aidan died last week."

He glanced down at the dark water. "I hadn't heard. Was he ill?"

Yes, *but* . . . Grandpa Jack whispered.

"She said he'd had the flu for several days. Wasn't getting any worse; wasn't getting any better. Then shazam! He's gone."

"Sorry to hear that. I knew he was anxious to have you redesign the entrance."

"His wife wants me to finish it and get it installed by the end of the month."

Jason glanced at his watch. Undoubtedly anxious to get back to tracing the B and E culprit.

"Couple of interesting things," I said, to recover Jason's interest. "First, *Ms. Reid* was Joan Summers twenty-three years ago."

Jason was puzzled, but only for a moment. "Your mother's been here in Annapolis all along?"

"She and Aidan, she said, started out in California. I don't know when they came back, but she's been Mrs. Reid for a while."

"I heard Aidan made some big money a number of years ago. Must have been about the time you were at the Naval Academy."

"Cops," I said, "learn things mere mortals aren't meant to know."

"Well . . . yeah," he said, smiling smugly. "Then Aidan

A Sardonic Death

made a bundle with a start-up importing prosthetics. That's when they built Ravenscroft."

"So when did you land the job of maintaining that monster pond?"

"They had that dug three summers ago. Right away, it started to go stagnant so they called me. First thing I had to do was convince their lawn maintenance guys to stop fertilizing around it. Last year I put in the bubbler and added marginal plants to take up the excess nutrients."

"So what I planted was the first of the marginals."

He nodded.

"I also want to ask you about a plant I didn't recognize. Mom called it Water Celery."

"It's still alive? She told me she and Aidan brought it back from Italy. Just a wimpy piece of root. When I first saw it, I doubted it would survive."

"It's now a good-sized clump," I said. "Beginning to crowd some of what I put in."

"It's obviously happy where she planted it."

"Did you smell the flowers?"

"It was just beginning to bloom the last time I was there. Looked a little like Queen Anne's Lace."

"They smell like wine. Did Mom tell you anything about it?"

"Just that she'd sneaked it through Customs."

"I'm surprised she didn't warn you. It's poisonous. *Very* poisonous."

His graying ponytail whipped as he twisted to face me. "Let me guess. You're thinking it's what helped Aidan slip his mortal coil."

"I think it's entirely possible. And, unfortunately, I'm guessing that it was Mom who put that root in his soup."

"Penny, that's terrible. You reunite with your mom after twenty years and find out that she's a killer."

"She's already engaged to another man, for God's sake."

"I can't do much about that," Jason said. "What's done is done."

"I'm going to ask her to let you rip out the Water Celery, no matter how pretty she thinks it is."

Back home, Curious Georgette pestered me until I gave up the drawing table and immersed myself in the mysteries of the East. At least for the afternoon. Cookie and Thaïs followed me to our little deck with my newest Feng Shui books.

An hour later, a tumbler of chilled chardonnay served to focus my mind on the intricacies of yin and yang, the flow of chi in a space, and the most auspicious placement of a bagua template. That involved positioning earth, air, fire, water, and metal elements in a garden. Of the five, my mother's red lipstick and flower represented fire. That made sense to me because when I was a kid, she was always full of energy, ready for action, anxious for adventure. My dad, now that I think about it, was pretty much the opposite: a sit-back and relax sort of guy. Spencer and I always had to beg him to even toss a softball. I'd bet it was Mom who planned that trip to Italy and Sardinia. And of course, it was she who had insisted on bringing home the Water Celery root.

Based on having the best of both Mom and Dad's sets of genes for myself, the *yin* and *yang* of my *chi* should be in harmony. And there I was, already thinking in Feng Shui terms.

By the time the sun faded beyond the western horizon, I'd listed the ideal elements in each segment of a garden bagua: Fire Pit in the North, Pond or Fountain in the South, Meditation

A Sardonic Death

Bench in the Northeast, a Patio in the South, etc. After another hour of Feng Shui study, I was suffering from a severe case of bagua-itis.

Grandpa Jack had always counseled me to test the water before I jumped into a new project. But I also remembered that Madison once suggested (with a cynical smile) that the best place to practice garden design was in a client's garden. So, in defiance of what Grandpa Jack would think, I phoned my web guru and asked him to add a page about Feng Shui garden design to the website. At the top of the page, I wanted, in italics, *We Also Speak Feng Shui*. Images of typical Feng Shui elements such as a waterfall rock and a fire pit would fill the page. I'd send him the text and photos tomorrow.

Cookie began whining for her supper. And no wonder. It was 6:00 P.M.

Chapter 5

I had hovered over my drawing board until oh-dark-thirty (Navy-speak for the middle of the night), and nearly drowned in two carafes of coffee in the process. I'd double-checked all the horticultural selections I'd made for Mom's new garden: mature size of the plant, bloom time, preference for sun vs. shade and all that. The center of the circular drive was what took the most time. I didn't want a circle of flowers with a little pond in the center. *Bo-o-ring!* And I shied away from an abstract arrangement. The middle of the circle needed to be attractive from every angle. Cars and limos would circle it to drop guests under the portico. I decided it would become a basin for a trio of spouting fountains illuminated after dark by underwater colored lights, a small version of one at a Las Vegas casino I'd seen online. On the periphery of the circle, flowering shrubs would be illuminated by in-ground LEDs with larger evergreens arranged behind. On either side of the front door, I specified large blue pottery containers, each with three Tropicana lilies with fire-engine red flowers and striped leaves that looked like they'd been swirled through all the colors of summer. They'd have to spend most of their days in the sunny conservatory and be rolled out when Mom expected guests. (Or her fiancé.) A small price to pay for the wow factor of those lilies.

One of the revisions I'd made from the concept was to re-compute the number of Tennessee Crab Orchard stone steppers from the circular drive up to the front stoop. Thanks to my new transit, I found that only three were needed.

I'd also solved the other problem that my mentor had found

by replacing shade-tolerant Snowberry shrubs with Mohawk Viburnums that preferred full sun.

I have to admit I was pleased with what I'd created. Maybe I *had* learned to imagine a landscape ten years into the future.

Madison, I hoped, would be proud.

This morning, after a quick brushing and serving of tuna for Thaïs, and food and a walk for Cookie, I poured myself an OJ and devoured a bacon sandwich that I washed down with the same rainforest blend coffee that had kept me designing all night.

I untaped the plan from the drawing board and rolled it carefully. At the Skipjack Copy Center, I dropped off the original and asked for three copies, one of which I would render in color like I'd seen in my Residential Landscape Architecture book. When you have a high-end client, I'd learned, colored plans are the norm.

A couple of hours later, I picked up the copies. But before heading back to Eastport, I stopped on State Circle and went up to check in with Tony, my day-job boss at Lewis and Gregory Public Relations. He looked up. "Penny! Thanks for stopping in. We've had a great time. Wish you'd been here."

"I kinda wish I'd been here too."

"How many bodies did you find?"

"Not funny. But if you must know—"

"No offense, Penny, but your little 'vacation' lasted longer than you asked for."

"I'll back-date another request and add the two weeks."

"Don't bother." Unusually magnanimous for Tony. "So when can you come back to us?"

"Since you're so generous," I said with a genuine smile, "How 'bout Monday?"

"I'll have a project for you I think you're going to like."

I wasn't looking forward to either a new PR project from Tony or the long hours I'd spend tonight coloring Mom's plan.

Headed back to the drawing board, I worried that I was beginning to get a reputation for mixing my gardening addiction with sleuthing. I won't belabor the point, but I wouldn't take any credit for solving the mystery of any of the deaths I'd been "involved" in. I'd been on hand when a solution presented itself. Or I'd recognized the elements that, in combination, illuminated the perpetrator. So I didn't really deserve the reputation, did I? I was a bit like Rhys Bowen's turn-of-the-century New York sleuth Molly Murphy who once admitted that most of the cases she solved were more due to luck than skill.

My top priority was to nurture my blossoming reputation as a landscape designer. But I did plan to be on the lookout for evidence that could explain Aidan Reid's demise.

I unrolled the copy of the plan that would be transformed with the wizardry of color. Staring at me, in black and white, it was as unfinished as the charcoal version of Edvard Munch's Scream on a tee-shirt. Which planted an idea: Could I learn if Aidan set off into the next world with a scream or a smile? Going from robust to dust in a couple of weeks was, in itself, suspicious.

I'd seen Mom's Grove Book of Memories with messages for Ophelia to meditate on after the service. *May Aidan rest in the Lord, One door Closes, Another Opens, To live in hearts we leave behind is not to die*, and on and on. Mom said she'd gag herself with a spoon rather than read anything in that book.

With Curious Georgette as my excuse for leaving the drawing board, I set off. The Grove Funeral home was at the end of a winding road—a Victorian mansion that overlooked a

A Sardonic Death

tiny Chesapeake tributary that was probably too small to have a name. I introduced myself to the man who came into the foyer.

"Welcome," he said. "I'm Doug Grove." In funereal tones, he suggested we sit and discuss my ideas for honoring my loved one.

"I understand you handled my stepfather's funeral . . ." I hoped this wouldn't be as uncomfortable for him as it was for me.

"And his name was . . .? He undoubtedly assumed I would want one as meaningful for my dead someone.

"Aidan."

"Ah . . . yes. Aidan Reid. Such a terrible loss for Mrs. Reid."

"Well . . . the thing is," my Pinocchio nose began to grow "—she's still very upset. She's worried now that she never really had a good-bye look before he was carried away. She was grieving so much that morning that she only knew her beloved husband was gone. Anyway since I was out of town at the time, she asked me to inquire if, in preparing Aidan, you had the impression that he had died peacefully. You know how it is . . ."

Doug Grove confirmed that they had picked up Mr. Reid as soon as his doctor had certified his death. "When we laid him out, our embalmer—"

"Did he mention anything to you?"

"Miss, I'm getting to that. *She* made a written note for Mr. Reid's file. What it said—hang on a moment, I'll pull that folder."

Mr. Grove opened a wide drawer in his opulent desk and pulled out a dark blue folder. "I'll read you her notes. 'Mr. Reid is an overweight 48-year-old. Death due to aggravated influenza. Body appears normal with the exception of rigidity in facial muscles giving the appearance of a grimace.'" Doug Grove looked up. "She said she hadn't seen a grimace like that before—on a deceased person, that is. Her assistant, when he saw Mr. Reid, said he looked to him as if he was grinning. Whatever it was, Ms. Summers, I guess you could conclude that Mr. Reid had as pleasant a death as could be expected. Ms. Reid should be glad to hear that."

"I'm sure she'll be."

"Please give her my best."

"Thanks, Mr. Grove. I'll be sure to tell her. It will certainly relieve her anxiety—Oh, just one more thing, while you have Mr. Reid's file open. Since I wasn't in town when he died, and I hate to ask Ophelia these details, can you give me the dates of his arrival and of his funeral?"

"We picked him up on May third and his funeral was three days later. The sixth. After the funeral, he was cremated per Ms. Reid's instructions."

"Many thanks."

Before I headed home, I leaned back and closed my eyes. Mentally, I checked off "Clue No.1: With the assistance of some Devil's Parsnip, perhaps added to vegetable soup, Mom had helped Aidan across the River Styx."

Grandpa Jack interjected: *I cannot believe my daughter killed her husband. In spite of the fact that she strayed from her marriage bed once or twice.*

Once or twice? Maybe once or twice a week. But Mom's culpability was as obvious as the jade ring on her finger. Wasn't it? I didn't want to think she had committed, if not murder, something very similar. Manslaughter? Maybe not life in prison, only twenty-five years? I was no lawyer, and I wouldn't ask my professor Madison's partner, Cheyenne who *was* a lawyer.

A Sardonic Death

On the other hand, Grandpa Jack continued, *perhaps it wasn't Joan. That extra ingredient in Aidan's soup might have been added by her fiancé.*

I barked a silent sarcastic *thanks* to Grandpa Jack for cutting my sleuthing down to *double.* Clue number one wasn't quite as crystal clear as I had thought.

But it was the idea of once again losing my mother—this time to prison—that made it hard to concentrate, even when I was back in my condo and staring at the copy of Mom's new entry landscape and my array of Prismacolors. Intent on getting the coloring done, I taped down the corners of the plan and chose two grays to blend, a warm gray and a cold gray, to render the concrete driveway and circle that disappeared under the porte cochère.

I'd learned from Madison that when part of your design is under a roof, it can be visualized on paper as a grayed-out "x-ray view." What needed to be "seen" under the porte cochère, in addition to the portion of the concrete circle, were the tan Tennessee Crab Orchard stone steps from the landing to the door, the blue vases flanking said door and the Tropicana lilies in said vases. Reaching for two shades of blue for the vases, my mind raced to imagine the finished fully-colored plan. It was hours in the future.

I had looked forward to seeing Aidan's pleasure in the finished design, so I must have felt a smidge of what had drawn Mom to flee her marriage from my father, a desire to please the man who had spurred me to actually begin my formal study of residential garden design. It seemed strange to think it, but I felt somehow less related to Mom now than I had been to Aidan. Of course, I still wanted the photos of the finished job in my portfolio, but I couldn't imagine that pleasing her was as important as it had been to please him.

My long-ago anger at her boiled again. I hadn't used any of my childish revenge plans but just possibly I'd have the chance to wreak my retribution now. If I found that Mom had sent Aidan across the River Styx, I could make sure she was indicted for his murder. I knew these were the musings of an angry adult child, but I indulged them for a few satisfying moments.

I needed to shake these thoughts and turn my attention back to rendering the plan. I began selecting colors for the plants. But even before I found the shades of green and turquoise Prismacolors for the evergreens, Chopin's mazurka blasted from my phone. If I couldn't keep my mind on the job, I'd never get it done. Maybe I should hire an answering service.

"Penny for your thoughts."

"Penelope?" *Like who else would it be?*

Although Dad greased my appointment to the Naval Academy, the old codger rarely calls since he retired from teaching and has never invited me to his bachelor hideaway on Arundel Island.

I tried, probably unsuccessfully, to mock him. "Dad, is that you?"

"How've you been?"

Since I hung up my uniform, he's hassled me for quitting the Navy in mid-career. I knew instinctively that he wasn't interested in my gardening or landscape design.

I made my answer short and not very sweet. "Just fine, Dad."

"Good, good." He'd never been much of a conversationalist.

"S'your nickel . . ."

"Do you have any idea how out of date that expression is?"

Engineers are so incredibly detail oriented. I refrained from

A Sardonic Death

allowing my irritation to show. "Dad, I have work to do." As in *what is this about?*

I heard a woman's voice in the background. Unintelligible.

"I called to invite you to go sailing."

"What?" It took a moment to register. "Where? When?"

"I've scheduled a maiden voyage in my new–well, new to me, sailboat on Sunday."

I hadn't been sailing yet this year and was having withdrawal symptoms. Sounded too good to be true. "Thanks, Dad, that sounds great."

There had to be a catch.

"The refit on the Samuelson's boat is finished and I'm thinking of making it a family reunion." *OhmyGod.* "Spencer and Janisse are coming and—," did I sense a hesitation? "My wife Laurel."

"Congratulations. I didn't know."

"*And* your mom."

This could be the family reunion from hell, Grandpa Jack whispered.

Which turned out to be the understatement of the year.

"I've never even been to your island," I said, trying not to sound reproachful.

"Just give your name to the guy at the gate. You'll be on his list. Come to the house for drinks about noon and we'll go down to the boat about one."

Although I had misgivings, I had to admit that at least the sailing part sounded like fun.

It was much later when I finished embellishing Mom's plan with the Prismacolors. I gave Cookie her last walk and wondered if the self-employed ever enjoyed normal sleep patterns.

Chapter 6

Almost ten Thursday morning, with my beautifully colored plan rolled loosely beside me and a hefty invoice for my design work in my portfolio, I wound my way through the Simms Creek estates to Ravenscroft. Before I could get to the microphone on the post, the Frank Lloyd Wright-inspired gates moved noiselessly apart. I assumed that my approach had been caught by a hidden camera and Mom had triggered the gates to open. Au contraire. A dark red Mercedes coupe with tinted windows rolled from the entry circle and squeezed out between the gates. I couldn't see the driver. Not that I would have recognized him. I knew none of my mom's friends.

Grandpa Jack, who sometimes plays the devil's advocate, whispered: *Doctor or lawyer?*

It's the wrong century for house visits, I countered, except of course for Aidan's doctor. I waited for the Mercedes to go by and approached the open gate. My ancient blue Chevy van with my picture on each side was an imposter in this neighborhood and certainly no match for the likes of the Mercedes that sped past me. I pulled through the gates to the entry circle and parked behind Mom's Ferrari.

She answered my knock in her bathrobe and slippers, her face flushed. She never used to stay in bed this late unless she was sick. Maybe the Mercedes driver *was* her doctor. When I was young, I'd never known her to be sick. She certainly bore no evidence of sickness this morning. Her cheeks were a healthy pink.

"Hi," I said, the plan and portfolio in hand. "I'm sorry if I

A Sardonic Death

came too early. I should have called."

"Give me a sec to get some clothes on." She waved me toward the kitchen. "Punch the espresso button on the coffee machine. It's automatic." On my earlier visits, Aidan hadn't offered this amenity. The button punched, the machinery made satisfactory purring noises, clicked twice and hissed as it filled the small cup. If this is how the upper-class lives, I thought, I could easily become accustomed. A tiny spoonful of sugar added the perfect touch to the inky liquid. The first sip took me back to when the *Enterprise* visited Palma de Mallorca. But today's espresso wouldn't be followed by a glass of Palo liqueur. After the second sip, I thought about swirling the semi-liquid glop at the bottom into an image of my future.

At a cafe in Palma, after I'd drained my first espresso, a fortune-teller had offered to read the future by flipping the cup upside down on the saucer, allowing the dregs of espresso sludge to slide toward the saucer. She twisted the cup three times and lifted it to create what looked like a meaningless map in the cup. After considering it for a moment, she said just two words: "Man trouble." She'd been right on the money.

On the counter beside Mom's coffee machine was an unopened envelope from a law firm I'd never heard of, Malakoff and Gratrix, Attorneys at Law blah blah blah. Curious.

What was also curious was that she hadn't identified her morning visitor.

She breezed back into the kitchen in a purple pants suit, put another cup under the spout and hit the button. "*Pearl la vostry salute*," she said, in what I guessed was mangled Italian. "Learned that last year. Means 'To your health.'" We sipped our espressos and grinned the silly smiles of friends who hadn't seen each other for twenty-some years.

This morning, her hair was brushed out and pulled together with a broad silver barrette in back. A younger look than Monday's. The red carnation over her ear matched her lipstick. Add a red fan, and she could understudy Carmen.

"There was a car just leaving when I pulled up. Lawyer?"

"Actually, that was my acupuncturist and massage therapist. He helps me stay in shape for tennis."

"Whatever he's doing, it seems to make you glow," I said.

"He does, indeed."

At the dining room table, I unrolled the colorful plan and put a napkin ring on each corner to hold it more or less flat. "Let's have a look at your design."

"Yes," she said. "Yes!" She pulled the plan closer, placed a fingernail on the flower beds bordering the circular drive where I'd indicated a profusion of color, and then noticed my artistic version of miniature Tropicana lilies in containers at the front door. "Lovely."

Mom continued making approval sounds, then looked up at me. "What's next?"

"The very first next thing is for you to initial your approval in the little box and write me a check. After that, I'll get with my friend Roy at Hillsmere Gardens to price out the plants and the installation cost. But I'll be here to supervise from start to finish."

I pulled out my invoice, she wrote me a check and added a smiley face in the corner.

"There's one more thing I need to tell you," I said, matter-of-factly.

"What's that?" she asked, upbeat.

I tucked the newly-approved plan and the check into my portfolio and back into my backpack. "That Water Celery—"

"It looks nice with what you and Jason planted." She

A Sardonic Death

glanced at her jade ring and smiled.

"It's very dangerous for you to have that in your pond, Mom. If I were you, I'd have Jason yank it all out."

"Oh no, dear. I couldn't do that."

"It's killed livestock in England."

"Let me know," she said with a mischievous smile, "if you see any cattle grazing in the garden."

"Mom, it's not funny. Suppose your neighbor's kid—"

"Our neighbors don't have kids. Only grandchildren."

"Then, okay, your neighbor's *grand*kids climb over the fence and start chewing on what looks nice and crunchy."

"We've never had children climb into our yard."

"Did you know the root's the most poisonous part?"

"Of course. It's a thin white carroty thing. What I kept in a sandwich bag all the way home."

"Please? Keeping it is just playing with fire."

You can't give advice to a fool, whispered Grandpa Jack. *He won't heed it. And a wise man doesn't need it. Joan was stubborn as a child, too.*

Grandpa Jack should know. He was her father.

I finished my espresso and rose to leave with a promise that I'd light a fire under Roy to work up an estimate for the installation. "I'll be in touch as soon as I have some figures."

"Penny . . ." Her pause was like on the phone when she was about to reveal that she'd been my mother twenty-three years ago. "A letter from Aidan's attorney came yesterday."

"What'd it say?" Pretending I hadn't noticed the envelope.

"Could you wait a minute?"

She went back into the house and brought the envelope back. I watched her peruse the letter.

A quick intake of breath. "It's about Aidan's will. I need to go to his office."

"What's going on? D'you want me to go with you?"

Mom wagged her head no but I couldn't help but wonder why she seemed so surprised. Must not have been good news.

"Okay." My mind jumped to the "not good news" in the pond. The more I thought about it, the surer I was that Mom had assisted Aidan into the next life. I rebuked myself for having an overactive imagination but vowed to keep my eyes open and my antennae a-twitch.

I turned right from the circle instead of toward the gate, drove slowly and parked in the caterer's spot close to the pavilion. Beyond the pond, I could see the dock on Simms Creek where Aidan's diesel yacht was moored. I'd never given it more than a glance. It was an example of what those of us in the sailing fraternity call a "stinkpot".

I made my way around the big pond to where the Water Celery crowded the Arrow Arum I'd planted last year. *Surprise*. A clump of the Devil's Parsnip had been chopped out. If Jason didn't soon yank it all out, the gap would fill in, but where and when had the missing clump gone?

Chapter 7

I hadn't seen Roy since before Madison and I had gone to North Carolina. I found him loading azaleas and nandinas into a van for an installation job. During my first plants course, it was here at Hillsmere Gardens that I meandered along row after row of plant material noting the Latin names, common names, and each plant's characteristics. Professionals use the term "plant material" to distinguish it from "hardscaping material," like retaining wall stones, stepping stones, river rocks, and timbers that can also often be found at garden centers. For a designer, there's no end of things to learn.

Roy doffed his cap, brushed his brow and did a double-take. "Speaking of my favorite designer!" He jumped down and gave me a brotherly hug. I noticed he had a silver ring on his pinkie. He caught me noticing it. "Oh, that—Holly and I are engaged. I haven't gotten it sized yet." Roy and Holly had been my classmates in the design course.

"Congratulations. You youngsters don't let any grass grow under your feet." I had ten years on him so I could play the elder aunt.

"Now if you're finished mocking me," Roy said, with the smile of a hopeless romantic, "tell me what I can do for you today."

"I have a plan and plant list for the Reid job."

"That's a good start. Let's go to the office."

I handed him a black-and-white copy of the plan and my plant list.

"When you get a chance," I began in my best auntie voice, "I need some numbers for Ms. Reid. The sooner the quicker?

She'd like to have her new garden in place for a do on the July Fourth weekend."

Roy pulled a pencil from over his ear and marked the plan and plant list: "Summers Breeze." With the pencil back behind his ear, he let out an exasperated breath. "Your mom and everyone else. Like they just realized they want to re-do their landscape. They couldn't have come in March. Oh no. Wait till June and want it yesterday."

My pouty smile has worked in similar situations, so why not now?

"For Penny Summers, though," he said, after a glance in my direction, "in honor of her new design business, I suspect we can move you to the head of the line."

I didn't doubt it since I knew Roy was a favorite at the Garden Center.

I pocketed my pout and gave him a genuine smile of appreciation. "I owe you, Roy. And please give Holly my congratulations."

"She's in the Garden Shoppe. Tell her yourself."

More than a year ago, the Chesapeake Sign Shop had crafted the images and lettering on my van. I stopped in and asked George, with his armload of tattoos, to add an image of a Phoenix and FENG SHUI SPOKEN HERE to both sides, near the bottom with my website address.

"I'll ring you when they're ready," George said. "Probably only take a half hour to apply."

When I returned to my condo, the answering machine was blinking rapid triplets. I sat at my desk, my pen hovering over an empty legal pad, and listened.

"Hi, Summers," the first caller said in an Asian accent. "I make fortune cookie and hope for auspicious garden behind

A Sardonic Death

shop. Preeze call as soon as possible." I noted the number and tagged it "Fortune Cookie." This prospect, although I was happy that someone had picked up my new specialty on my website, didn't seem auspicious at all.

The second caller was a woman with a shrill voice. Maybe elderly. "Hello, Ms. Summers. I'm Adele Winters, down near Galesville? I think the idea of an oriental garden sounds simply wonderful. I have a few rose bushes and two huge lilac bushes that I would not want to move, but I hope you can give me some ideas. Oh, and I think I'd like one of those koi-fish ponds."

This was depressing. An elderly lady who doesn't realize that a properly installed koi pond would cost her at least three months of Social Security checks. Sure. Just dig a little hole, drape a shower curtain in it, fill it with the hose, and go to the aquarium store for a sixty-five- dollar imported Japanese koi. If she had a rich uncle who just left her ten thousand, it might be doable. Koi ponds do not come cheap and there's only a couple of companies in our area that can install one properly. So much for what I'd learned from Jason when he taught the water-gardening module of our Master Gardeners training. I poured a substantial chardonnay to start the pre-prandial process and slugged half. Now for the third caller.

It was a gentleman with a slight accent. "Good afternoon, Miss. I am fascinated with the prospect of having a Feng Shui designer make a new plan for my garden." *Well-spoken, at least.* "My home is on Lake Drive in the Bay Shores area," he added. *Whoopee!* People in that part of town had disposable income coming out their ears. At least that's the popular conception. "I have an extensive herb garden for my Chinese medical practice," the caller continued. "Might I have the pleasure of your reply whereupon we might arrange a short meeting at my house? I should like to explain an idea that should be beneficial to us both."

As we used to say in the Navy (when a senior officer was not within hearing), "Is a frog's butt watertight?" Okay, you had to be there, but it's kind of like asking if the Pope is Catholic. I'd return the nice gentleman's call right after breakfast tomorrow when I'd be at least as lucid as what was left of my chardonnay. With a pen poised over the legal pad, I realized he hadn't left his name or a number.

The phone rang again but it was after hours. Pre-prandial medication having begun, I let the machine take it. It was the same man I'd just heard. "Miss Summer. Second time calling. I apologize I did not leave my name on your machine. It's Chinese, so I'll pronounce it slowly for you. Chun—Yang—Chen. Dr. Chun Yang Chen. I await your call. Thank you." Click. A few minutes later, he called again, this time to leave his phone number.

The doctor had a severe case of Can't Remember Stuff.

Chapter 8

The Bay Shores community where Dr. Chen lives is less than twenty minutes from my Eastport condo. But the metaphorical distance is more like a hundred miles—an enormous difference in incomes and lifestyles between Eastport and Bay Shores. In my condo block, a large percentage of owners look longingly out to the Bay and hope for an occasional invitation from a boat-owning friend to get them out on it. (Yours truly, for instance.) In the Bay Shores community, a similarly large percentage have piers that extend from manicured backyards into Lake Litchford with sailing yachts moored alongside. Yet they sail only a few times each year.

You expected life to be fair? quipped Grandpa Jack.

I turned into Dr. Chen's crushed oyster-shell driveway. Directly ahead was an empty garage and to the right was a small parking area presumably for his patients. I parked close to the open garage door and marveled that there was no luxury car in residence. His front garden definitely needed attention. It appeared to be the remnants of a "builder's special"—cheap plants, cheaply installed, several on the sick list.

The good doctor's hand-carved double doors stood open for me. A gentle breeze mixed with a whiff of clove wafted through from another pair of open doors on the lake side of the house. I knocked gently on the wood near the phoenix's tail-feathers.

"Ah, Miss Summer, please do come in." Dr. Chen was handsome, lanky, about my height, undoubtedly of mixed parentage, one of whom was Asian. He brushed black hair away from his face with his left hand and held out his right in welcome. "Thank you so much for coming." His white shirt, jeans, and running shoes suggested a forty-ish man about town. Potential running buddy?

No fraternizing with your clients, Grandpa Jack advised. I hate it when he suggests what I should or should not do, but, dang, if he's not usually right.

"Very nice to meet you, Dr. Chen. You have a beautiful home."

"Thank you. You care to have a walk-about?"

"I'd be grateful." Where had I come up with this blue-stocking banter?

Chen led me into the living room, fireplaces at each end, and motioned me to a magnum chair where I sank into a soft leather cloud. He took a chair near the French doors that stood open to his back deck. Steps from the deck led to a wide garden and to a pier into Lake Litchford, where a sailboat tacked its way toward the narrow channel out to Chesapeake Bay. For an instant, my heart yanked me away from my new client to imagining sailing Saturday with Dad and his new wife.

Dr. Chun Yang Chen's pier into Lake Litchford had no yacht on either side. Not that he couldn't afford one. His million-dollar home made that clear. One thing I've learned, though, is that people who live in expensive homes sometimes invest the whole enchilada in the house, and have only modest amounts to spend on accouterments.

On the interior wall and alongside the fireplaces, colorful broad-brush contemporary canvases paraded on bone white walls. My evaluation of his house went up a half mil. Above a fireplace, in contrast to the avant-garde art, hung a portrait of a beautiful woman. Her long black hair framed a smiling face. Her almond eyes invited love. He noticed me admiring her.

A Sardonic Death

"My ex," he said.

"She's beautiful." Her red lips and a red flower in her hair reminded me of Mom.

I turned back to the woman's portrait. "Is she here in the States?"

"She's in Taiwan," he said. Nothing more.

I nodded as if I understood.

"May I show you my office?" We went through a door beside the other fireplace into a suite of rooms with a separate entrance from the parking area for patients. Here, the walls were a soft sunlight yellow and the carpeting dark blue. On one wall was an antique cabinet with dozens of small drawers, all red like his ex's lipstick, each with a brass label and small knob. "This is my apothecary." He opened a drawer, invited me to sniff, and cocked his head, awaiting my impression. It was the scent of clove I'd noticed when I arrived. "You like?"

I smiled and nodded.

"You call it clove. I call ding zhang. Very good before making love. Also for helping chi move 'south.'" He laughed and indicated the direction from his mouth to his stomach. "Warms the kidney fire when the stomach misbehaves." He chuckled as if he'd made a joke. If he had, it flew right over my head, but I smiled to be polite.

"I grow most of these herbs," he said. "Would you like to see my garden?"

"Yes, of course."

Another chuckle as he seemed to remember my profession.

We went back to the living room and through glass doors onto the broad deck clearly furnished for relaxation and entertaining. Down a few steps, a pair of magnificent large herb gardens, separated by a swath of lawn, graced his broad terrace. On their left was a gazebo at the head of the pier that reached into the lake. I wondered if there was usually a yacht alongside. The two herb gardens, I guessed, together had more than a hundred different plants in various stages of leafing, flowering, and seed-forming. Grassy paths bisected and crossed through them so that, with a single step from turf, any plant could be tended or harvested. At the far end of the central path, a naturalized pond beckoned. In spite of my old horror of ponds and pools, I found myself drawn to it. My baby brother, Josh, drowned in a swimming pool when I was supposed to be watching him twenty-some years ago. My dread increased last year when I found a dead friend in a pond on my first gardening job. However, since Aaron Hunt and I had become engaged at my Great Aunt Zelma's swimming pool just two weeks ago in North Carolina, ponds and pools no longer held quite the dragons they had for so long.

Dr. Chen's pond had an array of blue and pink tropical waterlilies standing above the surface, pockets of yellow iris, a rainbow of Louisiana irises, Arrow Arum, Variegated Sweet Flag, Papyrus, Horsetail, and Chameleon Plant. "It's gorgeous," I said. "Do you maintain it *and* all the herbs?"

"I have a policeman friend who keeps the pond beautiful for me." He had to mean my friend Jason Keller, Annapolis's pond guru extraordinaire. In many ways, Annapolis is a small town.

"He's done a great job for you here."

But the Feng Shui of this pond was all wrong. If it had been where the bagua would have indicated, a water feature of some kind would have been the first element of the garden to be encountered, at the foot of the steps down from the deck. Where this pond was should have been a metal sculpture. I held my tongue as it wouldn't help our relationship if I became a Feng Shui holier-than-thou know-it-all. At least not yet.

A Sardonic Death

I admired a tropical purple waterlily standing above the surface that looked like its center was glowing from within. The contrast of dark purple and bright apricot yellow zazzed the color wheel in my brain. "I know some of these plants," I said, then pointed to a clump of the same Water Celery my mom had brought back from Italy. "But that one is new to me," I lied.

"Ah, Water Celery, from Sardinia. I borrow some from a friend and it grows very fast." The clump from Mom's pond. Could this man be Mom's visitor with the red Mercedes?

"Interesting," I said. But the possibility that Dr. Chen was my mom's friend seemed too much of a coincidence. Hadn't she said an acupuncturist and massage therapist kept her in tennis-playing condition? What were the odds of some other Annapolitan having Water Celery in their pond?

We started back to the house. The sky couldn't have been bluer or the breeze gentler. The sound of children playing was a happy murmur in the neighborhood. "Water Celery, I understand, is quite poisonous. Please don't let any children near your pond."

"Of course."

"Dr. Chen, if you don't mind me asking, are you an acupuncturist in addition to a traditional Chinese herbalist?"

He smiled, his face covered in happiness. "Ha-ha, you're a very smart woman. My medical school in Taiwan is the China Medical College. I have both M.D. and doctorate in T.C.M., Traditional Chinese Medicine, which includes acupuncture. Here, also I became certified in massage therapy." He chuckled again. "Many schools, many years, you see." Dr. Chen had the credentials to help keep my mom in shape for tennis and swimming. What an amazing coincidence. Mom's massage therapist had called me to incorporate Feng Shui principles in the renovation of his garden.

"You're a triple threat, then," I said as we went back up to his deck.

"Ha-ha, yes I have heard that. I make big money being a triple threat." He laughed at what he'd supposed was a joke. I wondered if I should interpret that laugh to suggest that he, in fact, did *not* make big money.

"I didn't see a treatment table in your office."

"Most patients I see in their homes. I only prepare instruments and prescriptions here."

"Ahhh."

"Will you have tea?" he asked.

"Of course. That would be nice."

Back on the deck, he motioned me to a chair while he continued indoors. I looked out at the wide panorama: Beyond the herbs, on the left side of his pond, the spacious gazebo offered shaded and cushioned comfort. Grand homes for the well-heeled ringed the lake. When I was at the Naval Academy, my roommate and I had sailed in the Severn and the Bay as often as possible but we'd never sailed through the narrow entrance to the lake. It would have made the perfect harbor to ride out a storm.

Dr. Chen returned with a china teapot and two cups. He settled in the chair next to mine, a small tile-topped table between us. "You see, you cannot rush the tea making. No hideous American teabags ever in this house." His face had an almost built-in smile that broadened as he poured our cups. "Very hot, you will see."

I groaned inwardly when I looked in my cup and saw what might have been a flower petal on the bottom instead of dark tan tea. Then I inhaled a sweet scent and sipped.

"Jasmine," he said, "best for new guest."

A Sardonic Death

"I'm honored."

After a second sip, he said, "Now I tell you why I called."

I set my teacup on the little table between us, the better to pay attention to my prospective client.

"I love my gardens," he said, "but not all Chinese peoples have Feng Shui talent. I am, how do you say, 'a case in point?'"

"I would be very happy to help you," I said. "I assume you're not thinking of re-making your backyard garden."

"Oh no, of course, no." Again, his natural smile. "I would like you to make a new front garden, make chi flow better, to welcome guests, and create 'open arms' for patients."

I sat back and took another sip of the most unusual tea I'd ever had. (Say good-bye to old teas, Penelope).

"That's a tall order," I said.

"Meaning?"

"It just means a big job."

"Big job is no problem?"

I pretended to consider the big job and perhaps too quickly decided that I could finesse my way through it. "No problem at all." I smiled.

"No problem then," he said.

I rose to get my portfolio from the van. The doctor's cell phone chimed something by Bach as I started into the living room. I heard him answer, "Angela, I will come to you later as we planned. My landscape designer is . . ." His voice faded as I walked through the house. By the time I returned with my portfolio, his phone was back in his pocket.

I handed him one of my new Feng Shui brochures.

"Very nice," he said.

I explained my schedule of design fees and how I develop a design in three phases. He nodded his understanding. Then I asked him for the information I needed for my Client Sheet and noted his contact information. On a Letter of Agreement, I filled in his name and address, a summary of what he'd asked me to do, and asked him for a signature and the first phase payment.

"Good," he said, handing me a check. "Money's no problem. I'm eager for you to start—as soon as possible." Roy was right. Everyone wants his new garden *yesterday*.

"Do you have a plat of your property?" I asked. "Like a small map?" He went to another room. I heard him pull out a file drawer and close it. He returned with a large folder.

"Probably in here." It was.

"If I may," I said, "I'll make a copy and bring it back."

"Of course," he said.

I tucked it in my portfolio and a stood. "It's been a pleasure."

"The pleasure is mine."

"I'll get back to you in a few days with a preliminary concept. And thank you for the wonderful tea."

Once behind the wheel of my van, Grandpa Jack muttered: *Did you sense anything strange about your new client?*

I always thought I had what men called "women's intuition" but I hadn't noticed anything strange, only that he was rich, charming, and serious eye candy.

Chapter 9

On the way to the Skipjack Copy Center with Dr. Chen's plat, I called Jason. "I visited one of your pond clients today."

"I have dozens. You want me to guess?"

"How many live in Bay Shores?"

"That does narrow it down. Dr Chen?"

"Bingo. It's a gorgeous pond."

"It ought to be. He can afford it."

"Ummm–did you transplant a clump of Water Celery from Mom's pond to his?"

"I assumed he'd helped himself to that clump. Your mom must be one of his clients."

"What a coincidence. He's asked me to design a new welcome zone for his guests and patients in the front."

Jason waited a beat. "Some of his guests are his patients."

"What?"

"You know, when hubby's out of town–"

"Meaning what?"

"Let's just say he seldom has patients come to his home. He usually goes to them and provides any service madam requires in addition to acupuncture or massage. If those services are remarkable, then madam comes calling socially."

"You have a wild imagination."

"He obviously hasn't invited you to see the view from his bedroom."

Maybe Grandpa Jack did sense something about my first Feng Shui client. "I'm a mere mortal, Jason. You know there's no way I could know what Annapolis's finest know."

"Dr. Chen has a bit of a reputation. That's why his wife divorced him."

"There's got to be more to that story."

"There certainly is, as in several divorces in the last few years triggered by the birth of an Asian-looking kid to a lily-white family."

"Really?"

"Stay tuned."

"I shall," I said. "Have you deduced all this by maintaining his pond?"

"Like a bloodhound, I keep my nose to the ground."

"Should I explain his extra-curricular activities to Mom?"

I heard from Grandpa Jack before Jason could answer. *Penny,* some *things folks have to learn for themselves.*

At the Skipjack Copy Center, I computed the percentage enlargement of Dr. Chen's plat to bring it to a scale of a quarter inch to equal one foot and gave it to Gary. He was inundated with orders for architects and builders but promised he'd have it enlarged for me in the morning.

Returning home, I remembered Aaron's suggestion that we would get properly engaged, as in exchanging rings, at the summer solstice. I searched the internet for a solstice party in Annapolis. Nada. Then I remembered that I'd first learned about solstices in the introductory unit of the requisite navigation class at the Naval Academy. From my subconscious, a seed buried since I was a midshipman thrust up a seedling. You might say I got lucky. Aunt Zelma would have attributed it to my psychic credentials.

Yep. As a graduate, I could bring a guest to the Naval Academy Officers Club Solstice Party. Well—ta-da! Neither of us would be in uniform which would be a good thing because

A Sardonic Death

the Club might frown at a guest who was enlisted, no matter how high he was on the ladder.

The event would be on Friday, a week from tomorrow. Perfect. My email to Aaron laid out the specifics:

> Dearest Nearly Betrothed
> I've found the only solstice party in town. At the Naval Academy Officers Club. Hors d'oeuvres at six, cash bar, at seven a toast to the solstice (in poetry) compliments of the Navigation Department (the actual time of the solstice will have been almost twelve hours earlier), and dancing until 2 A.M. I'll ask my psychic friend Gina for the best time to exchange rings. LOL!
> BTW, Please get your ring finger sized and tell me if you'd prefer gold or silver.
> When my practical self realized I could trade in the engagement ring I'd kept to warn away male predators after my engagement went up in smoke, I added:
> We can choose mine here.
> Love from Penny. PS - Can't wait!

Bursting with enthusiasm for Aaron's arrival and our pending formal engagement, I realized that I hadn't shared any of it with my oldest best friend, Gina McBee. I owed her a round at Harry Browne's since returning from North Carolina.

"Just closing up," she said when she answered. Her Flights of Fancy shop a block up from the City Dock carries minerals and semi-precious stones that she claims can cure any ill or block any mischievous spirit. Gina would disown me if she knew what I believed in my heart about the abilities of her stones to protect the wearer.

"Care to catch up at Harry Browne's?"

Fifteen minutes later, at the end of the bar upstairs, we waited while Bart finished pouring a pair of drafts, set them up and sidled in our direction. "What'll you two lovely ladies have today?"

"I missed your Dark and Stormies in North Carolina," I said.

"If I *haven't* been to the Carolinas and *haven't* missed your Dark and Stormies," Gina began, "may I have one too?"

"Comin' up." Bart swiveled to pick up a bottle of Goslings on the mirrored shelf.

Gina picked up a cashew from the tiny dish in front of us. "How was North Carolina?" Popped it into her mouth.

I retold the story of finding Madison's long-lost stepfather and summarized the Civil War flag scam. "The best part of the trip was getting acquainted with Madison and Cheyenne's kid. Kalea is the cleverest eleven-year-old you can imagine."

Gina assumes a mystic smile when she's about to give me advice. "So you're thinking you want one of your own? I've been telling you, you should get married." Advice she hasn't herself heeded.

"Here you go," Bart said, placing the tumblers on the counter and dropping in lime wedges.

I took a swallow. "One other thing. Aaron and I are semi-engaged."

"Semi . . . ?"

"He'll be here next week and we'll trade rings on the solstice."

Her smile grew a wicked edge. "You've always denied any interest in astrology and *now* you're going to get engaged at the moment of highest masculine energy in the year. *The* best time of year to focus on your life's purpose. Not to mention your

A Sardonic Death

Saturn Return."

"You and my Great Aunt Zelma! She hit me with the Saturn Return thing and I don't need any additional tutorials. Our timing, I assure you, is coincidental."

"You may think so, but you forget that you're governed by the stars and planets whether you like it or not. So, trust me, it's *not* coincidental." She picked up her glass and swirled it once. "I have just what you need. A labradorite pendant. And it'll go with just about anything."

For someone like me who spends most of her time in tee-shirts and jeans, what goes with anything is not a priority. "Perfect," I said, hoping it wouldn't bring down the wrath of the universe, not that I believed there was such a force.

"It'll boost your energy and intuition and help you through the Saturn Return transformations."

I could use an energy boost, I thought, slugged more of my Dark and Stormy, and realized I hadn't told Gina of my mother's reappearance.

"Something *else?*" Maybe she *was* psychic.

"You're going to find this as mystifying as I do. My mom has shown up again—"

"*What?*" Gina shrieked. "*Where? How?*" We had just started in fourth grade together when Mom disappeared.

"That design job for Aidan Reid . . ."

"Okay. And—?"

"His wife called. Said Aidan had died but wanted me to go ahead with the design. Then she hits me with the fact that she used to be my mom. I just met her Tuesday."

"What's she like?"

"You'd probably recognize her . . . from when she used to meet us after school."

"No. What's she *like*? Not what does she *look* like?"

60

"She probably killed her husband, Aidan Reid."

Gina's mouth dropped open. "*Whaaat?*" Gina and I have always enjoyed tossing information bombs at each other.

"See, she brought this poisonous plant back from Italy or wherever last year. It's growing in her pond. If you die from its poison, you die with a grin. And I talked to the funeral place. Aidan had the grin."

I hadn't realized this was so bottled up. Telling Jason was important but dropping it on Gina was positively cathartic.

"To tell you the truth," I added, "I think she's slipped a cog. Now she's already engagedto someone she's known for months. It's creepy."

"You were an English major," Gina said. "Sounds like you've got a book to write. Just change enough to call it fiction."

I slipped her my own sardonic grin. "If I live through it."

Gina tipped back the last of her Dark and Stormy. "We're going to the shop. I'm going to outfit you with that labradorite pendant right *now.*"

Chapter 10

Saturday morning, with my landscape measuring kit in the van, along with my new transit to accurately measure grades and a measuring wheel I'd just bought, I made tracks to Dr. Chung Yang Chen's home. Breezes off the bay reminded me that I'd be sailing again the next day. No dark clouds in sight. Only blue sky, the color of Dr. Chen's office carpeting.

Again, no car in his garage. He was probably working with a patient at home. Jason's information had made me wary of any speculations about my new client. Which also meant that I didn't need to know or care what therapies he might be using at the moment. Or where. I parked in his driveway facing the open garage.

I had rubber-banded the enlarged plat of the front of his house to a piece of pressboard. The footprint of his house gave me reference points. I measured from each corner of the house to the front door. I did the same to locate his patients' entrance and penciled in a symbol for outward-opening entry doors. Two mid-size weeping cherry trees were set slightly back from the two corners. Which left me almost a clean slate across the front of the house. I took several wide-angle photos over which I would sketch ideas on a sheet of tracing paper: trees, shrub groups, focal points, perennial beds, et cetera.

Taking my camera back to my van, I was surprised by a beautifully restored black Ford Falcon grumbling to a stop behind it. After a glance at the driver, I checked out the old base sticker on the windshield. The owner was a reservist who drills at Andrews Air Force Base.

"Hi," he said.

"Hello," I answered.

"Do you work here or are you visiting?"

"How about you tell me what this is about before I answer?" Cool. *Right?*

He broke into a smile, kicked an oyster shell off the lawn back into the drive, and leaned against his spotless car. "I'm Weems," he said. "Actually, William, known as Weems. Looking for Dr. Chen."

"His car's not here, as you can see, and I haven't seen him since I drove up, maybe a half hour ago."

"Every time I come by, he's not here. He's a hard man to corral." Weems had to be originally from somewhere west of the Mississippi.

"Sorry, I can't help you there. Are you a patient?"

"Nope. My wife is, and I just want to get answers to a couple of questions."

"Should I tell him you were here if he returns while I'm still here? What's your last name?"

"Doesn't matter."

Odd. Definitely odd.

"If your wife's name would register, I could tell him Mrs. Whoever's husband stopped by—"

"Thanks," he interrupted, "but that's not necessary either." He waved a quasi-military salute of farewell and went back to the driver's side, got in and revved his engine before he backed carefully onto the street and headed east. A great detective I am—I didn't get his tag number. Not my problem. He probably wanted free advice about massage therapy. Unless he'd been stationed in Japan and learned the benefits of traditional Chinese medicine.

Or, Grandpa Jack whispered, *could Mrs. Whoever be one of*

A Sardonic Death

the conquests Jason told you about?

Good question. If I saw that old Falcon parked in town, I'd surreptitiously wait to see if Mrs. Whoever perambulated with a baby-buggy and, if she did, try to sneak a look at the kid. I could (occasionally) think like a detective but I was hopeless as a note-taker.

Back to work. I used measuring tapes to locate the two weeping cherries and the diameter of their canopies on my base plan. And sketched them in using my ¼-inch circles template selecting the circle that represented twenty feet. Easy-peasy.

On my way back to Eastport, I stopped for lunch downtown at Chick & Ruth's Delly. From a wall peppered with dozens of menu items favored by local politicians, I chose a sandwich named for the Mayor of Baltimore: chicken salad, bacon lettuce and tomato on multi-grain. I gave my order to the same waitress who had called Aaron "Hon" a year ago.

"Anything to drink?"

"Regular please, no cream."

She muttered "the Navy way" and poured from her pot of regular. During my four years aboard an aircraft carrier during Iraqi Freedom, not a single officer, male or female, added milk to their coffee. Just one of those things that's not done in the wardroom, like discussing politics, religion, or sex.

Thaïs, my longhaired cat who normally flakes out on my desk and occasionally does mouse duty, has found a new favorite place to hang out. Of all the soft places in our condo she could have chosen, it's my drawing board, from which I had to remind her only five thousand times Friday afternoon to vamoose. Fitting a Feng Shui bagua with its eight segments, eight directions, eight colors, and four elements that should be represented in each of the segments seemed somewhat straightforward. That was probably because I was blissfully unaware of the myriad of interacting forces that might affect the free flow of chi in Dr. Chung Yang Chen's entry garden. But fitting the bagua over the plan was totally impossible with her lying on my work.

"Sorry, Thaïs, I don't need your help here. Hop down!" *Thalump*. I bribed her off with a dish of tuna, taped down my enlarged plat base with the sketched details, and corner-taped a sheet of trace paper over it. With a bagua template, I began to contemplate where the eight Life Sectors of Dr. Chen's front garden would be placed.

The point of designing a Feng Shui garden is to promote the flow of *chi*, by arranging five elements: Wood, Earth, Metal, Water, and Fire in appropriate locations. Since each of the Life Sectors has a color, I assumed that the flow of the *chi* in Dr. Chen's garden would be enhanced with an element of the designated color. For instance, in the Wealth sector, the placement of a wood element like a purple bench, or a flowering shrub with purple flowers like a Miss Kim Lilac, would help the flow of *chi* more effectively than just a plain wood bench. Likewise, a blue glazed earthen pot in the Knowledge sector would be more beneficial than some other earth element.

I considered variations of elements and colors until my brainwaves were totally tangled.

By evening, I'd finally decided on a bubbling stone in the forefront and a Lutyens bench near the patients' path from parking to the office door. I also realized that his front doors, as well as his patients' door, would need to be painted bright red, symbolizing fire, good fortune, and joy. The dragon carving on the left door and the phoenix on the right could both be left unpainted which would enhance the wood elements in the garden. By mid-afternoon, I'd also decided on a pair of tall dark green ceramic pots to grace the entry walk to the front door, a shrub-type bamboo (a very "auspicious" plant for a Feng Shui garden) and a bubbling boulder. I ticked off the Feng Shui elements on my fingers: water (bubbling boulder), fire (red doors), earth (the pottery), and wood (the bench), and the new plants.

Madison had been right: *The best way to learn garden design is in a client's garden.* Time for theory is passed. This is where the pencil meets the paper: the preliminary stage where soft pencil lines and a lump of gray kneaded eraser are useful. Kind of like thinking aloud. I changed to a fresh sheet of trace twice before I was satisfied.

Several hours after I finally let Morpheus carry me off, I screamed myself awake from a nightmare. Thaïs hopped from my bed and scampered to Cookie for protection. I'd been tormented by a dragon with a Water Celery flower in its claw. The dragon was wearing a Dr. Chen mask.

I grabbed my new labradorite necklace from the bedside table and held it tightly, trying my best to believe it would protect me.

Chapter 11

Dad was right. Sunday morning, I had only to show my driver's license to the Arundel Island gate guard. He gave me a map of the community with Dad's address circled in red and raised the barrier.

I had never been on the island, so it took me a while to follow the twists and turns and find Severn Street. I figured the black Lexus in the driveway was Dad's. Another car of indeterminate parentage was parked behind Mom's red Ferrari. I suddenly wasn't sure I wanted to be part of the first family reunion in twenty-three years. Grandpa Jack was right. This might very well turn out to be the family reunion from hell. On a sailboat of all places.

But family reunions can be the stuff of comedy, Grandpa Jack suggested.

Yeah, sure.

Dad's front door stood open. In the living room, surrounded by bottles of vintage wines and other home remedies of higher proof, Dad was holding forth on the history of his boat. "A few years ago, it was the Samuelson's. I sailed with them a lot." When he saw me, he gestured to the bottles and glasses. No hug, of course. Dad was on a roll and wouldn't be interrupted. I smiled back and nodded to Mom, Spencer, and Janisse.

"I guess it was four years ago last April," he continued, "they took off for the Caribbean. They sent me a couple of postcards, then nothing. They never returned. When I reported them overdue, it was too late. The Coast Guard never found them or their boat. Then a year ago, it came back to Annapolis,

A Sardonic Death

repainted, with a load of cocaine. The DEA seized it and, with my help, located their son, an attorney in New York. He had no interest in the boat and offered it to me. At a very affordable price, I must say."

I was incredulous. Without a drop of alcohol in my system, I felt that history was spinning in overlapping circles. This was the same sailboat on which my St. John's College friend, Katelyn, had found bricks of cocaine the day before she died. A year ago, when I went to her funeral, I met her boyfriend Aaron, who I was now on track to marry.

When Dad stopped yakking, everyone in the room sipped their poison of choice. I poured myself a glass of quinine water and went to hug my brother and his wife, she with a bulging tummy. It was obvious that Janisse and I would be the only sober sailors this afternoon. And, as far as I knew, she was not a sailor.

"Congratulations on your expanding family," I said.

"My doc thinks it'll be twins," said Janisse.

Mom had chosen a bright red rose for her hair. "Mom, I had no idea that you and Dad had stayed in touch."

"We hadn't, but last week Spencer spilled the beans to Matthew. Then he called and this was arranged so we could all reveal our surprises." She looked directly at Janisse.

"Not much of a surprise anymore," Janisse said.

"Drink up," said Dad. "We need to get down to the *Laurel*." She's named in honor of *my* surprise: my new wife, Laurel. She's gone for supplies."

Janisse finished her ice water and turned to Mom. "And what's *your* surprise?"

Mom grinned like the proverbial cat with a feather in her whiskers and spread her left hand to show off the green gemstone. "Jade, from China. He's a wonderful man. A doctor in town. I hope you'll all come to our wedding in August."

I raised my glass. "Cheers to you three." I didn't add that in the not too distant future I would follow in their nuptial footsteps. Not with a pregnancy, though, thank you very much. Spencer and Janisse raised their glasses.

Spencer must have already drunk more than enough. He rose and began stumbling through a toast. "Here's to our wives and girlfriends: May they never meet!" At which Mom and Dad shared an artificial laugh. Then Spencer urged us to sing, "For they are jolly good fellows, for they are jolly good fellows . . ." Janisse joined half-heartedly and out of tune. It was totally bizarre. I covered my annoyance by disappearing into the lavatory to change into my sailing togs.

Laurel arrived, a red-head in a white silk shirt and white shorts, not wearing a bra, a stunning specimen of mid-life Renaissance woman. My brother's wayward eyes spent a beat too many in admiration. Her pixie hair looked like a not-very-sharp lawnmower had just passed through. Probably done by the French artiste at Mademoiselle's Hair Spa. Where I would never be found, alive or dead, with my frugality in such areas. I'm happy with an occasionally-combed ponytail.

You might change your mind before Aaron arrives for the Solstice party, Grandpa Jack whispered.

Only if I scrap my sanity, I replied, no longer certain that my desire to go sailing would triumph over the agony of spending the day with my kin.

Laurel held the booty from her liquor store raid: chilled champagne. I was sure it was not to be sacrificed to King Neptune on the bow of the sailboat. Too valuable to share with jellyfish. But if I weren't planning to stay sober this afternoon I would've loved a long swig.

To Laurel, I introduced myself, my googly-eyed brother,

A Sardonic Death

Janisse and Mom. "Welcome to the family."

"Penelope," she bubbled, "I've heard so much about you." *Really?*

Dad embraced her with an old-fashioned smacker. Still no hug for the daughter he hadn't seen in months. "Laurel used to teach psychology at the Naval Academy." I wondered if their friendship may have had its roots back when Mom disappeared.

Dad led our little parade on foot the two blocks to the yacht club and nodded to two couples as they hoisted picnic baskets aboard a miniature replica of a Chesapeake oyster-dredging skipjack. Alongside a stub pier was the *Laurel*, refinished in white as it had been when it was the Samuelson's.

"Let's gather at the bow," Dad said. I was happy to see he hadn't forgotten boating lingo. "Laurel, would you be so kind as to do the honors?"

She kneeled on the dock and leaned over to reach the sailboat's stem (the part of a boat that cuts through the water, hence: stem to stern). "Oh, ship of dreams, you who have challenged the oceans of the world, or soon will—" chuckles all around "—may your seas be always calm and the wind at your back. I christen you the 'Laurel of Arundel Island.'" She nodded demurely and reached back as far as she could as if preparing to whack the bejesus out of the sailboat. Then, holding the bottle by its neck, she arced it in slow-motion toward the bow like a slo-mo replay of a baseball hitter and tapped it gently against the bow, the cue for us to make crashing and bubbling champagne shurshing noises. And applaud.

"Well done, milady," gushed my father.

We boarded the *Laurel* and stashed our sandwiches, sunblock, hats, and drinks. Dad started the engine. "Cast off fore and aft," he called in his macho sailor voice. Spencer and I coiled the bow and spring lines on the pier where they'd be ready to snag when we returned. Mom, who had probably traveled thousands of miles on Aidan's Harley, admitted she'd never been on a sailboat and stood waiting for someone to ask her to do something. Laurel cast off the stern line and Dad, at the helm with the single lever engine control, urged the boat into forward gear and accelerated gently. As we cleared the end of the dock and entered the channel out to Arundel Bay, he acknowledged a wave from the Yacht Club security guy. "Mike tells me he's pulled dozens of the 'gold-chain' sailors here off mud-bars when the tide is out. Says they've got more hooch in 'em than water under their keel."

It must have been funny at the time but didn't earn a chuckle now.

"Joan," Dad said, "you can haul in the fenders." She gave me a shrug so I went with her to the port lifelines and unsnapped one of the three fender lines to show her how it was done. She got the other two and we returned to the cockpit where Dad motioned me to the hinged seat under which the fenders were stored. Decided that I'd have to be Mom's dutiful sidekick today since she was clearly the "odd woman out."

We turned south after clearing the northern tip of Arundel Island. When the breeze picked up, Dad slowed the engine and turned into the wind. I showed Spencer the electric jib-furling control and how to crank up the main. Dad then cut the engine, turned to port, and we were finally under sail. "Laurel," Dad said, "you may as well get the feel of the boat." He motioned her to come to the helm and take the wheel. I'd learned long ago that a sailboat with a tiller where you can really feel what the wind and the boat are doing, hopefully together, is the only way to learn to handle a sailboat. The wheel on this boat would

A Sardonic Death

be like power steering. It will move the rudder whichever way you want, but you can't feel the pressure. Laurel, however, seemed to be a quick study. She had the boat heeled on a starboard tack without, I guessed, even knowing what a starboard tack was. When a gust heeled the boat further, Janisse screeched "We're keeling over!" Spencer attempted to comfort her, but I doubted if he'd ever sailed before either.

Dad called to Laurel, "Start that sheet!" which he must have learned by sailing with midshipmen. Laurel froze. Chesapeake waves roared past, only inches below the edge of the deck. Laurel was clueless. "Ease the mainsheet," Dad yelled. She still didn't know what he wanted her to do. He pulled himself to the cam cleat that held the sheet, snapped the line out from between the cams and payed out the woven line until the mainsail eased, losing some of the wind's pressure, and the boat regained her more upright stature.

Dad sat back on the cockpit cushions and took his scotch and water from the cup holder. Laurel looked up at the more upright mast, then back at Dad with a look that said get me out of this mess.

"Penny," Dad said, "you want to take the helm?"

I thought he'd never ask. "Sure. Why not?"

Laurel looked immensely relieved when I took over. She slid in next to Dad and grabbed her Bloody Mary from her cup holder. The first thing I did was to crank in the jib sheet. The luffing jib had nearly driven me crazy while I watched the incompetent leading the blind. At the Naval Academy, I had skippered our largest sailboat in the Newport to Bermuda race. That's just to say I knew a thing or two about handling sailboats.

Janisse took this opportunity to announce that she felt a little sick and went to the hatch and stepped gingerly down into the cabin. I told her it was the wrong thing to do. Down there, without a horizon to watch, seasickness could intensify and engulf you within minutes. Spencer soon followed her, and although I'm sure his last meal was threatening to re-emerge too, he soothed his wife as well as he could. She would probably never set foot on a sailboat again.

When we finally got to the Bay, the wind shifted to the north. As we had decided to sail south to Annapolis, I set the main and the jib "wing and wing" and announced to Laurel that we, indeed, now had the wind at our back.

Laurel doled out plastic cups of champagne as traffic thundered overhead on the Chesapeake Bay bridges. I declined the champagne as did Janisse when she emerged from the cabin, now that we had the wind behind us and the ride smoothed. Spencer, Mom, Dad, and Laurel downed their bubbly and proclaimed, "Hear, hear!" and breathed deeply of the sea air.

Dad leaned back and closed his eyes. Laurel took her broad-brimmed hat and a cushion and stretched out on the cabin top between the hatch rails. Mom moved closer so we could talk.

"Were you surprised that Dad remarried?"

"I wondered why he hadn't sooner."

"He could never find anyone to match you," I snarked.

Here I was, finally enjoying a day on the water and making light of my parents' divorce when I could be trying to figure out how Aidan died. Not that I could prove anything, but someone, presumably Mom, had doctored his last meal with a bit of Water Celery root.

For a moment, I considered surprising her with news of my new client and the coincidence that he was her therapist. In that same moment a gust threatened to douse Laurel's lee rail. I

A Sardonic Death

eased the mainsheet until the gust passed.

I basked in the joy of being at the helm of a sailboat and, at the same time, tried to ignore the struggle I was having with my conscience. On the one hand, I wanted to get Ravenscroft's entry makeover installed and get professional photos taken for my portfolio. On the other, the lingering anger for my twenty-odd years of motherlessness made me anxious to see Mom brought to justice. Then there was Grandpa Jack's hint that her intended new husband may have been the one to hasten Aidan's departure. All this flew through my brain as I adjusted the rudder a half-spoke of the wheel. The thought of telling Mom about my new client had passed. Maybe I could learn something more about him from her.

"So how did you know you were ready to marry again?" I said, feigning daughterly interest.

"It's so wonderful Penny. Aidan and I cared for each other all these years. Twenty-some-odd years ago, we thought we were part of a revolution. Like we'd reawakened to the Age of Aquarius and Woodstock. For a while, we lived the life. But this is different. Partly because it's new, of course, but it's so unbelievably wonderful. You'll understand when you see us together. When the time is right."

If it sounds too good to be true, Grandpa Jack reminded me, *it probably is*. I'd heard that so many times when he was alive.

As I cranked in the main to a close-hauled starboard tack to round Greenbury Point, the sky began to change. As soon as I could see up the Severn, I knew we were in for another surprise. Low on the western horizon beyond the Naval Academy was a dark line low in the sky. A dreaded Chesapeake summer squall. By the time I coaxed Laurel into the cockpit to wake up Dad, the squall line was closer, its dark tentacles stretching to entangle us. Sunday boaters raced for harbor. A pair of Naval Academy yawls jibed, lowered their sails, and started their engines in hopes of beating the storm back into the Academy's boat basin.

The sky turned squall gray. The jib had electric furling so I punched it on.

"Dad, get the engine going. Spencer, get the main halyard off the winch and haul it down." Since he'd cranked it up, I figured he could haul it down. I eased both sheets to allow the sails to luff. Spencer released the main halyard from its winch and began pulling the big sail down. Just in time for a gust to hit that might have knocked us down if the sails had been drawing.

"We're keeling again," Janisse wailed. So much help, my sister-in-law.

"Dad, where're the sail ties?" Stiff winds nearly swept my words across the Bay. But he caught the gist of my query and pointed to a cockpit seat. I lifted it and grabbed a bundle.

"Mom, you and Dad take these and tie one around the mainsail every couple of feet."

Rain began pelting us and choppy waves increased in size and effect. The roller jib was wound tight around the stay. Mom and Dad began tying down the main as Spencer pulled it down. Finally, it was bundled and tied along the boom.

We need a place to ride out the squall, Grandpa Jack yelled silently.

Right, I said to myself. Lake Litchford. I pulled the chart from a cubby in the binnacle, glanced at it and put it back. Through the rain, I could see the flashing green buoy that marked the channel entrance. I shoved the throttle forward until we seemed to dance through the waves, the rain and the wind toward the buoy.

A Sardonic Death

Dad's cupped hands made a megaphone. "Where're you going?" he yelled.

"Don't worry, I know a place," I called back, as we pounded through waves and lashing rain toward the buoy. Dad, Spencer, and Mom huddled, bedraggled. I hoped Laurel was comforting Janisse in the cabin. It was time to let Mom know where we were headed.

"Mom, you're in for a surprise."

She held tight to the teak trim at the edge of the cabin, an expectant frown on her face. The rose in her hair was taking a beating.

"I haven't told you, but I have a new client. Turns out he's your therapist."

Mom brightened up, smiling through the rain pummeling her. "You're sure?"

"Absolutely. He lives on Lake Litchford, right? We're headed to his pier. Hang on!"

We raced past the green buoy and into the channel. When the waves calmed, I throttled down, entered the lake, and motored through the rain to Dr. Chen's pier. Mom and Dad re-hung the fenders on the pier side and Spencer found spare dock lines. I nudged the pier and slipped the engine into reverse and then neutral while Dad and Spencer threw dock lines onto the pier. Spencer jumped to the pier just as Dr. Chen, wearing boxer shorts, ran from the gazebo onto the pier.

"You need help, sir?" he called to Spencer.

A movement in the gazebo at the head of the pier caught my attention, and what to my wondering eyes should appear but a naked woman with long auburn hair climbing into her clothes. Mom, Janisse, Spence, and Dad also witnessed the transition.

"Oh," Chen said, when he noticed me, "surprise, surprise."

He looked at the others on the boat as if he were going to introduce me to strangers as his Feng Shui landscape designer.

Then he recognized Mom. While his face morphed from surprise to horror, he gasped and ran back to the gazebo. He and the woman picked up remnants of their clothing and raced through the rain to the house. Not the surprise for Mom I had intended.

In that instant, she yanked the bedraggled rose from her hair, tossed it overboard, and crumpled into a cry that broke my heart. Chen was not only her therapist but her fiancé!

Mom shuffled the jade ring off her finger, turned her back to Lake Litchford and heaved the ring over her shoulder. It was still raining so I couldn't hear it *plink* when it hit the water.

I'd heard of daughters mothering their parents but never imagined I would become one.

Chapter 12

After the woman disappeared into the dusk, Dr. Chen, sheepishly but graciously invited our boatload of refugees into his house. He phoned out for a catered dinner while we took turns in his warm shower. And gratefully accepted terry-cloth robes while our soaked sailing clothes tumbled in his dryer.

At dinner, we were all nearly mute. Before digging into an array of Chinese carryout, we started with a soup he said he'd made using local vegetables and seasonings with herbs to ward off the flu. "An old family recipe," he said, with a wry smile toward Mom.

Neither Chen nor Mom spoke more than a dozen words. I had a pretty good idea of what was going on in Mom's mind but wondered what her now *ex*-fiancé was thinking. I also wondered if his lady friend was still in the house. *In his bedroom?*

After hearing Janisse's tale of seasickness, Chen offered her and Spencer a guest bed overnight. Sunday morning, they could take a cab back to Arundel Island and their car. Dad and Laurel chose to sleep on the boat in anticipation of decent sailing weather tomorrow. I had to admit that Chen, scoundrel though he was, under the circumstances, was being very gracious.

After all the carryout dishes were demolished, he made a large pot of Jasmine tea. "Best for new guests," I said, which earned me a Dr. Chen smile. We sniffed its wonderful essence, drank it slowly, and thanked him for his kindness.

I called a cab and Mom and I waited under umbrellas in his

driveway, behind the open garage where his blood-red Mercedes waited.

"He's outta my life," Mom whispered when we were settled in the cab. "He may be a good massage therapist, but he's a charlatan."

I couldn't help but empathize with her. I too had been jilted by my once-upon-a-time fiancé. And my message had been delivered nearly as dramatically—by email to me on the *USS Enterprise*, anchored just outside Barcelona's harbor.

"Great-Aunt Zelma says folks will be folks," I said, "and nobody can make angels out of 'em."

"He doesn't deserve to live."

"Mom, you have to be thankful you learned he wasn't an angel before . . . well, before he got his claws into your bank account."

"If I were the vindictive type, I'd tear him apart." Mom slumped and began to whimper. She cried almost all the way back to Arundel Island.

Which led me to wonder if she would be capable of physically harming this man. Just because I'd never known her to be violent didn't mean she couldn't be. Didn't someone say that, given the right circumstances, *anyone* could be a murderer?

Would the prospect of marrying a wealthy widow have been a sufficient reason for Dr. Chen to have killed Aidan? Was it possible that he had actually loved Mom but had a severely warped moral compass? It was too awful to contemplate, but Grandpa Jack was right. Chen had to be considered.

By the time our cab was permitted onto Arundel Island, I'd forced my brain in a more pleasant direction. For example, the call from Roy this morning that he'd finished the estimate for

A Sardonic Death

installing Mom's new design. "He also said your installation is scheduled to start the week after next, so it'll be looking great in time for your midsummer party."

Corners of her mouth began twisting upward.

"I'll come by tomorrow and bring the contract, okay? Try to get some sleep if you can."

I paid the fare as the cab rolled to a stop at Dad's house. After a quick hug, I trailed Mom's Ferrari back out the Arundel Island gate and south to the relative sanity of my four-legged housemates.

Chapter 13

Good morning, sailor," I said into my phone early Monday morning. I tried to whistle Reveille, but my inner bugler had gone AWOL.

"Hey," Aaron said, "how's the sweetest woman on the planet?"

"You're so good at silver-tongue you could teach it."

We laughed.

"So I've been thinking about the solstice party," I said. "I hope you got my email."

"Of course. You didn't get my reply?"

"Don't B.S. me, Mr. Senior Chief. You haven't sent one. Probably spending too much time at the Club trying to pick up lonely wives."

"Touché. All right, I have been busy. But with work, not wives. One of the things I've been busy at is getting a ticket for a flight to Baltimore. It's Wednesday."

"Great. Did you get your ring-finger sized?"

"Uhhh . . ."

"In case you haven't located a jeweler, I found a place for you. Alfred's, a couple of miles from your main gate. They'll be open this afternoon."

"Roger that."

"Decide if you'd prefer silver or gold. Then let me know, Mr. Hunt."

"Sorry I've been dragging my feet."

"As long as it's not about getting *cold* feet, you're forgiven. Just don't let it happen again or I'll come after you with the frying pan."

A Sardonic Death

"Again?"

I laughed, thinking how lucky to have met a man with a similarly warped sense of humor. "So . . . I'll meet you at Thurgood Marshall on Wednesday. Let me know what flight to meet, okay?"

"Yessir, ma'am, I will." I could imagine the snap of his heels.

"Can't wait to see you, Sweetheart."

"Talk soon, my love."

I didn't much feel like a run, but I'd been lazy for too long. My personal mantra has been "Weekends are for Running." I changed into my running gear and set out with Cookie on a short leash. Her slender Dobergirl legs can match any stride, casual or full bore. We made our usual round trip twice. Roughly six miles.

In the past when there was no mother looking over my shoulder, I've been known to rehydrate with chilled chardonnay after a run. Now, with Mom reincarnated, I headed for the shower, imagining *she* might already be on her second martini or Bloody Mary.

I had just yanked off my clothes and turned on the water when my phone's mazurka trilled. I recognized the number. It was my eleven-year-old C.S.I. apprentice, Kalea, who had assisted me sleuth a Civil War flag scam in North Carolina. She and her two moms had arrived back in town from Asheville.

"Hey Punkin. How's your Maddie-Mom?"

"She's okaaay—" My design professor, Madison aka Maddie-Mom, was recovering slowly from surgery after a Civil War reenactment "accident" in North Carolina.

I could tell Kalea was not her usual upbeat self. "What's going on?"

"Are you coming over to pick up the cushions Cookie chewed?"

"Soon as I have a shower."

"I need to talk," she said, sounding very grown up.

"Hold it together, Punkin. See you in a few."

I'd attended Madison and Cheyenne's wedding in January when Maryland's same-sex marriage law came into effect. Their adopted daughter Kalea (the brilliant "niece" I thought I would never have) had adopted me as a surrogate aunt and fellow sleuth in North Carolina. While we sleuthed the death of Madison's stepfather in the Tarheel State, my Dobergirl, apparently missing my devotion, used her pearly whites to tatter several sofa and chair cushions.

When I arrived, Kalea burst through the door and jumped to hug me. "Aunt Penny!"

I was barely able to hold her. (I need to increase my push-up reps.) I looked around. "Where're your moms?"

"Gone for groceries. We just got back."

"Then this would be a good time to talk." We took the two overstuffed chairs Cookie hadn't savaged. "So what's happening?"

"I'm not sure, but both Maddy and Shy've been snappy at each other. It's about the new intern at Shy-mom's law office."

"What about her?"

"I think Shy might like Christine more than Maddy-mom. Or *me*."

Like a concussion, warning stars blinked. This was way above my pay grade and even further from any of my areas of expertise. "They're married for heaven's sake," realizing, even as the words came out of my mouth, how lame I sounded.

Kalea pulled a face. "In case you haven't noticed, *married* people get divorced."

A Sardonic Death

Aboard ship, I had counseled sailors in my division on various problems, but never about the pending divorce of their parents.

"Okay, Miss C.S.I., where's your evidence?"

She gave me her youthful version of an evil eye. "They argued about her on the plane all the way to Baltimore."

I waited for more.

"Christine's just out of law school, prepping for the bar exam." Her tone shifted to cautiously confidential. "I honestly think they're both tired of me. If they get divorced—"

"You shouldn't worry about what might never happen." I knew my advice was about as useful as a pencil sharpener at a computer convention but as I said, this was over my head.

Kalea was quiet for a couple of seconds, then said, "I'll keep collecting evidence." She brightened. "How's that design job you wanted to get back to?"

"Big surprise," I said. "The job, fortunately, is on track." Then I explained it was for a man who died while we were in North Carolina.

"*Died?*" she said. "But it's on track?"

"Here's the surprise. He was my mom's second husband."

"*What?*" Who knew such a small jaw could drop so far.

"A week ago, I met my mom whom I hadn't seen in more than twenty years."

"That's *amazing*," she said. "Kind of balances out what's happening with me and my moms."

"Kalea, you're a great kid and your moms love you. None of us can know what's around the corner, but I guarantee you'll be fine."

Again, she demonstrated her ability to turn a conversation on its head. "Tell your mom I'd like to meet her."

"She's now a co-owner of the prosthetics company her

husband started."

"So she'll be so busy with that she won't miss him too much?"

I wasn't going to go there. "We can hope."

We put the three savaged couch cushions with a plastic bag of rescued stuffing in my van. Kalea hugged me farewell.

At McGonagle's Upholstery, Gus looked over the savaged cushions, shook his head in despair, but agreed to effect the repairs. For a handsome fee. It's a good thing I love that dog.

I'd promised Tony I'd come back to my day job today, but it was almost noon when I finally checked in at Lewis & Gregory. Tony was on the phone. He frowned and held up a finger. I nodded and sat facing his desk.

"Johnny," Tony said in a confidential tone, "you and I have known each other since Harvard and you know the reputation L&G has in this town, so it wouldn't matter to me if you wanted to sell ice to Eskimos—" (I cringed inwardly, supposing only English majors have an autonomous cliché alert) "—we could make it happen. You're opening a boating supplies franchise. This is the time, this is the place, and we're your team." I applauded noiselessly and waited for the schmooze to wrap up.

"This will be up your alley," Tony said when he'd hung up. I had no idea what he meant and, with my question-mark face pointed to his phone. He nodded. "Clean up your desk and meet me at Harry Browne's, say one?" Harry Browne's restaurant on State Circle is where I got engaged the first time—now ancient history. It's where Tony . . . that is . . . Mr. Lewis and I discuss projects he wants me to work on. I'll just say that there are a lot worse places to dine with your boss, and he always puts it on his tab. It also has the added benefit of

A Sardonic Death

being only two blocks from our office.

There wasn't much in my in-box so I checked in with our graphic artist, Steve. "You like boats, right?"

He looked suspicious. "So what's wrong with the one you're trying to sell?" I laughed.

I told him the insignificant amount I'd overheard about the boating equipment store project. My cell phone started "When the Saints Go Marching In." It was Mom. "I'll keep you posted," I said, and blew him a sisterly kiss.

"Mom?" She was crying. The reality of her broken engagement was sinking in. "Should I come and see you?" She sniffled a "please" and I promised I'd come as soon as I could after the five o'clock Naval Academy chapel bells rang. The Big Ben style bells could be heard every fifteen minutes all over downtown but probably not as far as the Simms Creek estates where Mom lived.

I was already in Harry Browne's sumptuous dining room when Tony arrived. The maître d' has learned that if I come in, he can expect Tony momentarily. "Always a treat, Mr. Lewis," is his standard line when he ushers Tony to my table. Tony glanced at me, giving me the opportunity to order.

"The usual, if you please," I said. (Roasted Veggie and Mozzarella Panini . . . and chardonnay.)

Tony asked for his usual: pastrami and Swiss on rye and a Black Jack Stout. While he unbuckled his military-style navigator's bag, I refreshed my memory of the old chandeliers, wall sconces, and the antique pressed tin ceiling. The first time I'd met Tony here, I was trying to find out who had killed my newest friend at St. John's College. Today my avocational responsibility was to figure out who was responsible for Aidan's ingesting poisonous Water Celery roots.

Unless designing landscapes is no longer an avocation,

Grandpa Jack reminded me from beyond the grave.

Oh that, I whispered silently. Soon to be my sole *vocation*, I hoped.

Tony pulled a folder from his bag and laid it between us. A waiter brought my wine and Tony's stout. Tony slurped foam and set down the glass.

"Our client," he said, "is Dylan Caque Brody . . . the third." Tony explained his friend's unusual middle name. "We called him Johnny at school, Johnny Cake. He wouldn't appreciate my mentioning that to you, so—"

I said it slowly. "Dylan Brody." The Irish name somehow carried ominous overtones.

Tony opened the folder.

"So why does he want to sell boat supplies?"

"He thinks it'll dovetail with his interest in ocean cruising. He's been some kind of salesman all his life. At Harvard, he imported Irish sweaters. When he bundled his profits, he began importing Irish fabrics, all kinds of doodads and—"

"Have you ever asked about his politics?" I was thinking IRA, but that's probably because I read too much.

"Penny, that'd be like asking someone what stocks he's invested in."

"Sorry. Curious Georgette was suspicious."

"Who?"

"It's my nickname from asking too many questions when I was a kid."

"What would his politics have to do with opening a boat supplies store?"

"Sorry," I said. "I watch too many BBC mysteries."

The waiter returned with our sandwich plates, both heaped with their famous sweet potato fries.

"Isn't it the merchant's decision what to do with his

A Sardonic Death

profits?" Tony asked.

I pondered that with a sip of wine. "Okay, what's he got in mind?"

Tony popped two fries and washed them down. "The name he wants to use is Brody's Boat Works. And the logo image he wants is an old boathouse with a sailboat hauled up on the railway."

Tony took a sheet from the folder. "Dylan made up the tagline: 'From stem to stern, Brody's got it.'"

"Makes him sound like an amateur." I lunged into my sandwich and surmised that Mr. Brody might not have a full complement of salesman DNA.

"Penny, will you take the lead on this one?"

I gave it a swallow of wine and winced at the memory of dealing with clients like the drug barons we had last year. "If you trust this guy to work with us in good faith, I'll take your word for it."

Tony gobbled half his sandwich, wrapped the other half in a linen napkin, and finished his beer.

Right on cue, my sandwich ejected a pickle into my lap. It had happened before. "Don't laugh," I said as I rescued it and put it on the plate. "You should be used to this little diversion of mine."

Tony laughed and handed me the project folder. "I've got a meeting in ten minutes. Check this out and let's talk again." He picked up his wrapped sandwich and handed me a bill with a portrait of Ulysses S. Grant. "Leave a decent tip," he said, "and save me the receipt. Tell the waiter I'll return the napkin."

I had mixed feelings. I needed this job and, at the same time, hoped my Summers Breeze Gardening business would take off so I could kiss this whole ridiculous public relations gig goodbye.

Chapter 14

I finished my panini slowly, perusing the single sheet in the folder Tony had given me. There wasn't much more information about Mr. Brody's project in it than what he'd said.

As I tipped up the dregs of my chardonnay, our waiter reappeared. I handed him the fifty-dollar bill and explained the missing napkin. "Not to worry," he said and a moment later returned with the check and change. I left most of it on the table, pocketing the check and some of the remnants of the fifty dollars for Tony. The folder went in my backpack as I waved "Bye" to the maître d'.

On my way back around State Circle to our office, my mind was a blank. I couldn't think of how to approach my new project. "Goddess, grant me an idea," I whispered into the Chesapeake breeze. How on earth I could make Brody's BoatWorks stand out from our myriad of boat supply stores? Annapolis, after all, is not only a genuine colonial-era town but a sailing center for the entire East Coast. I'd need to come up with a unique gimmick. That's what we'd be paid for, right?

By the time I walked through the Lewis & Gregory door, the Goddess had a suggestion: visit boating supplies stores and divine how they might be improved.

By mid-afternoon, I'd visited two and started a list. I was browsing in a third when a woman who looked to be about my age, dressed like a Vogue model, approached.

"Aren't you Penelope Summers, the landscape designer?"

"Well . . . yes." I gave her what I hoped was an agreeable smile. "Have we met?" Then a flash of panic. I might not have

89

any Summers Breeze business cards in my backpack. So much for my marketing skills.

"I'm Thalia." She smiled broadly. "I've seen your picture on your van."

I chuckled. Steve, our L&G artist, had taken the shot of me holding a blue Salvia ready to plant. I have to admit that it enlarged nicely.

"Dr. Chen told me you were applying Feng Shui principles to a new design for his entry garden."

That's when I realized this was probably the same woman we'd seen in Dr. Chen's gazebo. I hadn't had a good look at her as she fled, but her stature and hair color looked identical. Our circles of acquaintances, I imagine, overlap more often than we're aware.

"That was kind of him. Are you thinking of improving *your* garden?"

"Oh no. My husband and I are live-aboards. Our sailboat is the *Haleakala,* up Spa Creek. It's the tallest mast you can see from the bridge. Our only garden is a pot of basil, I'm afraid."

I relaxed a smidge when I found cards in an inner pocket of my backpack. I pulled one and handed it to her. "It's nice to meet *you*. If you decide to install a roof garden, please call." I was only half joking.

"I may do that," she said. Then, "If I may ask, what brings a landscape designer to a boat supply store?"

I explained that my love of sailing didn't involve boat ownership, but my day job had a lot to do with being here. She asked if we could get acquainted over coffees.

We met at City Dock Coffee. Thalia, looking like a Victoria's Secret model with her long auburn hair hanging to her shoulders and I in my jeans and a Life is Good tee shirt sat at a bistro table on the sidewalk.

"Have you known Dr. Chen long?" she asked.

Could Thalia have suggested coffees to discover if we were competitors for Chen's affections?

"It's been only a few days since he asked me to work on his garden," I said. "You?"

"Since last fall. Charles travels a lot so the doctor and I play a lot of tennis."

Tennis may not be the only game they play, Grandpa Jack whispered.

"Hey," I said. "It's a great way to stay in shape. So what's your interest in boat supplies?"

"Simple. Charles leaves me a honey-do list before he leaves. This week it's a broken cabinet latch."

The Goddess had an idea. "You must've bought boating supplies all over this town," I said. "Based on the best features of the ones you know, if you could design your ideal boat supplies emporium, what would it be like?"

We chatted for nearly an hour. Some of her ideas I had already considered. One that I had not was to have a sailboat race video game in the store with terminals for two virtual sailors. Another, I thought, was even more brilliant: During Boat Show weeks, offer free rides from the dock to the store in golf carts converted into boatmobiles. We tossed those ideas around for a while before I decided I'd schmoozed long enough on my boss's nickel. On a gorgeous summer day. Who could wish for anything more?

Tony was back in his office when I dropped in to explain where I'd been. And a few of the ideas Thalia and I had come up with.

"Nice," he said. "How soon would you like me to arrange a meeting with Mr. Brody?"

"How 'bout Thursday?"

A Sardonic Death

I spent the rest of the afternoon sketching floor plan ideas. It was almost five when I waltzed into our graphics studio and asked Steve to make a three-dimensional sketch of my proposed floor plan that Tony and I could take to Mr. Brody. Along one edge, Steve would add boatmobile sketches of street-legal six-person golf carts modified to represent a classic wood Chris-Craft, Chesapeake Skipjack, the Queen Mary, and an aircraft carrier complete with little F-22s ready to launch on miniature catapults.

The five o'clock chimes from the Naval Academy chapel carillon rang out. But before heading to Ravenscroft and my tearful mom, I visited the Hillsmere Garden Center. Roy dug out the paperwork he'd prepared for Mom's renovation, complete with pictures of each of the plants I'd specified, all in a dark green binder. Then he explained the contract for the installation and Hillsmere's requirement for a series of three payments.

"If Mom signs it and writes a check tonight," I said, "you'll have it in the morning."

"Then I'll pencil in next Monday as our start day, okay?"

"*Wow,* you weren't kidding when you said her installation could be done earlier."

"We aim to please."

"While I'm here," I added, "I have another client you'll probably be working with."

"Tell me."

"He's a Chinese doctor and I'm designing a Feng Shui garden for him. I'm going to suggest a bubbling boulder. You could probably get Jason Keller to help with it. He taught the water-gardening module of the Master Gardeners' training. Day job is detective."

"Tell Sherlock I'll be calling."

Chapter 15

I pulled up to the small stone post at the Ravenscroft gate and pressed the button. I loved to watch the big bronze center circle in the iron gates split, the two halves sliding sideways.

Mom met me at the door, her eyes weepy and red. I hesitated only slightly, then hugged her as she drew me in. I could say only, "I am so sorry Mom."

She nodded into a tear-flooded hankie.

"Here's some news that might cheer you," I said. "Roy plans to start work here next week."

A tiny sparkle shined through her tears as she beckoned me into her spacious living room. A cocktail shaker alongside an empty martini glass (except for the uneaten olive) told me all I needed to know. She picked up the shaker, poured the second martini (from that mix, at least), and sipped.

"What can I get you, dear?"

The elegance of the room conjured the last chapter of a Sherlock Holmes story in which I would star as the detective sipping a sherry while leaning on the dark mahogany mantle and dissecting the alibis of the several gathered guests to finally reveal who had dispatched Aidan Reid to the crematorium. The mental image dissipated almost as quickly as it had formed. "A chard?" I suggested.

She gazed into her martini as if expecting to find wine instead of gin. Then looked up. "Could you get it yourself? It's in the fridge."

I returned with the wine and sat at the end of the couch nearest her chair. She continued to stare into her martini. "I

A Sardonic Death

wish I'd waited till you could go with me."

Seems I was still in the Mothering Mom business. "You visited your lawyer," I guessed.

"Not *my* lawyer. Jeff Gratrix was Aidan's lawyer."

"So tell me."

Dabbed her hankie at the corner of each eye. "We're in trouble."

"*We're* in trouble?"

"Okay. *I'm* in trouble."

Mom wasn't a sailor in my division on the *Enterprise* who'd gotten herself pregnant. Not *that* kind of trouble. "Can you be a little more specific?"

She finished most of her second martini and put down the glass. "His will leaves essentially everything to the business. Jeff said Aidan wanted his company to prosper so that I would continue to benefit."

"That's not a *good* thing?"

"Okay. Let me go back a bit. Ten years ago, I think. Maybe eleven, Aidan started importing prosthetics. That's how Prosthetonics was born. With all the Middle East vets returning without legs and arms, the business has done quite well." She picked up her empty glass and looked into it as if it held the essence of the wealth she had referred to. "So when Tanya came along, an ex-Army reservist with a prosthetic arm—the ambulance she was driving took an IED—anyway, her family has big money . . . and connections. She talked Aidan into allowing her to buy in and she became a co-owner. Now, of course, she's the sole owner—whom I've never trusted. With the exception of her friend, Colleen, her *assistant*. I'll tell you about *her* later."

"Mom, could you get to the point? What about insurance? Did Aidan have life insurance?"

"Well, of course. Thank goodness. That'll keep me going until her big idea—"

"What big idea?"

"It's supposed to become the next technological breakthrough in the industry. Tanya's dad is heavily invested and she's convinced it'll work. It's a method of connecting brain impulses directly to mechanical fingers or whatever. Jeffery explained that if the patient wants to, say, pick up his martini glass, his brain triggers the embedded Bluetooth thingie and it sends the impulse to the prosthesis." She demonstrated by reaching in slow motion for her glass and wrapping her fingers around it.

"Sounds like NASA could use it to get robots to conduct research on asteroids," I said. "Except, of course, Bluetooth signals can't travel that far."

Mom stood and faced the hall. "I'm going to mix another martini. Can I refill your wine?"

I picked up my half-full glass and followed her to the kitchen. "How often do you see Miss Nowick or whatever?"

"Novak. Tanya was at the funeral but she was actually here with her assistant, Colleen, the day he died. Said they needed to plan some strategy or something and since Aidan hadn't been at the office for a week, joked that they'd bring the mountain to Mohammed."

While Mom poured gin into the shaker and added a few drops of vermouth, I opened the fridge and pulled out the chardonnay. "Did Tanya visit very often?"

"I first met her at last year's pool party."

"Tell me about her."

"Early thirties, gorgeous. She's been a model for the prosthesis she uses as her right arm. Looks like something Hollywood could have dreamed up for a humanoid alien."

"Brains *and* beauty."

A Sardonic Death

"I'm convinced Aidan was in love with her," she said, "or at least *thought* he was in love. Isn't it strange," she said, "how love can get interrupted?" Martinis were helping her wax philosophical.

Was she thinking of Aidan and Tanya or of Dr. Chen's shamelessness? Or of Aidan's apparent loss of interest in her?

"Did you say Tanya now has an *assistant?*"

"She persuaded Aidan to hire Colleen as her assistant just a couple of months ago."

"Was Aidan was attracted to her too?"

"I met her for the first time at the 'Mountain to Mohammed' meeting. I doubt if she was attractive to Aidan. She's nice enough but rather plain compared to Tanya."

"So, what *about* Aidan's *will?*"

"Jeffery says there's nothing to be done now. The will stands and we just have to keep our fingers crossed that Prosthetonics prospers."

It occurred to me that, aside from Mom and Dr. Chen, given the promising new prosthetics technology, the new owner of Prosthetonics might have had reasons to want Aidan out of the way, leaving the business solely in her hands.

You're never going to learn how Aidan died, Grandpa Jack warned, *if you keep adding to your list of suspects.*

"Mom, if all the Prosthetonics staff was at Aidan's funeral, can I borrow the Memory Book with the sappy sayings?"

She rose unsteadily and left the room. "I almost tossed it," she said when she came back. "I'll never need to remember who wrote, 'When the Angels carried him away, they Scattered the Stardust of Memories.'" She jabbed a gag-me finger at her mouth and handed me the book, too glad to be rid of it to ask why I wanted it.

On the cover, MEMORIES was woven through the purple

clouds of a tropical sunset. I dropped it in my backpack and pulled out the Hillsmere Gardens contract. "Here's Roy's contract for the installation. He plans to bring his crew to start a week from today. He's thinking it'll take three days at the most. So it'll be finished in plenty of time for your party."

Mom signed the contract and wrote a check for the first payment, adding the smiley-face under her signature without batting a blue-tinted eyelash. A smile broke out across her tear-stained cheeks. The prospect of getting her new entry garden installed had raised her spirits.

I returned to my van wondering if her tears had been bogus. Or could she be genuinely concerned that she might lose her mansion and her lifestyle?

Chapter 16

After the revelations at Ravenscroft, I returned to my condo, fed and walked Cookie, then sat at my desk with the memory book from Aidan's funeral listing all the "mourners." After adding Mom and Chen to the list, I assumed I had a complete catalog of suspects. Like any good detective worth her salt, I would have to eliminate them one by one.

Then I picked up my latest gently-used bookstore find from Peter Robinson, poured two fingers of Laphroaig, and lost my way somewhere in Eastvale. I managed to sleep through my alarm the next morning, finally awakening to Thaïs gently pawing my nose.

I dressed quickly, attended to my menagerie, and raced downtown. With a mug of coffee from our break room, I went to inspect Steve's work on the BoatWorks floor plan.

"What brings you to Steverino's emporium?"

"Do I need a reason to visit the artist at work?"

"Five bucks to watch, ten if you try to help."

I moseyed to his side until I could glimpse over his shoulder. His version of my BoatWorks floor plan looked good. I zipped my mouth shut and gave him an emphatic thumbs up.

At my lunch break, I sent Aaron a panicked email:

> Dear Aaron - Annapolis is no longer the peaceful town we knew last year. A poisonous plant has invaded—called alternately Water Celery, Water Dropwort or Devil's Parsnip. Mom brought it back from Sardinia. Verrry

poisonous! The hell of it is that I think she may have used it to hasten Aidan's death.

My schedule, except for an L and G project at the moment, is totally crazy. Fortunately, neither Cookie nor Thais seem to be affected. I hope I can regain an even keel before you get here. Stand by for a lengthy briefing on the ride to Annapolis. After that, my attention will be totally on you.

What flight? What time?

Love you! Penny (mmmm)

Frenzied but determined, I called Jason to ask if I could visit him that evening.

"Might not be home until six," he said. I said I'd be there.

I jogged back to my Eastport condo, fed and walked Cookie, and put out fresh tuna for Thaïs. Even brushed out her undercoat which resulted in contented purrs. (That's what you sign up for with a longhaired cat.) Just for fun, before I left, I put a Sherlock story open on the couch and turned on a reading lamp in case either of my housemates cared to study the famous detective's work.

Headed out of town, at a stoplight when it was safe to check my iPhone, I checked my mail for the fifth time. Still nothing from Aaron. When I looked up, the light was still red. Cheyenne, Kalea's lawyer-mom, and a younger woman were crossing Rowe Boulevard from the District Court to the Court of Appeals. This had to be Christine, the intern Kalea was worried about. Almost as tall as Cheyenne, with dark hair and a cute face, was all I could register before the light turned green and I turned toward the Severn River bridge. I could understand Kalea's concern. My heart ached for my CSI-wannabe "niece," hoping her home wouldn't fall apart.

I'd been to Jason's place once, a year ago, to pick up the

A Sardonic Death

supplies for the Reid's pond planting job. He'd said he'd pay me for my time but I blew it off, having garnered the design job for Aidan, and grateful for Jason's help in the past. Plus, I wasn't interested in doing pond chores. I didn't think messing about in ponds would ever be in Summers Breeze Gardening's repertoire. I still don't.

Jason came to the door in shorts, pulling a tee-shirt over his head. "Care for a brew?" he asked.

"Whatever you've got."

He ducked into the house and I did my best to erase the glimpse of his six-pack abs. The screen door banged as he returned with two Yuenglings and handed one to me. We took the two ancient yard-sale chairs on either side of an old varnished stump that could have been split for firewood if it hadn't found its calling as a porch table. He took a swig and set his bottle on it.

"What've you got?"

"I'm worried."

"You need help with a pond?"

"Probably, but that's not why I came."

"First things first, then."

"Okay." I sipped the beer. "First, I gave your name to Roy at Hillsmere Gardens so you may find yourself building a water feature for a client of mine. I'm suggesting a bubbling boulder for your Doctor Chen's front garden."

He took a long swallow. "Should be fun. Have to check my catalogues." He lifted his eyes, his mental gears grinding. "And maybe buy a diamond drill bit." He lowered his gaze. "And what's the real reason you came all this way to talk with your pond guy?"

"Remember the Water Celery in Mom's pond?"

"How's it doing?"

"Like a weed. I've pleaded with her to have you yank it out."

"She hasn't called."

"She insists it looks interesting among the other marginals. Which of course it does. She's not at all concerned about how poisonous it is." I sipped again. "Which brings me to a dilemma."

"Don't tell me—"

I reminded him of the derivation of the term *sardonic smile*.

"So if I get a call about the mysterious death of anyone who knows Dr. Chen—*or* your mom, I should check if the victim is smiling." He grinned in a gruesome imitation of a death grimace.

Jason picked up his brew and turned the bottle. "We have to consider the evidence. Just that Aidan died with a sardonic grimace doesn't prove that any particular person provided the—what is it—Water Celery?"

"So you'll concede that Aidan was likely poisoned, but as far as whodunnit, you don't care that he may have been murdered?"

"Penny, I care, but—really—do you think I could investigate what might have been a murder when all I have is hearsay?"

I hadn't yet tried my pouty face on Jason, so I gave it a shot.

Jason swigged the last of his beer and set the can on the stump. "Okay, Curious Georgette, I'll play. Who profits from Aidan's death? If he had life insurance worth a bundle then the beneficiary could come under suspicion."

"His prosthetics business gets the lion's share."

"Not your mom? Is she going to be okay?"

A Sardonic Death

"As long as Prosthetonics prospers. The co-owner—"

"Anyone I know?"

"Tanya Novak."

He glanced into his memory circuits. "Does this Tanya have a prosthetic arm?"

"That's what Mom says."

"Does her dad own Novak Laboratories?"

"No idea, except that he's invested in prosthetic device development. And might have given Tanya the money to buy into Aidan's business."

"I think she was on the cover of a fitness magazine recently."

"Matches what Mom says."

I savored my beer and wondered how this might be connected to Aidan's death.

"Well, for your mom's sake," Jason said, "I hope the business prospers."

"You don't mind if I sniff around? He was, after all, my stepfather, even though I never realized it."

"Be my guest," Jason said. "But if anything comes up I should be aware of—"

"Right."

And that's where we left it. Jason wasn't interested and I couldn't blame him. There was nothing, really, that definitively pointed to murder. Aidan's death could have been planned or could have been an accident. Anyone might have put Water Celery root in a salad, a stew, or in almost any kind of vegetarian recipe. But on purpose? And make it look like Mom was at fault?

The sixth time was a charm. Aaron had shot me an email with his arrival time.

Chapter 17

Wednesday, I briefed Tony on the ideas that Steve would be illustrating for our meeting with Dylan Brody the following day.

When four o'clock rolled around, I had only one thing in mind: meeting Aaron at the airport in Baltimore. I ran to where I'd parked in the West Street Garage, jumped in my van, and headed north. At a stoplight, I checked online and found that Aaron's Delta flight was on time. I also primped a little if you'd call finger-combing a ponytail primping.

When I turned onto the I-195 spur to the airport, Aaron phoned. He'd already picked up his baggage and was waiting at the ARRIVALS level. Four minutes later, I spotted him and pulled to the curb, blocking in a car rental bus. We met at the rear of my van where we hugged, kissed, hugged again until the bus honked, and opened the back doors for Aaron's luggage. In that order.

After I'd found my way back to I-95, we noodled over our engagement ring exchange at the Solstice party on Saturday, my plan to have him meet my mom, and my Brody's BoatWorks project. Then he asked how I felt about meeting my mother after all these years. I said she seemed like the one I knew long ago in some ways (like wearing a red flower in her hair) but she was mostly a stranger—with the emphasis on *strange*, "hearing" Aidan in the house and "seeing" him on the pier.

Aaron then wanted to know if I had considered that I might have inherited her gene for weirdness, imagining, I supposed, our lives forty years in the future when he might be faced with

A Sardonic Death

handling an eccentric partner. I couldn't blame him. Who knew?

At the condo, I walked Cookie while he unpacked. We began the pre-prandial hour with wine and Aaron's favorite dark rum, the Gosling's I'd picked up for him, water on the side. A blissful hour later the doorbell rang. Aaron insisted on throwing on his clothes and answering the door to the Great Wall of China delivery guy.

After we tucked the leftover Kung Pao chicken in the fridge and tossed on the rest of our clothes, we headed to Zellender's Jewelers. I'd already confirmed with Mr. Zellender that he'd take my ten-year-old engagement ring in trade for Aaron's ring. Mr. Z examined the old ring with his loupe, looked up and smiled. "Your former fiancé didn't skimp. This is a Hearts and Arrows cut diamond. That cut takes a long time, so it was expensive and it's still valuable."

I didn't ask for his estimate of trade-in value since it would probably hinge on what we would buy. First on my list was a ring for Aaron. He found one with an onyx stone that I approved of, and I bought it while I sent him to find an engagement ring for me. I didn't want him to see his again until Saturday.

He was like a kid in a bicycle store, happily picking out a shiny new one that would be the envy of his classmates. "Penny, look at this." He'd found a gorgeous emerald-cut solitaire diamond in the vintage cabinet. Mr. Z slid behind the counter, unlocked the cabinet and brought the ring on its black velvet stand up to the counter. My heart rate jumped.

"It's beautiful. May I try it?"

With a genial tip of his head, "Of course, Miss."

I slipped it on and held up my hand. It looked perfect and, surprisingly, it nearly fit. Probably only a single size adjustment.

"It's just right," Aaron pronounced. "It really is."

"Aaron, my sweet, I agree." I grabbed his face and planted a kiss.

Mr. Z noticed the size problem. "We can resize it for you. No additional charge." He slipped the ring onto a sizing stick and I chose the ring that fit. "Tomorrow afternoon okay?"

"Okay," Aaron said, "now you go find something to entertain yourself—" he grinned at Mr. Zellender "—while we settle this."

I hadn't wandered far when Mr. Z called me back. He held up a small calculator. "I have good news, Miss Summers. The diamond you brought in will more than cover the cost of both your rings."

"Sweet . . ." I whispered.

"Would you like a check for the balance?" I said that would be fine and gave him my address and phone. Grinning like fools, we turned to leave.

The same young woman I'd seen with Cheyenne was looking into a display cabinet across the store. I pretended to look in other display cases in order to keep my back to her. As I prodded Aaron toward the door, I overheard her ask about unisex engagement rings.

Outside, "Why the quick exit?" Aaron asked.

On our way back, I filled him in on the Cheyenne-Christine-Madison triangle. Arranging a meal with Kalea and her moms was going to be dicey. I knew Aaron and Kalea wanted to see each other, but after the family reunion on the water, I'd had my fill of awkward family dynamics. Still, it had to be done.

Last on my to-do list was to invite Mom to dine with Aaron and me. She accepted enthusiastically and we agreed to

A Sardonic Death

confirm it the next day.

Over nightcaps, I entertained Aaron with stories of our family sailing debacle. More stuff he needed to know before he met Mom.

With another summer storm brewing, I opened the bedroom windows. Soon, I was too busy to count the seconds between the lightning flashes and the ensuing crescendos of thunder.

When we finally disentangled, it was well past midnight and thunder still rumbled gently from somewhere on the other side of Chesapeake Bay.

Chapter 18

Thursday morning, I walked into L&G a half hour late. Krysta, Tony's administrative assistant looked up and tapped her watch. I responded with what I hoped was a wouldn't-*you*-like-to-know smile. "Are we still on to meet with Mr. Brody today?"

Krysta assumed an exaggerated nose-in-the-air pose. "It'll be on his yacht—" she pronounced it yaa-ott "—at noon. The *Lizzie*, his 'tendah' will meet you at the dock at 11:45."

Grandpa Jack whispered his surprise. *Tender. Not a dinghy. Meaning the yaa-ott is huge.*

Oops. I would have to reschedule lunch with Aaron at Harry Browne's. He was at the Naval Academy hobnobbing with friends from his time as a teaching assistant and we had planned to rendezvous on Maryland Avenue at 12:30. I texted him: Client meeting with Tony at noon. Sorry. See you about 5. Love, P. He could eat at the Drydock in Bancroft Hall or on the quad with the burgers for lunch bunch. I'd make it up to him tonight.

I picked up the zippered binder Steve had loaded with sketches for the project: the BoatWorks logos, the storefront, the 3-D store layout, and the three boatmobile ideas that Thalia Johnson had dreamed up. I showed the pages to Tony and he bestowed his blessing. "*Verrry* nice, Penelope. Good job."

The *Elizabeth's* tender was on time. Craig, her First Mate, as he identified himself, wore a Greek fisherman's cap and epaulets on a military-style neatly-creased short-sleeved white shirt. "Welcome," he said in a distinct upper-class English accent. He took my hand as I stepped into the beautiful wooden

A Sardonic Death

tender that could have graced the cover of WoodenBoat magazine. Tony and I introduced ourselves as Craig steered out to the yaa-ott in the harbor. I suddenly felt underdressed in my black pants and boat-neck sweater.

Tony spoke over the small outboard's muffled putter. "Have you seen Captain Brody's yacht?"

Now it was *Captain* Dylan Brody. I shook my head.

"If you like to sail, ask him when he plans to do another circumnavigation," Craig said. "You might wangle an invitation."

Ask if I can go, Grandpa Jack whispered.

We bumped against a padding-edged platform at the base of a folding stairway that led up to the *Elizabeth's* deck. A clever boatswain had covered the boarding ladder railings with intricate ropework all the way to the quarterdeck where Captain Brody greeted us. Tony held out his arm for a shake. Instead, Brody grabbed him in a bear hug. "Tony!"

"Good to see you again, Johnny." Tony was muffled in the embrace.

The *Elizabeth* was larger than any sailboat I'd ever been on, more than twice as long as the Naval Academy sloop I'd skippered in the Newport to Bermuda race. It looked like it had been transported from the era of the America's Cup races in the 1920s. As if it were a Navy ship, I almost requested permission to come aboard and salute the flag that hung demurely from a polished flagpole at the stern. I scanned the luxurious details: bright bronze fittings, polished teak trim, and underfoot, a huge rope mat woven in a Celtic design.

"And who is this delicious young woman?" Brody asked.

I'd never been called delicious, but I figured there's a first time for everything. Dylan Brody was in his forties, clean-shaven and handsome in a world-traveler sort of way. *I'd need to watch myself with this debonair rogue.*

"Penelope, our idea wizard," Tony said.

I no doubt reddened as I shifted the portfolio to my left hand and reached to shake his hand. But instead of taking it, he pulled me into an embrace of sorts where I got a whiff of some exotic aftershave.

"A pleasure to meet you," he said as he released me.

The embrace had so unhinged me that I stumbled over my rejoinder. "I'm, uh—honored to meet you, sir."

"My dear, please call me Dylan."

Unlike his first mate, he was hatless. No prideful captain's cap with gold braid scrambled on the brim. His red hair was fading toward sandy, his striking features weather-worn. I wasn't sure if either *Yessir* or *Right-o* would be appropriate so I pasted on a discreet smile and nodded.

"Well," he said, "let's go to the cockpit."

He led us aft to where two steps down landed us in a party-sized cockpit. In the center was the helm: a four-foot wheel embellished with elaborate ropework and a Turk's head where each spoke met the wheel. Easy to grip in a storm. The binnacle that housed the compass was a polished brass dome. Over us, an awning stretched over the boom from port to starboard, shading the entire cockpit.

"Sir?" said a waiter who materialized from the hatch.

"What would you like to drink?" Brody asked us, gazing at Tony and then to me. "The sun's not quite over the yardarm but, as the captain, I decree that it shall be for purposes of enjoying the afternoon."

"Scotch and water would be great," Tony said.

"Laphroaig," Brody said to his waiter, pronouncing it *la frog*. "Nothing but the best for my brother." Then he turned to me and explained the reference to his 'brother.' "Adelphi Dia

A Sardonic Death

Bios, Brothers throughout life. It's our fraternity motto. And for you, my dear?"

"Chardonnay is my summer preference," I said.

"Karim, break out a bottle of Chateau Genot-Boulanger 2009 for Miss Penelope."

"Sir."

"Please also bring us a Veuve Clicquot La Grande Dame '93 . . . and three flutes."

This whole adventure was way over my pay grade . . . and my comprehension. I'd never heard of these vintages. After today, I'd probably never hear of them again.

"I went ashore this morning," Brody said to Tony, "to get acquainted with your commercial real estate offerings."

"Anything promising?" Tony said.

"A couple of possibilities, but Raymond has several more for me to visit tomorrow."

Karim returned with the drinks and the champagne, its lattice of wire over the cork partially loosened, and a tray of lobster sandwiches. Brody handed me a softball-sized wine glass and poured the French chardonnay far north of where a bartender would have dared. It took no more than a single sip of this full-bodied buttery nectar to send me to Nirvana. Entranced would be a better word. The gentle kiss of a wayward Chesapeake breeze may have enhanced the effect. The *Elizabeth's* galley obviously included a wine cellar because the sip had precisely the right amount of chill. After the second sip, I was ready to fly. I'd missed lunch so, even after tucking into a lobster sandwich, I knew the countdown to lift-off wouldn't take long. I heard Tony and Dylan's voices, as if at a distance. Their conversation drifted in and out of my consciousness until I heard Tony say, "Penny, Johnny'd like to see your ideas."

Brody refilled his own tumbler of Scotch, took a swallow and beamed at me with the kind of warmth that could melt a marshmallow. "What've you got for me?" he asked. I hoped he wasn't reading my mind.

Grandpa Jack wondered if the question was a double-entendre. Was Brody asking for the drawings, or for *me?*

I have no idea, I replied silently. I needed to get a grip.

I unzipped the presentation binder while my imagination leaped to where I'd last heard that sound.

Grandpa Jack punched my arm. *What is wrong with you?* I had no answer.

Dylan's gorgeous eyes burrowed into mine. What was happening? What *had* happened? My normally unflappable self seemed to have been sucked into an alternate reality in which I was a whimsical schoolgirl.

The binder lay open in my lap. I moved closer to him and opened it to the first page where Steve and I had developed three variations of his "Brody's BoatWorks" logo. His aftershave was rapidly derailing my train of thought.

"That's the one," Brody said, tapping his forefinger on the first one, smiling into my soul.

Tony slugged his Scotch. "Brilliant choice," he pronounced, as much, I thought, for Brody's selection as for my ideas and Steve's artwork. He wore a smile a mile wide. Brody's project would keep us all in clover.

Our client flipped a page to our impression of a BoatWorks storefront, a contemporary version of a vintage store. "Magnifico," he exclaimed.

So far, I had all the right answers. I had the feeling as if I were on the stand to win this man's love rather than approval of a project design.

You're losing touch with reality, Grandpa Jack whispered.

A Sardonic Death

I must have been because I wasn't paying attention. My Great Aunt Zelma's North Carolina term for what I was feeling was *bumfuzzled*. I knew I had to make it through this tribunal and get back to real life before I lost the plot. I was already worried about how I would describe this meeting to Aaron.

The next page was Steve's 3-D rendition of my store layout ideas. "Dylan," I said, enjoying the taste of his name on my tongue and losing track of the explanation I'd prepared. "Mr. Brody, we've looked at all the boat supply stores around Annapolis, and . . . and, we think we've created something better than all of them." I was afraid to draw more attention to myself by saying "the ideas I found." But Brody's endearing smile told me he knew it was *me*, not *we*.

Which made it harder to continue the performance.

"I think it's a wonderful plan," he said, "although we'll need to make adjustments when we have a space selected."

"Of course," I said. "We'll work with your designer."

The last sketches were of the boatmobiles, the golf carts decked out like a vintage Chris-Craft, a Chesapeake skipjack, the Queen Mary, and an aircraft carrier. "To take boat-show guests to and from Brody's BoatWorks," I said. It was all I could say. I was exhausted. Not by my show-and-tell, but by the charm and charisma of Dylan Brody.

I felt a physical relief when he finally turned to Tony.

"You and your brilliant protégé have proved to me that I want to work with you. We'll make Brody's BoatWorks the best upscale marine supplies market in the city."

Tony glanced at me and I gave him a quick grin. We'd nailed it.

Dylan stood to pop the champagne cork. I mimed poking fingers in my ears. "Wait till you hear my starting cannon," he said. So he was into sailboat racing or the *Elizabeth* had served as a Committee Boat or maybe both. He poured bubbly into the three flutes. We all clinked. "To Brody's BoatWorks!"

Without a doubt, it was the most magnificent champagne I'd ever tasted, served by the most intriguing man I'd ever met. "My, this is good," I stammered in my best Junior League voice. Three beats later, I tipped the flute up to savor the last drop.

Brody grabbed the bottle. "There's only a bit left," he said. "You deserve to celebrate."

If you can visualize the scene, you'll understand that I really had no choice. He poured another half-glass for me. He then buzzed Karim and asked him to bring up a red cymbidium from the lounge.

Brody grows orchids on the Elizabeth!

Grandpa Jack broke the reverie. *It's time for you to get back on terra firma.*

When the waiter returned, Dylan handed me the little orchid. "Come calling any time," he said.

No doubt my face reddened to the color of the perfect little orchid. "Thank you," I said. "It's beautiful."

As we started down the ladder, Brody asked, "May I accompany you to the dock and, perhaps, to dinner at Reynolds Tavern?"

"I'd love to go with you tonight," I said, "but I've promised to take my mom out this evening." For some reason, I neglected to add, '*and* my fiancé.'"

"Penny's stepfather died recently," Tony said, lending gravitas to my regrets.

Craig had secured the tender against the padded platform. Brody offered his hand to help me across the non-existent abyss. I actually needed it since I was beginning to feel that good old rock and roll that can be expected after imbibing on a

A Sardonic Death

nearly empty stomach.

"Thank you, Dylan," I said.

Tony stepped in and sat. Dylan released the lines to the platform and seated himself beside me. "Land Ho," he said to Craig.

Assuming that I, too, was in mourning for my stepfather, Brody offered his condolences. "Perhaps another day?" he said, his expression hopeful.

"Sure," I said, nurturing excitement as well as foreboding and knowing I'd face an onslaught of admonitions from Grandfather Jack.

I found a Summers Breeze card in my wallet and handed it to him. Just in case he wanted to follow up on his offer of "perhaps another day."

With an arm around me, he said, "Please tell your mom I'm sorry for her loss." Then, "Could we invite her to join us for that *other* day?"

"I'll ask her," I said, knowing I wouldn't.

Craig killed the motor as the tender's fenders kissed the seawall. "Here we are, then."

Dylan rose and handed me onto the dock. "*À bientôt*," he said.

"*À bientôt.*"

On the Spa Creek Bridge to Eastport, I scanned the harbor but the *Elizabeth* was too far beyond the yacht clubbers. A single thought, *What if?* followed me home.

Cookie and Thaïs greeted me at the door. Aaron hadn't yet returned from the Naval Academy.

Chapter 19

I put two bottles of chardonnay in the fridge and removed the three-quarters full one I would need to make it through the evening. A poor substitute for the nectar I'd been served on the *Elizabeth*. After two swallows, I opened a bag of pita chips. Such is life, I said to myself without the faintest idea of why I'd said it. Or what it meant in light of today's events.

I was completely flustered by Dylan Brody's attentions. I couldn't figure what he saw in me, and I didn't know how to react. He was handsome, congenial, considerate, single, and . . . yes, wealthy. His most recent affair, Tony had told me, was with an actress who had returned to her husband, an Italian count. This was a new kind of feeling for me. Nothing like a teenage flutter over an actor or musician whose poster was on my bedroom wall. I had been instantly drawn to this remarkable man, and he seemed to reciprocate my feelings. In contrast, Aaron and I had drifted together in the wake of our mutual loss of my St. John's College friend and Aaron's girlfriend, Katelyn. For me, it certainly wasn't love at first sight. But over time, Aaron grew on me. His agreeable nature, integrity and good looks couldn't be denied. Now, reflecting on my reaction to Dylan, I had to wonder if I was actually committed enough to marry.

Aaron would be back any moment for our evening with Mom, which, at the moment, I dreaded. One or the other of them, probably both, would notice I was, as Grandpa Jack used to say, *off-kilter*. But there was nothing I could do to forestall it. I just hoped Mom's mental balance would be somewhere close to normal.

A Sardonic Death

I phoned her to confirm our dinner plan, wishing that it'd miraculously been canceled. She answered on the second ring with a voice that had barely survived tee many martoonies. "I've made us reservations," she said, "at Reynolds Tavern. It's on the corner—"

"Mom. I know where Reynolds Tavern is. Thanks for making the reservation. What time?" She told me and I said I'd pick her up—

"No just come on over. We'll go in the Ferrari."

I rang off and imagined a worse outcome, if that were possible, than Sunday's sailing party. I hoped Dylan and Tony would have finished by the time we arrived or at least be in a different room.

You've fallen, Grandpa Jack whispered.

Fallen? I wondered. Fallen for Dylan? Between a rock and a hard place? Out of love with Aaron? Into a swamp? Off the suspension bridge of life?

I decided to use my trepidation for Aaron meeting Mom as my excuse for hitting the chardonnay early. If I could drink enough before Aaron arrived, he might attribute any weirdness to the alcohol. Not a great plan, but a plan nevertheless.

Very clever. Grandpa Jack spoke again, this time so clearly that I was glad Aaron wasn't in the room. *What will you do if Aaron doesn't buy your wine-buzzed brain?*

I'll be in a deep pile of manure.

Two raps on the door. Aaron. I stood and instantly felt unsteady. "Come in," I called, but sat back down instead of going to the door. My soon-to-be husband looked like someone I'd known in the distant past, but his image didn't displace Dylan's in my mind's eye.

Aaron saw my empty wine glass and the bowl of pita chips. "I've been preparing for the outburst of craziness we're likely to witness this evening," I said.

Nervousness must be contagious. Aaron went straight to the kitchenette. I heard him pour himself a couple of fingers of Goslings with a splash of water.

As the Ravenscroft gates rolled apart, Aaron said, "I'll try my best to be on good behavior. I promise not to do my screech-owl imitation." We both laughed.

A minute later, we stood at Mom's front door. I knocked.

With the door still swinging open, she said, "Who is this handsome young man?" and half-stumbled aside to let us in. I hoped she couldn't tell that we, too, had lubricated our tonsils.

"Aaron, I'd like you to meet my mom, Ophelia." Mom wore a droll smile.

"My pleasure, Ms. Reid." Aaron smiled and reached for a handshake.

"Have you come all this way to ask for the hand of my daughter?" Mom said.

I shuddered. She was starting already. It could only get worse. "Mom, can we sit down?"

"Oh. Of course." With a small lurch, she led us to her living room. "Help yourselves," she said, nodding to her bar with its hanging wine and martini glasses.

Aaron and I exchanged a glance. Amber rum would have to suffice for my devotee of dark rum. I was afraid to try anything stronger than the chardonnay from the dorm-size refrigerator below.

Aaron set his drink on a coffee table. I raised my wine toward Mom and nodded. What I wanted to say would have ruined the evening before it got started. I tried to formulate something innocuous but was too slow.

"Well, young man, have you?"

A Sardonic Death

"Mom," I said, "that's no longer a requirement."

Aaron swirled his glass and looked at me an awkward smile and what-should-I-say splashed across his face. Mom's petulance was precisely why I would have preferred to cancel our dinner date. If she wasn't passing judgment on Aaron before getting to know him, her pique was directed at me. I was now almost the same age as she'd been when she took off with Aidan. How on earth could she think of becoming a vindictive mother this late in my life after being an absent one for most of it? The wine had reinforced my capacity for indignation. It would be a long evening.

She seemed to have forgotten the question she'd just asked. "You'll love Reynolds Tavern."

"I've heard it's a great place," Aaron said, apparently hoping to wend his way into her good graces.

"Their Cajun Shrimp and Sausage is to die for," Mom said. We have twenty minutes, but they'll seat us even if we're a few minutes late."

I wanted to delay our arrival as long as possible to avoid crossing paths with Dylan and Tony. "It only takes a few minutes to get there," I said, knowing it was close to fifteen and even more if you factored in a walk from a parking garage. "So we needn't rush." I took a slow swallow of wine to demonstrate not rushing.

Forty-five minutes later, instead of going to a garage, she pulled her Ferrari to the curb in front of the restaurant and handed her keys to a valet. Inside, while we waited for a greeter to show us to a table, Dylan and Tony walked past us on their way to the door. Tony had conquered too much scotch to notice me.

Just as the greeter picked up menus and asked us to follow, Dylan's voice rang out. "Hold up, Tony. Our genius is here."

They both turned back and, in an effort to keep the evening on an even keel, I said, "Mom, Aaron, this is my boss, Tony Lewis. And our newest client, Dylan Brody." I nudged the floor for a trapdoor before Dylan could tug the silken strand between us.

The greeter waited impatiently with one foot in some kind of ballet pose and Dylan tugged. "Penny, a treat to see you again so soon." If there *had* been a trap door, I'd have disappeared right then. "And this fine lady must be your mother." He held out his hand. Mom took it and fluttered her eyelashes. Aaron was confused but said nothing.

Deal with it, I told myself. *Que sera, sera.*

"Dylan, please meet my mom, Ophelia Reid."

"I'm pleased to make your acquaintance," he said. "I was sorry to hear of your loss."

Then Aaron offered Dylan his hand, reluctantly comprehending that I'd broken our lunch date to spend the afternoon with this handsome stranger.

"This genius," Dylan said, nodding to me, "has laid the foundation, so to speak, for my new marine supplies store."

"I'm sure I'll hear all about it," Aaron said, glancing at me with a hopeful expression.

"*À bientôt*, Penny," Dylan said, affectionately. He and Tony disappeared through the door.

This was where the tracks got muddy. All through dinner, I tried to keep the conversation on a side road where I explained what I'd dreamed up for Brody's BoatWorks. There was no way I could explain Dylan's obvious attraction toward me or mine for him, but I felt sure Aaron sensed it. I simply said that Tony and I had met Mr. Brody on his yacht to discuss preliminary ideas and that Brody had decided to use our firm to handle the publicity for the opening of his new store. And, of course, that we'd meet with him down the road from time to time. Fortunately, I wasn't asked for a detailed description of the yacht, or I'd have undoubtedly betrayed my awe of the lifestyle I'd enjoyed for an hour and a half.

Grandpa Jack had an old expression: *You're wearing your heart on your sleeve.* Meaning one's emotions were on public display. I was quite sure mine were on full display and both Mom and Aaron had quite easily caught sight of them.

As my first bite of Trout Amandine headed mouthward, Grandpa Jack began to hum the old tune, *"Why do fools fall in love."*

Smart-aleck!

Chapter 20

Aaron and I woke up together Friday morning but didn't engage in what Mom would have called "hanky-panky." My hangover undoubtedly had something to do with that, but there was the Dylan Brody factor too. One of my dreams had involved an exploration of the *Elizabeth's* captain's suite with him.

While Aaron showered, I ground the beans and started heating water for the coffee press and fed both Thaïs and Cookie. I found the breakfast pastry I'd stashed in the fridge and had it sliced and served when Aaron, doing his best to wear a smile for me, strolled in. After a tentative kiss, I offered him a deal. "If you'll walk Cookie this morning, I'll be showered and dressed by the time you get back." Aaron didn't seem to mind that I was the primary beneficiary of the deal.

Over our second cups of rainforest coffee, I ventured into the day. "I'll be at L&G most of today," I said. "But we could meet for lunch at, say, noon?"

"Making up for standing me up yesterday?"

"Sorry. But it was a meeting I couldn't ditch." In an attempt to inject humor, I added, "I would have had to swim in from Brody's sailboat."

"Let's go to Chick & Ruth's instead of Harry Browne's," Aaron said.

I readily agreed. Far fewer ghosts for me than where my first engagement had begun. "Noon?"

"Sure thing," Aaron said. Then, obviously probing, "Your Mr. Brody sounds like an interesting client."

My Mr. Brody? I didn't like where this might lead and

wanted to be careful not to trigger any speculation that could undermine our planned engagement. On the other hand, I had a decision to make, and soon. Before tomorrow's solstice party. I felt hopeless in the face of this life-changing decision, like none I'd ever had to make. Unless you count that foolish idea of getting engaged the day I was commissioned. Fortunately, that one solved itself with his Dear Penny email when the *Enterprise* was anchored off Barcelona.

"He's a bit of a gambler," I said, "wanting to open a new boat supplies emporium in this town."

"So, his yacht where you had your meeting yesterday. It's in the harbor?"

"Out at the mouth of Spa Creek."

"The huge one I saw yesterday from the Naval Academy?"

"The *Elizabeth*."

"Does the size of a man's boat reveal the size of his ego?"

Here was another direction I didn't care to go. I chuckled, probably self-consciously. "Tony and I didn't measure either one."

"From the size of that sailboat, I'd guess he's got money to burn, so planning a new store here's probably a lark."

"Whatever," I said. "It's our bread and butter. So I need to head downtown."

"You don't sound very happy," Aaron said. "Anything happen yesterday to upset you?"

Another non-discussion zone.

I grabbed my back-pack. "See you at Chick & Ruth's. Let's talk tonight. We'll pick up our rings."

I used the fresh air between Eastport and State Circle to clear my head. When I arrived, unfortunately, the elephant was still in the room. Tony asked me into his office. "I'm sorry you couldn't eat with us last night. Dylan and I had a great dinner and a good chat."

"It was a coincidence for our paths to cross," I said, as lightheartedly as I could. "Mom made the reservations."

"He couldn't say enough good things about your ideas."

Not anything that needed a response. "Did he come up with any other ideas?"

"He wants you to work for him. Full time."

"That's ridiculous."

"More money than you make here."

"I'm curious, Tony. What on earth would he want me full time for?"

"My personal take? I think he's in love."

Could three and three make eight? Talk about facing a life-changing decision. Feelings? Mine were in free-fall. Even if I had a week, which I did not, I wouldn't be able to make the fateful decision about exchanging rings with Aaron tomorrow. In a microsecond, what flitted through my mind was that engagements are broken right and left. Why not ours? Or we'd go through with exchanging rings but postpone any wedding date. That would give me time to check in with Grandpa Jack as well as with my friend Stephanie, my compatriot from Master Gardeners training, and Gina. Steph had become a mom to me when my own was only a ghost from my past. She sees auras that I wasn't interested in even trying to see, but for the purpose I had in mind, that might be an advantage. I couldn't predict what I'd hear from Gina. She'd probably consult her crystals.

"You've got to be kidding," I said. "He doesn't know the first thing about me."

"Forgive me, Penny, but I assured him your beauty was more than skin deep."

A Sardonic Death

"Now *you're* making me blush."

"It's true, though."

I gestured to his family photo on his desk. Two cute kids. Gorgeous wife. "I'm going to my desk. I'll try to keep my mind on the project and not the man."

But that was impossible. At quarter to noon, I suppressed the idea of leaping over a building or two and marched around State Circle to the narrow walkway to Main Street and Chick & Ruth's, where I forced an image of Aaron to replace Dylan's and stepped inside. Aaron had commandeered the second booth and waved when he caught me scanning the place. A quick kiss and we made our sandwich selections.

"Hi, hon . . . you too sweetheart," the waitress said as she skidded to a stop. She memorized our choices and scurried to relay our orders to the chef.

"How was your morning?" Aaron asked.

The rubber met the road with a mighty squeal that could be heard in the next county. I heard the sing-song echo of my brother when he was twelve: *"Prevarication takes coordination . . ."* That was before I knew what the word meant. Now I knew quite well.

Nonchalantly, "Oh fine. Tony and I talked about the Brody project. Mr. Brody's with his realtor today, looking for a location." At least the last part was true. "You?"

"I went back to the Academy and out to the practice field. Took another look at Mr. Brody's sailboat. You and Tony had your meeting on that thing?"

"Yep. I nearly saluted the flag and asked permission to come aboard."

Aaron laughed.

"The size of that boat reminded me of what the early America's Cup boats must have been like. Well, not quite *that* large. D'you know the masts of some of those J-boats were so tall that today they would barely fit under today's Chesapeake Bay bridges?"

I could tell that my attempt to distract Aaron from Brody and his sailboat was unsuccessful. He couldn't care less about the dimensions of Captain Lipton's *Shamrock*.

Louisa brought our sandwiches, each with a huge kosher pickle and, thankfully, our discussion of sailboats ended.

After work, Aaron and I shared a paella dinner at Las Hermanas, at which Aaron never raised the subject of "talking tonight" about whatever might have upset me yesterday. A second pitcher of white sangria at dinner didn't improve my attitude but Aaron was oblivious.

When we got to Zellender's jewelry store, instead of a pleasant anticipation of married bliss, I felt myself sinking further into a swamp of deceit.

Chapter 21

The Naval Academy's Officers Club's blue canopied entrance was as I remembered it. After Tim and I were engaged, we'd come to the club a couple of times for drinks and dinner in the magnificent dining room. This evening, a banner displaying a smiling summer sun surrounded by curling fiery tendrils hung on the canopy. Below the image, it read SUNNY SOLSTICE. The antithesis of my mood.

I wore a deep blue cocktail dress. Aaron's stylish blazer and blue and gold rep tie could have marked him as an Academy alumnus, but no one challenged him on what year he was commissioned. No one even asked for our ID's.

Other couples in the grand foyer appeared to be mostly faculty, civilians and a smattering of military in their dress white uniforms with their spouses. I glanced around for Dr. Lapham, the calculus professor I'd had as a midshipman. Fortunately, he was nowhere to be seen. In my plebe year, I was foolish enough to offer to sleep with him in return for a passing grade. He'd declined but squeaked me through with a C, only because he was a nice guy. Not something I would have been proud to explain to Aaron. Then I did the math and realized that that particular bit of history was nearly twelve years old.

Tempus fugits whether you're having fun or not, whispered Grandpa Jack.

As a matter of fact, I saw no one I recognized, so Aaron and I paid our respects to the vice-admiral superintendent of the academy and wandered into the huge dining room under glowing chandeliers. We gravitated to the bar, where I pointed out a model of the sailboat I had skippered in the Newport to Bermuda race. An orchestra on a platform at the end of the room segued from something I didn't recognize to *Dancing in the Street*.

Aaron ordered a Pusser's rum and a splash, and, thinking of the Brody meeting on the *Elizabeth*, I ordered a Laphroaig single-malt that set his wallet back more than he'd bargained for. We sipped and smiled amiably.

On our way to a table, Aaron patted his jacket pocket where he'd stowed my engagement ring. "You've got *my* ring?" he asked.

I tapped a pocket then, with widening eyes, opened my tiny black purse, gawked into it and said, "Oh my," which Aaron knew was only an attempt at theatrics.

"*Holy Christoph—*" Aaron squawked *sotto voce* looking beyond my left shoulder.

"*What?*"

"Elana Sturgis," he choked. An attractive woman, slightly older than me, was coming toward us. She and Aaron managed an embrace that they must have hoped would appear casual. It wasn't. She also wasn't wearing a ring. He turned to me. "Elana is an adjunct professor in the electrical engineering department. We . . . umm . . . worked together."

Grandpa Jack was quick to interpret: *And perhaps a lot more.*

"Aaron," she bubbled, "please introduce us."

I'd never seen him tongue-tied.

"*Us* . . ." With a single word, she'd excluded me from the cozy twosome that she and Aaron had apparently once been. This was not boding well. On the other hand . . . .

I stood and extended my hand. "Penny Summers. I don't remember you from when I was a midshipman."

A Sardonic Death

"Well, I wouldn't expect that you would." *Was I imagining condescension?* "I started teaching here just three years ago. Back when Aaron had just come from the fleet." And to Aaron, "I thought you'd left us for good, dear. What brings you back?" Then she looked at me with a realization that *I* was what had brought him back. "I . . . well . . ." he stumbled, "I met Penny last year, just before I got orders to King's Bay. She and I . . ." And here he faltered. He stared at Elana. The fireworks between them were hotter than anything he'd displayed for me. I felt invisible.

"Aaron, *dear*," I mocked, "should I leave you two alone to catch up?"

He was still tongue-tied. Whatever they'd had going had reignited with a vengeance, so I took the helm. "Grab a chair, Elana. Join us," I said, with a smile, in an attempt to gain the upper hand of righteousness while I marveled at the timing of this intercession. Out of the proverbial blue, I'd been granted the option of not exchanging engagement rings. I had no idea if Stephanie, who could see the unseen, would have an explanation for this. I certainly didn't.

Elana smiled icily and copped a chair from an adjacent table. "Thank you," she said. "I'll be back in a jiff. Need anything from the bar?" she asked, as if more alcohol could pave over this earthquake-sized rent in the pavement of our lives.

"Not for me, thanks," I said in as deceitfully-chipper a voice as I knew.

It was a pleasant evening as I left the club alone and walked out the Maryland Avenue gate straight into downtown Annapolis. Fifteen minutes later I was home and left the door unlocked for Aaron, assuming he might need to use my condo as a base for a day or two while he shifted gears. Venus glared at me from the dark sky beyond my narrow deck. Even if marriage was not in our stars, would it be possible for us to remain friends? That might have to be up to Aaron. My conflicted emotions of the last couple of days left me drained as I silently wished Aaron happiness, wherever his future would lead.

Chapter 22

O n my phone. "Steph, hi . . . it's Penny." It was Sunday. The morning after.

"For heaven's sake, young lady. Where have you been keeping yourself?"

"Are you receiving visitors today?"

"Only if their name is Penelope Summers. I'll put a bottle of chard in the fridge. What time?"

"Noonish?"

"Come hungry for lunch," Stephanie warned before I tapped the phone off. Steph and I had met in Master Gardeners training two years ago. Not that she needed the classes. She could have taught most of them. Her townhouse garden in the historic center of Annapolis was on all the charitable garden tours. I'd signed up for Master Gardener training on a lark but soon found that I enjoyed the playing-in-the-dirt part of it. It had been Steph who suggested I establish Summers Breeze Gardens, starting with an old Chevy van and a few tools. Initially, I only planted and helped harried homeowners with small gardens, but then I lucked into the design job for Aidan Reid who I had no idea had married my estranged mother. Funny how stuff works out. Tomorrow, the renovations I designed for her front garden would begin.

Stephanie's seventy-something housemate Lionel answered the door. "Welcome, Penny. Come in, come in."

I had seen neither Lionel nor Steph since before Madison and I had left for North Carolina. I hugged Lionel and followed him to the kitchen where Steph was working her culinary magic. I handed her a jar of fig preserves I'd brought from

North Carolina. "From my Great Aunt Zelma," I said. "We stayed in her pre-Civil War mansion."

"You were eager to study classical garden design in some old garden down there. Did it work out?"

"It was kind of like, 'Other than that, Mrs. Lincoln, how was the show?'"

Lionel looked confused, and Steph, as she garnished a platter of chicken salad sandwiches, said, "Go on."

"The first day in the garden, I found my professor's stepfather—" My phone began playing Peace Frog.

"Excuse me. Gotta get this." As I accepted the call, I whispered, "Aaron."

"I came over this morning to try to straighten out things with you," Aaron said. "Can we get together later?"

"I'm at Stephanie's. How about dinner?"

"Meet at your condo?" he said. "We can walk to the steak place on Severn Avenue."

"Roger that," I said. And hung up.

Stephanie, watching, had that beatified smile that puts me in mind of the Mona Lisa. "What happened with Aaron?" she asked.

When I started to explain last night's solstice party debacle, Steph interrupted. "I know."

Stephanie's insights are usually on target but my practical side leaves me skeptical. So, I tried not to sound deprecating. "What is it that you know, Steph?"

"Aaron's girlfriend, Arlene? Elaine? Ellen? Something like that—"

"Elana."

"Elana, then. Their thing was smoldering when he met Katelyn. And then he was captivated by you. I'm not saying you were his rebound affair, but you have to realize that your

A Sardonic Death

attraction for each other was rather insubstantial. The mutual grief after Katelyn's death that you shared was, at best, a precarious foundation for love."

Like I said, Steph's intuition is impressive.

"So his attraction to Elana was rekindled when they met last night," Steph said. "It's a man thing. Their brains are wired differently."

"But—" I was ready to explain that I was actually relieved about the break-up of our unofficial engagement.

"You've made a new acquaintance. Damon? Darren? Dalton?"

"Dylan."

Lionel chose that moment to suggest that we go to the garden for lunch. Steph carried the platter of sandwiches and I followed with plates and napkins, the wine in a chiller and three goblets. Lionel brought a jar of bread and butter pickles and a bowl of chips.

Steph's garden in midsummer is a treat for the senses. Patches of purple, white, and pink blooms sent up a myriad of perfumes. Bees and butterflies animated the scene while a covey of cardinals bickered for the privilege of feasting at her sunflower seed feeder.

Once our plates were filled with sandwiches, chips, and pickles, I asked Steph to tell me about Dylan. I shivered involuntarily, wondering what I might hear.

"I should say that he's quite infected you."

I chuckled. "He's infectious, for sure." I described Dylan and attempted to explain my insanity.

"I believe, whatever becomes of your, may I call it *infatuation* with Dylan, you and Aaron should remain friends. After all, it's possible that he may come back to Annapolis when he retires."

I was hoping that Stephanie might see the future for me and Dylan, but apparently, that wasn't clear for her. At least not yet. It certainly was anything but clear for me. Would I even stay in Annapolis? Or would I be tempted to sail straight on till morning with Dylan?

"Your aura, young lady, has a strange vibration today."

I'd never been able to see the auras that Steph described and, even if I had, it's probably impossible to see one's own. My God, I thought, Stephanie's insights and seeing auras . . . what happened to everyday reality? Just then Grandpa Jack gave me a nudge. I had to chuckle. If Steph was crazy, then so was *I*.

Lionel slid the pickle jar to me and I forked out another half dozen.

Steph nibbled a chip and washed it down. "There's a worry line that breaks your aura pattern. What's going on?"

I smiled. Part of me knew this was all malarkey but I preferred to suppress my disbelief and retain Steph as a friend. "You can see Aaron and Dylan and how I've been affected, but you can't see what's causing the worry line?"

"I don't need to see it," she said, "because you're about to tell me all about it."

I laughed self-consciously and munched another pickle. She was right. Again. I told her about Aidan's death, and my willingness to suspect my mom. That led to my triangle of primary suspects: Mom, Dr. Chen, and Tanya Novak. And then the possibility that *any* of the Prosthetonics people could be a suspect.

Stephanie turned to peer into her big red Japanese Maple, the focal point of her back garden. Intently focused for several beats.

Finally, "Your mother was not involved," Steph intoned

A Sardonic Death

from afar. "She's not to blame."

One part of me wished that were true. Mom hadn't set out to be an evil person. Abandoning her family was simply her way of responding to what she might have called her "life challenges." If she ever acknowledged the pain she caused us, perhaps I could let go of my anger and distrust. But, for now, I would keep her near the top of my suspect list.

❧

It was nearly five when I got home. Aaron smiled wanly from the armchair where he nursed a dark rum over ice. As soon as he opened his mouth, I could see he'd started on the rum some hours earlier. "I might be drunk."

"I see."

"You're way too good for me."

I smiled, perhaps too coquettishly. "That may be."

"I know because I shcrewed up royally last night."

"You would have run into her again, probably sooner than later," I said.

"S'ppose."

"You don't need to explain, Aaron. What happened . . . happened."

He gave that idea some consideration.

"I'll survive," I said, "and you will too."

I went to him, held out my hand, and pulled him up. "We both need something to eat. I'll check the freezer."

"I thought we'd go to the steak place," he said.

"Let's say it was an idea that's been overtaken by events, shall we?"

He stumbled away and went to the lavatory. I pulled out the freezer drawer and realized my cupboard was nearly bare. But under a bag of frozen shrimp was a box of frozen lasagna. Twenty minutes later, I pulled it from the microwave and served it onto two plates that we took to the little bistro table on my deck. Aaron only brought his drink, so I went back for silverware and napkins.

"You're way too nice."

"Aaron, please just say what you need to say."

He picked up his rum and twirled the glass, ice cubes dancing in the amber liquid. "I'm so sorry I let us get to this point. Elana and I thought we would get married. But I told her we should wait until I retired. Then I met Katelyn. You know the rest."

I sampled a forkful of Mama Caramba's lasagna. It wasn't as bad as I'd expected. After a wash of chardonnay, I awarded it a passing grade. "So, hand me the engagement ring from Zellender's before you give it to Elana."

Aaron laughed politely. "It's still in my blazer pocket." He took another bite of lasagna and gave me a serious stare. "Friends? Still friends?"

I looked away, and thought briefly of my mom, wondering how many of the invitations to her Fourth of July pool party would be sent to friends she considered real *friends*. "Of course."

"By the way," Aaron said, "Elana has a friend she wants you to meet."

"Oh, *really?* "She's going to fix me up with another one of her sailor friends?" Like it was her way of shutting me out of Aaron's life.

"It's a woman. Astrid Bradley. She also works at the Naval Academy. She's a psychologist."

"So, this Astrid is going to offer me grief counseling to help me deal with the breakup with this sailor?"

"Wrong again."

"Then explain, please."

A Sardonic Death

"She thinks Astrid could help you understand your mother."

"Mother/Daughter self-help psychotherapy. No thank you. And don't try to convince me you were out all night discussing my crazy mom."

"Actually, Astrid apparently has a diagnosis for your mom. Something like schizophrenia."

I had to ponder that. If Mom had a diagnosable mental illness that contributed to her poisoning Aidan, perhaps I *should* learn about it. It might allow a judge to go easy on her if she's convicted of murder.

"I'll bite," I said. "Where would she want to meet? Bar? Restaurant?"

"I'll get back to you."

Chapter 23

Detective Jason Keller phoned early Monday. I was already on my deck after a good night's sleep and still on my first coffee. Aaron was packing his duffel bag. It had been his second night on the couch.

"Your client, Dr. Chen," Jason said, "took a bullet last night."

My pulse bounced. "Was he hurt? Is he alive?"

"He's okay. In the hospital, but okay."

"Thank God." I don't know why my Feng Shui client's well-being was my concern, but I was shaken. "How did it happen?"

"He and . . . I shouldn't tell you, but it'll be in the paper . . . a woman named Thalia Johnson—"

My BoatWorks brainstorming buddy. *"Thalia?"*

"You know her?"

I must have mumbled an uh-hunh.

"She didn't survive."

I leaned forward and put my head between my knees to keep from going wonky. Somehow, I managed to keep the phone against my ear.

I didn't need to know any more, but Jason didn't let go. "The doctor's Mercedes was Annapolis-bound on Muddy Creek Road," he said, "headed north from Pirate's Harbor, and apparently took several rounds. The state police are trying to identify the gun. They think it might have been an AR-15. Chen had surgery overnight to remove a slug from his right shoulder. He lost control and the car was totaled." Jason didn't need to mention what he thought the motive might have been.

137

A Sardonic Death

"Any leads on the shooter?" I asked.

"The owner of a plant nursery near where it happened reported that the entrance alarm at his place woke him up just after midnight."

"And . . .?"

"He didn't pay it much attention because the alarm is triggered whenever anyone uses his drive as a turn-around. Says he's been meaning to move the beam further in from the road."

"Tire tracks?"

"Aren't *you* the detective." A smile in his voice. "Penny, there's still time to apply for the police academy this fall." He paused. "No tracks. Gravel drive. But he caught sight of the car as it careened out of his driveway."

"That's good? Right?"

"Maybe."

"What?"

"The county cop who interviewed him tells us it was a car like your mom's."

"Well then," I said, using flippancy to cover my alarm, "all you've got to do is round up all the Ferrari owners around here who own AR-15's."

Jason coughed, almost self-consciously.

I said I'd visit Dr. Chen at the hospital.

"When you go . . ."

"*Yesss?* I knew he was going to ask a favor."

"We haven't interviewed him yet," Jason said, "but if you talk to him, let me know if he mentions anything that might hint at a threat."

"Don't you need to deputize me?"

Jason laughed. "Forget it. Just let me know if his anesthesia has worn off."

At the front closet, Aaron was folding his blazer into his duffel. He reached into an inside pocket and pulled out the velvet pouch that held my engagement ring. Looking sheepish, he handed it over.

I took it without looking. "You ever fired an AR-15?"

"You're still mad at me?" he said. *Two nights on my lumpy couch and he still had a sense of humor.*

"That was Jason on the phone. My Feng Shui design client was ambushed last night. Wounded. Not killed. He's at the Medical Center. They think it was an AR-15."

"The military version is the M-16. Only issued to military."

"Apparently they could tell the type of gun the shooter used from the bullets in his car."

"Okay, yes, I've fired one. What d'you want to know?"

I pocketed the pouch with my prize for side-stepping what would have been a doomed engagement. "How far could the shooter be from a moving car and be accurate?"

"A few hundred yards."

"Wow!"

"Those bullets travel more than a half mile a second."

"So . . . it looks like a marksman attempted to kill my client. And *did* kill the woman beside him."

"Sounds like your detective friend's got another murder to solve." Aaron returned his attention to the duffel, tucking in his toiletry kit.

I could tell that he didn't want to discuss it. I didn't blame him. The death of his St. John's College girlfriend, Katelyn, a year ago had hit him hard. He obviously remembered Jason had been the detective on that case too.

I didn't ask where he was headed. Maybe back to King's Bay. None of my business. When he was gone, I'd be left with a wounded client and a PR job that I would have loved to ditch except for our fascinating new client. And . . . oh yes, a

A Sardonic Death

landscape installation job for Mom that would begin in an hour.

I phoned Tony on my way to the Medical Center and told him I needed to work at home for a couple of days. Tony didn't ask, just said okay. I relaxed but knew I'd have to come up with something to account for my "working at home" time. Until then, I'd visit Dr. Chen, check in with Roy and his crew at Ravenscroft, and attempt to discover if Chen could have assisted Aidan Reid into the next world. I mean, if Mom hadn't fed Aidan the Devil's Parsnip soup, who else might have? Chen would have had a motive, the poisonous Water Celery was undoubtedly the means, but . . . opportunity?

You could have been working on this, Grandpa Jack whispered, *since I mentioned the possibility more than a week ago.*

Too many pots on the fire, I snapped back.

Chen's room was on the surgical recovery floor. A uniformed police officer stood beside the door. Her badge read RAYNOR. She looked me over. "And you are?"

I'd seen her before. She was one of the officers who responded last year to Jason's call after I found my friend Katelyn dead in a garden pond. I introduced myself and explained that Detective Keller had alerted me to Dr. Chen's accident. It seemed ironic that this handsome ladies' man had a female cop to attend him while his latest conquest was gone forever.

"Keller asked us to guard the room," she said. "He must think whoever fired at Dr. Chen's vehicle might try to pay him a visit here. Didn't want any more fatalities." She waved me in.

Chen's vital signs wavered on wall-mounted monitors that emitted intermittent beeps suggesting he was alive if not yet quite ready to resume his liaisons.

"Doctor Chen," I said, and announced myself.

He turned slowly toward me. "Hello." His eyes were open but seemed unwilling to believe his landscape designer had materialized in his hospital room.

"I heard you had an accident." I had no idea if he'd even been told that Thalia was dead. I wouldn't mention it. Unless Thalia had told him, he wouldn't know that she and I had met.

"I didn't have an *accident*," he said, bitterness stronger than his accent. "It wasn't an *accident*. It was an ambush. Attempted murder. Very different."

I felt deputized. "What makes you say that?"

Chen mumbled something unintelligible.

"Dr. Chen, I want to thank you again for your hospitality a week ago. Your hot shower saved our lives and your veggie soup was delicious."

Another undecipherable mumble. Then, "When am I going to see your plan for my front garden?"

His question could have benefited from a more conversational approach, but I deserved point-blank. I should have been in touch right after I'd stretched a bagua across his enlarged plat and assembled some ideas for its elements. "As soon as they let you out of this den of doctors."

A grin began to play around his mouth and a smile began to crease his cheeks. I found his left hand and squeezed it, a promise.

The Ravenscroft gates rolled apart to reveal Hillsmere's Garden Center van in the driveway. The roll-up door was open and Roy with two of his crew was jockeying balled and burlapped shrubs onto the lift-gate. A pick-up with an empty trailer was parked behind it. A small backhoe was excavating a planting hole for one of the Green Giant arborvitaes I'd specified. Three laborers were wheel-barrowing bags of compost from the pick-up to the beds where they would be roto-tilled in to amend the soil.

In Madison's landscape design course, a visiting professor from the University of Maryland lectured on the importance of soil chemistry. "It's basic," he'd said, emphasizing with alliteration: "Poor soil produces pitiful plants. Always amend with as much compost as your client can afford." I'd told Roy to bring plenty.

My mom walked out from under the porte cochère. "Isn't this exciting?"

It was at least as much for me as for her. It was my first landscape design coming to life. "Just wait till it's all in."

"I'm so happy, Penny."

That was a big change from her despair over her ex-fiancé what seemed like only hours ago. "Sorry I was late this morning. I just came from the hospital. Dr. Chen was in an accident last night."

"The snake?"

I nodded.

She rubbed her chin. "What on earth happened? Not that I really care."

"Someone shot at his car. He survived . . . with a bullet in his shoulder. They operated on him overnight."

"Don't look at me," she said. Followed by a Mona Lisa smile. "I was home all night."

She must have thought it was funny, but I didn't laugh. Something about her declaration made me ponder the truth of it. Maybe it was the enigmatic smile. Perhaps she spoke a little too quickly. Perhaps her tone of voice was a bit too glib. Although I'd never known her to tell a lie, I hardly knew her. Time would tell.

I shepherded her to where Roy had lowered the lift-gate with its collection of shrubs onto a drop cloth on the driveway. The perfume of the flowering shrubs mingled with the rich scent of freshly-turned soil would be what I would always remember of this day.

"Mom, this is Roy Schaffer—" Roy doffed his cap and reached for her hand "—my classmate from the design course."

"It's a pleasure to meet you, Ms. Reid."

I explained to Mom that it was my friendship with Roy that had helped nudge her installation to the top of Roy's job list.

"*Thank* you!" Mom said. "Can I bring you all something to drink? Cokes maybe?"

A memory from my childhood was homemade cookies hot from the oven. I guessed there would be oatmeal raisin cookies served with the drinks.

We walked slowly back to the house. At the front door, Mom commented on the two royal blue ceramic containers I'd selected at the garden center. In a day or so, they'd grace her entrance with bright red Tropicana lilies.

In the kitchen, she began mixing her famous cookie dough. I went to the coffee machine and cued its machinery to make me a cup of regular. I put a Chesapeake Bay Bridge commemorative mug under the spigot. After a few seconds of grinding, several clicks, and gurgling, I savored my third cup of the day.

Mom had pre-heated the oven. After she stirred in two cups of golden raisins, we spooned dollops of dough onto a pair of cookie sheets and slid them into the oven. At her coffee machine, she requisitioned a cup for herself into an Annapolis Boat Show mug. We sat at her small breakfast table.

"When I saw your ex this morning," I began, "I thanked him for his hospitality last weekend."

"Nice of you." I'd brought the subject around to where I

A Sardonic Death

wanted it.

"After he's out of the hospital, I want to get his recipe for that soup he served."

"Mmmm." She took a sip of coffee.

I felt like a detective who only asks questions for which he already knows the answers. "Did he ever make it for you?"

"We made it together once."

As I sipped my coffee, the nostalgic aroma of cookies baking crept from the oven.

"You and he made it here, in your kitchen?"

"We picked up all the veggies at Whole Foods and he brought the herbs and seasonings from his place."

"Sounds quite romantic."

She frowned. "Pull*eese*. Don't remind me."

"Where was Aidan," I asked in a tone of voice that I hoped would suggest it was idle curiosity, "while this soup kitchen was in operation?"

"Oh . . . that was when he was in New Jersey for a couple of days."

I focused on the tennis court through the window over her sink while Roy's little backhoe grumbled into the compacted soil out front. It was hard enough to envision Mom in a love nest, but nearly impossible to imagine it happening here in the home she'd shared with Aidan.

"Did you have any left over when Aidan returned?"

"There was enough for the next Saturday's lunch. Aidan said it reminded him of the soup we used to make in the commune."

"It had to be a healthy concoction."

Mom smiled at the bittersweet recollection.

"Might have helped him get over the flu," I said.

She opened the oven to check on the cookies, allowing the

delicious fragrance to dance around the kitchen. "It should have," she said, closing the oven and returning to the table. "Chen made a batch with added healing herbs and brought it over the day before he died. I reheated it and Aidan had a small bowl mid-day, but later he refused any more. Tanya and Colleen also brought their versions of chicken soup for the flu. But then he died during the night."

The sadness when she shook her head looked genuine.

Temporarily trading my deerstalker for my designer cap, I carried a plate of cookies and a dozen cold Cokes out to Roy and the crew. He called a mid-morning break and we sat around using the backhoe trailer as a communal bench. Although I had taken beginning Spanish in high school, I could only stumble through a couple of half-baked conversations with his crew. But we teased Roy amiably when he insisted on showing us photos from his engagement party. I told him that I'd missed him in North Carolina, but that he wouldn't have enjoyed the discovery of Madison's step-father.

By the end of the afternoon, the Hillsmere crew had dug and amended all the beds with several cubic yards of compost mix. They'd be ready to plant and mulch the next day. And I had delivered Mom's second check, due at the start of the installation.

The crew arranged all the plant material on the driveway, watered everything, prepped for tomorrow, and got the backhoe secured on its trailer before they left, and I went back inside.

"They've finished?" she asked.

I said they'd be back before the cock crowed the next day to start the actual planting.

Mom, energized by the anticipation for her new garden, began mixing the dough for her second most famous cookies, my personal favorite—snickerdoodles.

Chapter 24

I'm off to Old Vines," Mom said. "We need a couple of bottles of champagne to celebrate."

When I heard the Ferrari's resonant mufflers head out the gate, I decided to explore the mansion. I thought it might be possible to play the role of a classical detective and search the rooms for some trace of evidence left by Aidan's murderer. When I first heard of Locard's exchange principle, I was fascinated. Even weeks after the deed, I thought, today it might be possible to find a nugget of the poison root that could have fallen, unnoticed, as it was added to Aidan's food. Even then, though, unless it had fingerprints, I wouldn't know who had dunnit.

I examined the conservatory and living room, the kitchen across the back, and the dining room to the left where we'd spread my design for its final approval. I opened a door I hadn't noticed in the kitchen and discovered it led down. Presumably to a utility room, furnace, air conditioning equipment, and the like. Then, from the hall, I climbed the curving stairway to the second deck. (Navy types don't use the word "floor" or, for that matter, "stairs," at least aboard ship where the term is "ladder.") In this house, it was *terra incognita* as far as I was concerned, since I'd never had the opportunity or a reason to ascend. Both the master bedroom above the living room and the guest bedroom above the kitchen appeared as if their occupants had recently decamped, the bedclothes unmade and personal articles in both adjoining baths. If Aidan breathed his last up here, I needed to pull out my imaginary Sherlockian magnifying glass to search carefully.

When the distinctive roar of Mom's Ferrari approached and then shut down on the circle, I traipsed back down to the conservatory and opened my notebook to my list of Aidan's funeral mourners. Nada. I'd found exactly nothing. No thing.

Mom sailed through the foyer, noticed me, and stopped at the bar. A moment later, a champagne cork smacked the glass ceiling and a moment after that, she sat beside me, placing two full flutes and the opened bottle on the glass coffee table. "Well, isn't this a great day," she bubbled. We clinked our flutes and swigged till the tiny bubbles tickled my nose.

She noticed my notebook on the coffee table. "Whatcha got there?"

"Thinking about Aidan," I said.

"What's there to think about him?"

May as well fire both barrels. "I'm worried that you could be accused of murder."

She smiled sorrowfully as if I were an alien from somewhere beyond the Van Allen Belt.

"Mom, after you told me about the Water Dropwort in your pond, I wondered if it could be connected with Aidan's death. I talked with the funeral director. He read me the embalmer's notes. They documented that Aidan had a rictus, you know, a grimace that looks like a horrible grin. Isn't that what you said the old Sardinians looked like who were sent to their death after eating Water Celery soup?"

Mom's eyes enlarged, her eyebrows shot up. Had she not seen Aidan's face after he died? She nodded excruciatingly slowly. "My God," she finally said. "I had no idea."

In that moment, I wanted to believe her, but wouldn't have bet money that she hadn't fed him the Water Celery. It would have been a simple matter of assisting a man she no longer loved to make way for a man she had fallen for.

A Sardonic Death

If she hadn't, someone had. "How many people have you told about the Devil's Parsnips?"

"Good Lord, I don't know. I thought it was kind of a joke that I'd imported a plant that was poisonous in Sardinia."

"Mom, I feel stupid telling you that it's just as poisonous in Annapolis as it is in Sardinia. What you're not saying is that quite a few of your friends knew about the water celery."

Her face registered no reaction. She was obviously stunned.

"I think you said that Aidan's doctor, a Dr. Brennan, was here that evening. He wrote the death certificate?"

She just nodded, seemingly still in shock.

"Did you see Aidan before he was taken away?"

"No. Doc Brennan asked if I wanted a final goodbye, but I didn't want to see him."

"Mom, I've copied a list from the Memories Book of everyone at the funeral. Can you tell me who was here the day Aidan died? Besides Dr. Brennan and Tanya, and her assistant, Colleen, who else from Prosthetonics?"

"Oh God . . . how am I supposed to remember? It was all too awful."

My gut feeling was that Mom had probably had too many martinis to remember much.

"There were several others from the office," she said. "Give me a couple of minutes. Or, maybe, if I take a look at your list, it would jog my memory."

I opened my notepad and let her read the names.

"Stanley Hunter? No. Brad Wentworth? I don't remember, although he's the whatever-you-call-him, chief operating officer, and probably was here for the meeting."

"The 'Mountain to Mohammed' meeting?"

"Exactly. Tanya called to say they needed a meeting with Aidan to respond to an opportunity her father had presented, and Aidan, sick as he was, agreed. So they went up to his bedroom about three o'clock to discuss whatever it was. They were up there for almost an hour."

She turned her attention back to my list. "Colleen Clemmons. Yes, she was here. Generally, she and Tanya travel together. Aidan was always deferential to both when I was around, but Tanya is strikingly gorgeous. I assumed she'd become his lover as well as his co-owner."

"Back to my list . . ."

She refocused. "Shirley Calhoun. Nope. Herman Novak. He's Tanya's father with the money. He wasn't here that day, but Tanya introduced him to me at the funeral. I met several people from Prosthetonics there I hadn't met before."

"Jeff the lawyer?"

She nodded.

"What about neighbors?"

She examined the list.

"Dr. Chen, of course. He brought his soup."

"Any others?"

"Aunt Ida, on my mom's side, came up from Richmond for the funeral. But that was after he died."

"But you had a houseful the day Aidan died," I suggested.

"I think there were just five besides me: Chen, Tanya, Colleen, Brad Wentworth, I think, and Dr. Brennan. And Jeffery." She slugged the last of the champagne in her flute and refilled both of ours.

I slurped mine before the bubbles overflowed. "So the meeting was about three in the afternoon?"

"Like I said, they were with Aidan for maybe an hour. When they came back down, since it was nearly happy hour, I invited them all to join me for drinks. Tanya and Colleen took me up on it and we had martinis. I think Mr. Wentworth left at that point claiming he'd promised his wife a restaurant night."

A Sardonic Death

"Did they come to a decision for whatever they had the meeting for?"

"I didn't ask but I assumed so. Tanya and Colleen seemed happy and toasted each other with their martinis."

"How was Aidan at that point?"

"I went up to see if he wanted to have a drink with us even if he didn't feel like coming down."

"And . . .?"

"He seemed worn out from the meeting and said he'd rather not. He seemed out of breath, but I figured it was from the exertion and he needed to rest."

"Did Dr. Brennan check on him?"

"Doctor B didn't come until later. After I called him. Probably close to seven, about the time we were sitting down for supper."

"What prompted you to call him?"

"I'd gone up to ask Aidan if I could bring him more of Chen's soup, but he declined. That worried me, so I called Dr. B. He came right away, checked on Aidan and said his lack of appetite was typical for someone with the flu. Doc then joined us for supper."

"So you had Dr. Chen's soup?"

"No, dear, I knew Aidan might want it later. We had Mediterranean pizza. Lots of feta, olives, shrimp, and calamari. And a vegetarian for Tanya and Colleen."

"You made them?"

"Sweetheart, you know I never make pizza. I had them delivered from Paradiso. They're a new place but really good. And they're the closest."

I took a long last swallow of my champagne that was no longer fizzy. And finally got to the point. "Mom, we need to think how the Water Celery got to Aidan that night. Did Aidan eat any of the pizza?"

She didn't answer but went to the bar and pulled the second bottle of bubbles from the little fridge and brought it to the table. In Mom's case, I was pretty sure that more champagne wouldn't do her memory any favors. I needed to extract as much information as possible before the second bottle left her even more fuddled.

"Sweetheart," she said, "will you pop this cork? I don't want to ruin my nails. My next appointment isn't till Thursday."

I did the honors, but the cork didn't explode. Just landed at my feet. Mom laughed. "What's so funny?" I asked as I refilled her flute.

"Reminded me of Aidan's, ahem, last performance." She chuckled again at her private joke. "Don't ask," she said and guzzled at least half of what I'd poured.

"Mom. Aidan died with a sardonic smile. He had to have ingested Water Celery that evening and we need to figure out how it got into him."

"Dear, that isn't what Dr. Brennan said. He told me . . . he said that he died from . . . what was it?"

"Some complication of the flu or pneumonia?"

"That's it, whatever it was," she agreed, either remembering or becoming more forgetful, I couldn't tell which.

"Then how would you explain his sardonic smile—?"

"How on earth should I know?"

"Mom." Emphatic now. "Water Celery was the cause of his death. Now, you said you ordered two pizzas. Did Aidan eat any?"

"Didn't I tell you I tried to get him to eat something but he didn't even want Chen's soup? That was unusual because he'd liked it only the day before and earlier in the day."

A Sardonic Death

"So you and Chen, Jeff and the two Prosthetonics women and Dr. Brennan were down here in the dining room, eating pizza while Aidan was in your bedroom, having trouble breathing, and eating nothing."

"Actually, he was in the guest bedroom. After Dr. Brennan's first visit when he diagnosed Aidan, I moved him to the guest bedroom. I'd had a flu shot but I didn't want to take any chances catching whatever strain of it he had."

"What were you all drinking?"

"Curious Georgette is asking too many irrelevant questions."

"Mom. They're *not* irrelevant questions. I'm trying to discover how your husband died. Did Dr. Brennan see Aidan after dinner?"

Mom fidgeted with her champagne flute, turning it round and round until I was afraid she'd spill what was left in it. "As I recall," she said, "Tanya and Colleen tried to offer Aidan some soup they'd brought. I don't think he had any of it. When we'd finished our pizza, we poured more wine and raised our glasses in a toast to Aidan's recovery. Tanya and Colleen refilled their glasses and went up to get Aidan to at least share the toast to his health. Then—" Mom stopped abruptly.

"Then *what?*" I knew instinctively that this was when the evening turned upside down.

"When Tanya got to him, she screamed. All of us ran up. Except Dr. Chen. Aidan was dead. He'd vomited and was lying half on top of the quilt, turned toward the wall. I thought maybe he'd had a seizure. Tanya's broken glass and her spilled wine were on the floor. It was horrible. I remember feeling dizzy and Tanya and Colleen helping me back downstairs.

"Chen made vodka martinis for us. *Double*-dry. Not even a whiff of vermouth.

"Tanya and Colleen wanted to stay and comfort me but I said I'd be fine with Chen and Dr. B. To tell you the truth, both women kind of rubbed me the wrong way. Nothing specific, but I knew I'd be better if they didn't stay. Chen and I finished the martinis and then he brewed some herbal tea that he said would calm my jangled nerves, but I don't think anything could have been much help that night."

"Dr. Brennan stayed upstairs with Aidan?"

"He called an ambulance. When the ambulance got here, he asked if I wanted a few minutes alone with 'the deceased' and I said absolutely not."

"By that time, you were totally wiped."

"Aidan and I had never talked about either one of us dying, so Doc called the Grove Funeral Home for me and said he'd take care of the paperwork. Like you said, I was too wiped out at that point to be useful."

"Mom, people don't usually die from the flu."

"Aidan died from pneumonia, Penny. The flu had morphed into pneumonia."

"Pneumonia patients under a doctor's care, I think, don't usually die. Did Dr. Brennan say anything about that?"

"He did say that he was surprised that Aidan's pneumonia had worsened so quickly. He thought he might not have recognized when the pneumonia started to affect his lungs. The symptoms of flu are much the same as pneumonia."

"Last question. Did you keep the leftover pizzas?"

"It's beyond me how you can hope to find out how Aidan died by asking silly questions." Mom's frustration with my questions had finally boiled over. "For your information and edification, Miss Curious Georgette, I ate the last two slices of the veggie pizza the night before last."

I hadn't heard anything to implicate Dr. Chen in Aidan's death yet, and I couldn't blindly accept Steph's pronouncement

A Sardonic Death

of Mom's blamelessness at face value. There was also the possibility that Tanya had maneuvered a bit of Water Celery root into her chicken soup recipe, but there didn't seem to be any way to know if Aidan had ingested any of it.

It might have seemed cruel to leave Mom with her memories of Aidan's last day, but it was getting late and I had two animals at home that depended on me. I promised that I'd see her the next day when Roy would be back for the planting phase of her new garden.

Jason phoned as I triggered our condo gate open. I pulled in, let the gate close behind me, and stopped. "Penny for your thoughts."

"Do you know where your mom was last night?" Jason asked.

"Am I my mother's keeper?"

"Just thought you might know."

"Matter of fact she said she was home all night. I told her that Dr. Chen was wounded and she said something like, 'Don't look at me. I was home.' So does it matter?"

"The county police interviewed the grower and his best guess as to the car he got a glimpse of was that it was a dark Ferrari. Like your mom's. And since Dr. Chen isn't in your mom's good graces, I naturally thought—"

"Jason, your so-called *thinking* sounds like profiling to me. You know someone who drives a Ferrari therefore—"

"Penelope, I'm not accusing your mom, but there aren't many Ferraris in this part of the world."

"Don't all cats look alike in the middle of the night?"

"Fair enough. But you can let her know that she's likely to be on someone's interview list."

"The guy *thinks* he saw a Ferrari. When?"

"Just after midnight."

"Wasn't it Mark Twain who supposedly said to not believe anything you hear and only half of what you see?"

"A wounded driver, totaled car, and a dead passenger are not subjects for humor, Penny."

"And it's also not appropriate to profile Ferrari drivers as pot-shot takers."

Hang on, Grandpa Jack said. *So* now *you want your mom to be eliminated as a suspect in Chen's shooting? Even if she didn't kill Aidan, she could very well have shot at Chen.*

Chapter 25

Although her stripes hadn't changed their hues of light and dark gray, Thaïs was as livid as a cat could be for my having missed her appointed mealtime. As quickly as I opened a can of fish mix, she lunged into it without a single mew of a thank you. Cookie expressed her appreciation by vibrating her stub of a tail as she made short work of her evening ration. After a quick tramp around a dozen blocks of our Eastport neighborhood, we returned so I could microwave a one-dish supper for myself. Mid-wine-slurp, I was surprised by a call from Aaron. His friend Elana had responded to my willingness to meet her friend, the Naval Academy psychologist, Astrid Bradley.

"How about tomorrow?" Aaron asked. "She suggested the Paradiso Pizza place. It's new so it's relatively quiet."

"I'll be at Mom's during the day, but I could meet you, probably by seven."

"See you then."

Tuesday, I was at Mom's at eight in the morning, but Roy and his crew had beat me. Many of the plants, in nursery pots or balled and burlapped, had been moved to their assigned places on the beds. With my plan in one hand, Roy directed his crew as they set them out, one by one, then acknowledged me when I stepped into view.

"Glad you're here," he said. "Take a look at this." He referred to a group of shrub pots sitting in their places. "Now check the 'Green Giant' behind them." I immediately saw the problem. The arborvitae was smack dab centered behind the shrubs rather than spaced properly with its brethren in a classical semi-circle as I had intended.

"Can you get another 'Green Giant' and space them a little tighter?"

"No problem," Roy said, "if your mom's up for the increase."

"Don't worry about that," I said. "She'll cough up whatever it takes to make it perfect."

I intervened a few more times to adjust the positions of the plants ensuring the plantings would look right from every viewpoint.

Jason and a helper hired for the day were busy digging the crater which would become the centerpiece pond. Three submersible pumps, their fountain nozzles aimed skyward, sat nearby with a trio of bronze submersible lights.

Mom and I lunched in the conservatory: tuna salad sandwiches on whole grain bread, dill pickles and full globes of white wine that was a little too sweet for my taste, but I didn't complain. A scarlet bee balm bloom pinned over her ear was a sure indication that her *joie de vivre* had returned.

"I heard from Aidan again this morning," Mom said, after a preliminary sip of wine.

Her auditory imaginings no longer surprised me. "Tell me about it."

"And it wasn't just Aidan."

"Okay."

"He was in the guest bedroom next door with one of his mistresses. Probably Tanya. They were whispering lovey-dovey to each other. I couldn't hear their words through the wall but it was obvious they had missed each other."

"Mom, you know that was some kind of hallucination, right?"

"You're suggesting I'm going nuts?"

"Nooo. I'm only saying that, since Aidan's dead, you should realize that he can't be in the guest room. And therefore—"

"I know it doesn't sound rational, sweetie, but I heard them. I know it was Aidan."

There was no point disputing what she believed, so I asked about her plans for her pool party.

"Most of our friends who were at the funeral are planning to be here."

"The Prosthetonics people?"

"Of course."

"Jason?"

"Of course. Since our discussion yesterday, I've been half expecting him to arrest me."

Hate to say it, but she must be feeling guilty, Grandpa Jack whispered.

"Are you worried?"

"Not specially, but since I had nothing to do with Aidan's death, I'll have to hire a lawyer."

"Not *specially?*"

"Since I know they're after me, I'm assuming that would be Jason."

"Mom. *Who* is after you?"

"Specifically? I have no idea. I just feel it. Something ominous."

I found myself hoping that this friend of Elana would have a label for her condition. Something other than early dementia.

By mid-afternoon, everything, including the extra 'Green Giant,' had been planted. Watering and spreading mulch around the new plants took Roy and his crew until 4:30, which meant each of the crew would earn an hour overtime so the job could be wrapped up.

I got Mom to write the completion check to Hillsmere and find five $20.00 bills to tip the crew, which she delivered personally while they flattened mulch bags and loaded wheelbarrows, forks, and rakes into their truck. She was rewarded with broad smiles all around.

It was almost quarter after seven when I finally got to Paradiso Pizza in the Westgate Mall. Aaron and Elana, with her friend Astrid, were at a table near the back.

"Sorry I'm late."

"No problem whatsoever," Aaron said. "We just got a head start on our beer. Pizzas are on the way."

I thanked Aaron for convening the meeting. And the two women for making time to meet me.

"I'm here just to offer a hearsay diagnosis," Astrid Bradley said, "and refuse to take responsibility for anything I may say." She chuckled. I smiled. I liked her casual attitude.

"D'you work with a woman named Laurel at the Academy?"

"I used to," Astrid said, "until she took early retirement last fall. Said she had an offer she couldn't refuse."

"Small world," I said. "She's now my dad's second wife. And learning how to sail."

"Good for her," Astrid said, "She deserves a second chance."

A waitress approached with two pizzas on a pair of swirled wire stands. "Here you go," she said, "One Seafood Deluxe. And a Super Veg."

"When you get a chance," I said, "I'd like a pint of the Oyster Stout."

"Yes, ma'am," she said as if she were practicing military etiquette prior to boot camp.

A Sardonic Death

"We trust that one of these pizzas will suit you," Elana said.

"Either, or both, actually," I said. "May I start with the Veg?"

Aaron rolled the cutter through indentations and managed to stretch the cheese to the breaking point before sliding a wedge onto my plate at about the same time that my beer landed.

"Thanks," I said, clipping my tongue before adding *dear* or *sweetheart*.

Aaron had appointed himself Chief Pizza Server, as he duplicated his dexterity three more times, leaving me the choice of either variety for my second wedge.

"Aaron told me about your stepfather's death," Elana said, "and you think your mom may be to blame."

That, I thought, was the nicest way possible to convey my problem. I wasn't too thrilled about Aaron sharing so much of my personal life with his girlfriend, but I needed all the help I could get. "That's about the size of it," I said.

Astrid, meanwhile, had made short work of her first mouthful of seafood pizza. "According to what I've heard, your mom has exhibited some unusual behavior."

"*Unusual* hardly covers it," I said. "Try *bizarre*."

"Examples?"

"She hears her dead husband making love in the guest bedroom."

"Now that *is* unusual," Astrid said, "but what does she actually hear? Words? Or sounds? And does she think she knows who is with him?"

"She said she couldn't make out specific words, but she was certain he was in the room and she only assumed who the woman was—one of the women he worked with."

"Anything else?"

"One afternoon she saw him, down on their dock, motioning to her. When she got closer, he'd vanished."

Astrid pooched her lips in thought. Then, "Does your mom drink?"

"She loves her martinis."

I turned to Aaron, "You saw her the night we went to Reynolds Tavern. How would you characterize her drinking?"

"It seemed like she'd had quite a bit before we got there," he said. "She really scared me a couple of times, but fortunately the drivers she should have collided with had quick reaction times."

"And . . . at dinner?"

"More than you and me put together."

I eyed Astrid. "She surprised the shenanigans out of *me* driving back to her place without a fender-bender."

"Other episodes?"

"Only hearsay. And this was before his death. She was sure Aidan had been cheating on her and that he once had tried to kill her."

"Typical."

"Okay, here's one I witnessed. We were in her living room when she heard him calling her from upstairs. I hadn't heard a thing, but she went half way up, answering him. 'Aidan, dear, I'm coming. Hold your horses. Be there in a sec.' When she came back down, she was wide-eyed, apparently realizing that what she'd heard was only in her head."

"It sounds similar to schizophrenia," Aaron said.

"Some psychiatrists," Astrid said, "used to call it late-onset schizophrenia."

"What causes it?"

"Alcohol . . . drug use . . . maybe a genetic connection."

"I never met my grandmother, but there was nothing weird

A Sardonic Death

about Grandpa Jack."

Astrid nodded understandingly. She'd finished the pizza slice and was nursing her beer. "How old is your mom now?"

I did a quick calculation. "Mid-fifties."

"Has she ever had a stroke?"

"Not that I know of. But I haven't seen her for twenty-some years."

"Does she smoke weed?"

"Mom and Aidan lived the latter-day hippie life when they hooked up twenty years ago. Who knows what they may have smoked. But I've never gotten a whiff of it in the house."

"Okay," Astrid said. "Without being able to rule out THC, here's my totally worthless diagnosis."

I was listening but also prying a slice of mushroom from my pizza, imagining how easy it would be to insert a piece of pre-cooked Devil's parsnip under the cheese. It would be easy-peasy. A couple of seconds.

"*Paraphrenia.*" Astrid pronounced it slowly. "Like I said, it used to be called late-onset-schizophrenia, but it's different in that there's no deterioration of the brain. Some psychologists describe it is as a 'schizophrenia-like psychosis,' or they lump it under *psychoses not otherwise specified.* It can present as delusions of various kinds. The reason I asked about a stroke is because paraphrenia can sometimes be associated with physical changes in the brain. Mostly it's associated with auditory hallucinations. Usually no visual hallucinations."

"Sounds like an interesting condition to have," Elana said.

"But not," Astrid said, "if the apparitions are frightening."

"What I'm most interested in," I said, "is if the condition could have contributed to her decision to kill Aidan. Now, I'm not saying that she *did* kill him. There's no way to prove it one way or another, but I'm guessing . . . or, I should say, I think there's a high probability that she did."

All eyes went to Astrid.

"In a nutshell," she said, "There doesn't seem to be a whole lot of difference between paraphrenic people and so-called 'normal' folks. Since researchers haven't found anything unusual about paraphrenics with the exception of their hallucinations, I doubt seriously if those would translate to murderous tendencies. Sorry. But, as I said, my diagnosis isn't worth the papyrus it's written on." She snickered. "So you can draw your own conclusions."

Steph and Astrid versus me made it two to one. I'm not much of a believer in probability, but the odds suggested that I should focus on my second tier suspects: Chen and Tanya.

Back home, I had just uncorked a cheap chardonnay and settled in with a slab of Swiss gruyere when Kalea phoned. "What's up, Punkin?"

"You said your mom owns a prosthetics company, right?"

"She's kind of a *co*-owner. Why?"

"I'm going to put Shy-mom on. She heard something at work today that might have something to do with your mom's company. Hang on." Her cellphone clunked as she put it down while I heard her search for her Shy-Mom. I didn't have a clue what this was about, but I didn't have long to wait.

"Penny?"

"Yes?"

"Hi. Kalea's gonna make a great spy."

"You've got my curiosity gauge glowing. What's up?"

"I can't imagine this would be considered corporate spying, but let's just agree that you'll forget about this call and never mention my name in connection with anything I might say."

"I had a clearance for classified material when I was in

A Sardonic Death

uniform if that helps. I promise to keep anything I hear to myself and never mention you. But you're sounding secretive. What's this about? Kalea said you heard something about a prosthetics company?"

"Your mom's invested in one, Kalea says."

"More like she's a co-owner."

"I didn't catch the name of the company, but if this makes any sense to you, you're welcome to it. Under our arrangement of course."

"Okay. One of our managing law partners is Jeffery Gratrix. Don't know if you know the name."

"Small world. Mr. Gratrix was my step-father's lawyer."

"Well, Jeff was spinning tales with one of our senior partners and he mentioned a prosthetics company that had contacted him about a reorganization."

"Prosthetics?"

"Could have been prophets something. I couldn't hear clearly—they were behind a door. But the way the conversation was sounding, and I only caught a few words, it sounded as if something was close to the line of legality. Like a bit shady?"

"Any specifics? Any names?"

"The only name I remember but I have no idea if there's a connection, was Herman. Might have been one of the company's principals or a lawyer friend."

I recalled Mom saying she met Herman Novak, Tanya's wealthy father, at Aidan's funeral.

"Sounds like Kalea's skills are rubbing off on you. Thanks, Cheyenne. I'll check that out."

"You'll have to figure out where to suggest the info came from."

"Of course."

164

"Just one other thing, but no idea if it's connected. Middle of the morning, Jeff was sequestered with a client in one of our consultation rooms. I was on my way down the hall to our library and heard the client say something that I couldn't make out. But the voice was female."

"Thanks, again, Shy. Tell Kalea I said thanks."

I made a mental note to call Mom tomorrow. It was probably something to do with a simple reorganization since Aidan's death.

Chapter 26

It was a fine morning, no rain in sight, but before I started for my office, I rang Mom. I knew nothing about corporate business management. "Were you and Tanya Novak co-owners with Aidan?"

"I don't think he ever explained exactly what I was in the company. All I know is that I'm supposed to get monthly checks based on their income in the previous quarter."

"Mom, I think you mentioned that Aidan's lawyer is a Jeff somebody."

"Gratrix."

"Is he the company lawyer too?"

"As far as I know."

"I think you and I should pay Mr. Gratrix a call. We need to know the details of your relationship with the company."

"That's actually a very good idea."

"You probably remember Grandpa Jack's mantra about not believing anything you hear and only half of what you see?" I said. She said she did. "Then, will you make an appointment for us?" She would.

From Eastport to our L&G office on State Circle in the center of historic Annapolis is a mile, give or take, about a fifteen-minute jog depending on how many lights I catch. The benefit of jogging is that I can clear my cranial circuitry for the day—unless I encounter a friend, which is unlikely since I don't have many. This morning I thought about Dylan Brody and his relayed message to work for him. Like Tony said, the poor guy was probably smitten, a case of infatuation at first sight, because working for him made no sense. I had no

166

marketable skills beyond the writing and PR stuff I did for Tony. Not that Dylan and his beautiful yacht had no attraction. They did. But that wasn't the stuff that a real relationship could be built on. For crying out loud, I had more in common with Aaron than with Dylan. And that hadn't worked out too well. If Dylan ever got around to asking me directly, we'd have to sort it out on neutral territory, not aboard the *Elizabeth*. Probably named after his first wife or first conquest and I had no interest in competing with either.

Tony's assistant caught my eye as I walked in, only slightly out of breath from my more or less mile run and jogging in place at red lights. "He wants to see you as soon as you get your coffee," Krysta said. Tony's co-owner brother-in-law had installed one of those ultra-posh coffee machines like Mom's where you could choose your brew: anything from decaf Americano to caffè macchiato to Ghirardelli hot chocolate. If you became fully conversant with the instruction book, you could undoubtedly pilot an F-35. I had finally memorized the sequence of button-pushing required for a bold regular Navy-style, i.e., no milk or sugar. I carried it into his office.

"What's up, boss?"

"You get your mom's new garden planted?" Tony asked.

"With a little help from the Hillsmere Gardens team."

"Great," he said like he meant it. Normally Tony's only concern is how our projects were proceeding. Was it possible that he cared, even remotely, about my avocation?

"Tell me about your homework for L&G." Or was his concern actually a snide observation on my excuse for asking for Monday and Tuesday away from the office?

"Scraped together a few more ideas for Mr. Brody's BoatWorks."

"I won't ask for a recitation, but when you have time, could you drop me a memo outlining them?"

A Sardonic Death

"This afternoon."

Fortunately, I'd prepared. Yesterday, as Roy and his crew were spreading mulch at Ravenscroft, I sat between the Tropicana lilies with their gorgeous deep red blooms and researched sign carvers online. It seemed that every yacht yard on the Chesapeake competed for the most colonial-looking carved wood sign, even if they weren't all actually carved from wood. But I knew Dylan would want only the most authentic representation of his logo for his premiere location. I found several sign carvers who had made signs for boat-related enterprises, insurance companies, and counseling firms. Phelan Hurst's was a one-man shop, with a slew of high-profile clients and a long list of commendations that attested to his skill and reputation. I determined to take Dylan Brody's BoatWorks sign work to Mr. Hurst's sign emporium in Shadyside a few miles from downtown.

I went first to Steve's graphics shop and asked him to print me a half dozen line-drawing copies of the BoatWorks logo with the antique sailboat. I returned to my desk with a kind of kindergarten mindset, trying various color schemes with my Prismacolor pencils. It wasn't as easy as I had imagined, but then creative work never is. Finally, I had three versions ready for our client's consideration. I asked Steve to make copies for Tony, along with my selection of three sign-makers that actually carve their signs in wood.

After receiving Tony's blessing, I called Dylan and was invited to meet him for lunch at Café Normandie near the City Dock. Seems Dylan had adopted the Café Normandie like Tony had adopted Harry Browne's. Jean Louis himself greeted us with hearty French bonhomie and a wine recommendation to accompany the crepes we intended to order. "This red zinfandel, I tell you, Monsieur Brody, is simply su*perb*."

168

I had wondered how awkward it would be to meet with Dylan after he'd supposedly told Tony he wanted to "hire" me. The idea was so insane that I was sure he must have been in an Irish whiskey haze when it had been uttered. I didn't bring it up and he didn't mention it either. He was certainly a handsome man, but today we were simply a public relations consultant and a client at a lunch meeting. The vestige of our apparent attraction for each other had eddied around my separation with Aaron, but now that I had a bit of perspective, I understood that our breakup was inevitable, not the result of my attraction to L&G's charming client.

By the time the first pourings of the zin had been swirled, tasted, and commented upon, Dylan had selected my rendering of his BoatWorks logo on a dark purple background with the image and lettering in bright lemon yellow. His comment on my other two color combinations, dark Navy blue and gold, and Kelly green and silver, was "Nope. Too much like everybody else's."

The only modification he suggested was that the hull and mast of the boat on the railway be gold-leafed.

Why didn't you think of that, Grandpa Jack teased, while I revised upward my initial impression of Mr. Brody's marketing aptitude.

I jogged home to get my van for the visit to Phelan Hurst's sign-carving studio.

A table saw screamed through his open door. The whine kept him from hearing my footsteps through a room stacked with cedar planks of various thicknesses and widths. Along one wall were thicker pieces, presumably for two-sided signs. His workroom beyond had the delicious scent of cedar sawdust and shavings. He glanced up from the saw, finished the cut,

A Sardonic Death

switched it off, flipped off his safety goggles, dragged his hearing protectors down to his neck, and brushed sawdust from his bib overalls.

I introduced myself and reminded him that we'd spoken yesterday. "Well then," he said, "let's see whatcha got."

I pulled out the color copy of the design that Dylan had approved and added a notation that the silhouette of the boat's hull and mast was to be gold-leafed. I explained that the purple and yellow color scheme would be used on every sign our client would need in the store, but the gold-leaf would be only required on the big sign over the store's entrance. After I gave him the dimensions we needed, Phelan nodded. "That'll right shore grab yer attention," he said, and promised that he would have the big sign carved, painted, gold-leafed, and triple-coated with urethane, ready to hang in less than a month.

I was afraid to ask for the cost for such a large sign, so I didn't, knowing that whatever the cost, it would be worth every penny.

Chapter 27

Dr. Chen, his right arm in an elaborate sling, was released from the hospital the next morning and took a cab directly to Fiore's Fabulous Flivvers to rustle up a new Mercedes. When I arrived after work with my preliminary plan, there was a shiny new black Mercedes coupe in his garage.

Instead of *hello*, he said, "The police are still searching my red Mercedes, trying to learn who fired at me."

"Why would someone shoot at *you?*" I asked, keeping my suspicions to myself.

"You'll have to ask him when they find him," he said, motioning me into the house. "Unless we're talking about kids playing at shooting at cars like ducks at a fair, the shooter was someone who knew I'd be on that road at that particular time."

Jason had come to the same conclusion.

Dr. Chen suggested I go through the living room to the back deck while he put the kettle on.

I liberated four pebbles from his pond to hold down the corners of my plan on the coffee table and noted that the Water Celery clump from Mom's pond was flourishing. A few moments after his kettle whistled, he brought out a steaming teapot and a pair of cups. Instead of pouring the pungent tea, he sat mesmerized for several minutes over my design. Since colors are critical in a Feng Shui design, I'd hastily sketched in suggestions of color for each of the elements. Earth tones for the bubbling boulder, a pleasingly purple meditation bench with nearby beds of purple blooms at one end of a stone patio. Instead of a firepit, I'd suggested a contemporary sculptural

A Sardonic Death

representation of fire combining three shades of red to stand between the primary house entrance and the patients' entrance, echoing the bright red good fortune color of the doors. Five fountain-shaped clumps of bamboo placed strategically would engage with the natural stone of the small patio as well as the bubbling boulder. One gray and tan stone jutted up to complement the upward thrust of the little bamboos. Beside it a prone boulder slept and behind them was a boulder island, my nod to classical Oriental stone arrangement.

Both red doors of the house would be flanked by pairs of dark green ceramic containers, tall ones at the main door and a mid-sized pair at the patients' entry. Each pot would have, as I sketched in the plan's margin, a trio of complementary colorful plants, one spiky, one mounding, and a third trailing over the lip of the container. Chen's eyes darted from one section of the drawing to the next, siphoning each detail into his imagination.

While I waited for a comment, I felt much like I assume Ernest Hemingway must have felt as Gertrude Stein mulled his first story. In a word, *anxious*.

In a few moments, Chen's expression transformed. He looked up. "I don't like to have someone be guilty without a trial, Penny, but I think your mom was the 'man-behind-the-gun' last Sunday."

That was the feather that nearly knocked me over. "You *what?*"

"Maybe you didn't know that Aidan made your mom learn to use a gun."

Another feather. "I had no idea she even owned a gun."

"Small-sized for a woman to protect herself if a burglar comes. One day I talked with her about safety in her big house and she showed me."

"What makes you think she would want to kill you?"

172

"Don't you Americans say, 'Hell has not a fury like a woman?'"

"Something like that."

"We were coming back from Pirate's Harbor when it happened. Your mom and I had made that same trip after dinner back to Annapolis many Sunday evenings."

Jason's concern about a car resembling Mom's Ferrari being noticed at the attack site began to make sense. The possibility throbbed in my headache zone. Grandpa Jack mused that if Mom had killed once and not been found out, perhaps she felt untouchable.

I did my best to shove this all under my mental rug. "Dr. Chen," I said, "What Mom may or may not have done last week isn't anything we need to discuss but I'm sure the police will work it out in due time. I'm sorry for what you've been through but thank goodness you're recovering quickly."

He nodded and attended to pouring the tea, then raised his cup to mine. "Perfection, Miss Penny. This is a wonderful plan. I am, you know, wanting to know what the costs will be."

"Of course," I said. "I'll refine the plan with the details and costs for each element. But you must allow me a few days to get this together. At that time, I'll need a second payment that will allow us to move ahead."

"That," he said carefully, "will be perfectly acceptable. I will await your call. And perhaps by then we won't be burdened with this gunfire attack mystery."

Grandpa Jack whispered, *I wouldn't count on it,* while we shook hands and I promised to be in touch as soon as possible.

But as soon as my foot hit the accelerator headed back toward my condo, I called Mom. Her answering machine picked up. "Mom . . . if you haven't set up a meeting with Mr. Gratrix yet, I'm free after work tomorrow."

Chapter 28

Friday morning, Cookie sat expectantly as I filled her bowl and set it at her eating place. My phone chirped out its Chopin mazurka. I gave her a quick pat along her back as she dug in and answered. Mom had arranged for us to meet Aidan's lawyer, Jeff Gratrix, at his home at 5:30, and suggested we meet there. I told her that I'd prefer to ride together to give us time to chat before the meeting.

So, after a slow day at L&G, a few minutes after five we were on our way to Mr. Gratrix' waterside estate near Londontowne, a bit south of Annapolis. Mom had never been to his home, so I navigated with my trusty GPS. We were on the long bridge over South River when I mustered my courage to broach the subject. "Mom," I said, "remember that Jason told me the night Dr. Chen's car was attacked, there was a report of a car like yours in the neighborhood?"

"Jason's probably getting ready to arrest me."

"Mom, I didn't ask about your nightmares."

She glanced at me and smiled, seemingly returning from her paraphrenic imagination. "Of course, I remember what you told me. And do you remember what I said?"

"New question: May I borrow the little pistol Aidan bought for you?"

"If you get gun safety training."

She didn't seem surprised that I knew about the gun. Maybe she thought she'd already told me.

The GPS prompted a last turn onto a gravel driveway that led to a lovely old home on a promontory overlooking the South River. Except for our footsteps on the gravel, the only

174

sound was the honking of a broad "V" formation of geese on their way to Canada. We watched until their babble faded out over the Chesapeake Bay.

Mom lifted the bronze fist on the front door and let it fall. Approaching footfalls, then Mr. Gratrix opened the door with a welcome. "You found me," he said to Mom.

"With the help of my daughter's GPS." And turning to me, she added, "I'd like you to meet Penelope, my daughter, recently returned from helping the Navy in the Middle East."

Her introduction wasn't exactly true, but close enough.

"Welcome," he said, and gave Mom an avuncular cheek kiss, with a handshake for me. "You have my condolences on your dad's death."

Also not exactly true, but I saw no necessity of clarifying my convoluted relationship with the late Aidan Reid.

"Mr. Gratrix," I said, "Mom suggested that we talk to you about her new situation with Prosthetonics since Aidan died."

"Just call me Jeff. Your dad and I've been associates for years." Then, "Please come on in." He led us to a bright living room with a pair of old brick fireplaces, several beautifully carved and decorated ducks on each mantel. "Decoy carving is a dying art," he said, noticing my interest. "These are from carvers on the Eastern Shore. I try to afford a new one every year at the show in Salisbury." He chuckled as if to allay any concern that he'd have to save his pennies for each new decoy. He added, looking from Mom to me, "The sun's over the yardarm, as we say, so may I get you a sherry?"

I nodded and Mom said, "That would be lovely." I was sure that she'd had at least one martini before I'd arrived at Ravenscroft.

Jeffery Gratrix went to a beautifully renovated colonial cupboard and poured three glasses of what appeared to be

A Sardonic Death

Amontillado. A moment later, a quick taste confirmed that it was, indeed, a delightfully complex one.

"Ophelia," Jeff began, "I had a visit a few days ago from Prosthetonics' new co-owners."

"Really," Mom said. "How did it go?"

"Tanya and Miss Clemmons wanted to explore possibilities for restructuring the company."

"Would that restructuring," I asked, "be related to the meeting at Aidan's bedside the day he died?"

"In part," he said.

"Aidan told me you all would be coming to the house for a meeting," Mom said, "but he never said what it would be about."

"What we all agreed to was bringing in Tanya's father, Herman, as a board member. Since he's the link with the new technology they want to incorporate."

"What can you tell us," I said, "about this technology? What's so important that it prompted thoughts of restructuring?"

Jeff sipped his sherry and set his glass on the side table. Then he bent forward as if to share a confidence. It seemed that what he was about to explain was the crux of the situation. "I don't pretend to be fully up to speed on this," he said, "but, as I understand it, the technology that Herman has been funding will revolutionize the prosthetics industry."

"Meaning," Mom said, "that they expect to multiply the company's income."

"That's one way of looking at it," he said.

"Is there another way?" I asked.

"As I understand, it's something of a gamble, but, yes, if it works as they hope, Prosthetonics will be at the forefront of the industry."

I rubbed my thumb and forefinger together: *money, money.* Jeff nodded.

"Okay." Mom was smiling now. "Tell us about it."

"Are you at all familiar with how artificial arms and hands are activated?" Jeff asked.

"Aidan once explained to me that various muscles can be attached somehow to a prosthesis to make it move," Mom said. "And he said Mr. Novak's research has something to do with harnessing brain waves. That's all I know."

"I know nothing at all," I said.

"The research and trials Herman has been funding have to do with connecting brain functions directly to the prosthetic machinery using what they call *neurothetics.* In other words, if a patient thinks about grasping a glass of sherry, for instance—" he said, reaching for his glass "—his artificial hand will grip the glass." Jeff's fingers wrapped around his glass and held it up for inspection. "Then, responding to the patient's wish to bring the glass to his lips—" Jeff's arm swung the glass to his mouth, "—the prosthetic arm will respond appropriately." He sat back. "That's all new. Never been done. Their research involves using volunteers with missing limbs who have brain activity sensors either in a head-net or, eventually, implanted under the scalp."

"Obviously," I said, "a gamble with a fortune at stake."

"And Aidan was willing to take that gamble," Jeff added.

"Did the company have money to buy into that research?"

"Aidan's gamble was to bring in Tanya Novak. With her father's millions."

"That's what I figured," Mom said. "Prosthetonics was doing okay, but not making us millionaires. So, Mr. Novak, trading on his daughter's notoriety in the field of prosthetics, chose our company to, shall I say, *exploit?*"

A Sardonic Death

"Ophelia, the prospectus talked about the *opportunity* offered to Prosthetonics to forge ahead and profit by neurothetics technology. So, no, I don't think anyone considered bringing in Tanya and her father as *exploitation*. I wouldn't have given Aidan my blessing if I felt Tanya offered anything less than a unique opportunity for Prosthetonics to prosper."

"I assume the Novaks offered proof of the validity of their research in this *neuro*-technology," I said.

"Aidan authorized me to have a corporate sleuth make private inquiries and she confirmed neurothetics as a sound investment, that is to say, that the results of the research as of two months ago was all positive."

"I'm not sure I understand," Mom said. "Tanya and her dad offered Aidan a plum. He had nothing to lose and a lot to gain if this new system worked."

"Prosthetonics has been a solid company for ten years," Jeff said. "The Novaks knew that your company would have the panache to bring credibility to this revolutionary shift in the industry. Simple as that."

"I'll be blunt," I said. "Do you think Tanya and Herman would try to keep Mom from sharing in the future profits?"

He hesitated. "That's the other side of the restructuring question. The way the corporation is presently set up, your mom is a profit-sharing non-voting board member." He turned to her. "On the other hand, with restructuring, her portion of future profits could be reduced."

"Is there some way," Mom said, "to stay on top of any efforts in that direction?"

"As long as I'm their corporate lawyer, it could only happen over my dead body."

None of us smiled. "That means we need to hire you a

personal bodyguard," I said.

Jeff smiled. "May I refill your sherry?"

"Sure," Mom said, obviously rattled. And more sherry would probably make it worse.

I glanced at my watch as if the time would make a difference in my reply, then said, "I'm in."

When my sherry was refilled, I asked, "Is Tanya *the* owner for now?"

"Actually," Jeff said, "a month or so ago, the ownership was shared four ways, adding Colleen Clemmons as a full partner."

"Was Mom involved in that decision?"

"Your mom's a *non-voting* board member."

"What talent does Colleen bring to the company?"

"I actually don't know precisely but Tanya spoke very highly of her."

"Tanya's the Golden Girl, then," Mom said. "Whatever Tanya wants, Tanya gets."

"Basically."

"So, as of this moment, what is Mom's position? She said she never completely understood how Aidan had set it up so she could share in the business if he were not in the picture."

"Your mom is technically a non-equity partner. It just means that she didn't pay to become a partner. Bottom line is she shares in the profits without requiring her to attend board meetings . . . like the one when Aidan agreed to add Tanya's father to the company board."

"Wasn't it understood at the time Tanya joined that her father would also join the decision-makers?" I said.

"Perhaps unofficially."

"That means, if I understand you," Mom said, "that now he and Tanya, with Colleen, make all the decisions."

A Sardonic Death

"You're right. It's arranged so that your percentage of the profit from the preceding quarter is paid monthly directly into your joint bank account. I had Aidan set that account up as a 'joint tenants with right of survivorship' so it should be painless to switch it to an individual account in your name. I feel a little protective of you since Aidan and I go back a long way, so I can help with that if you'd like."

On the way back to Ravenscroft, Mom hit the bullseye. "Sweetheart, you're the one who suggested we should see Jeff. And then you told him it was my idea. Somewhere you'd heard that something wasn't kosher at Prosthetonics . . . that Tanya and Herman were maneuvering to cut me out of the profits. Tell me how you knew about that."

I hadn't told Mom about my eleven-year-old C.S.I. assistant and wanted to insulate Kalea from any potential nastiness. "Just something my professor's partner mentioned in passing. She's a junior partner at Jeff's law firm and overheard Tanya talking with Mr. Gratrix."

Mom frowned but accepted my explanation which was, after all, as close to complete honesty as she was going to get.

I declined a drink at Ravenscroft and hightailed it back to my condo with thoughts of another meeting with Jeffery to inquire about the relationship between the two women who might be looking for a way to separate Mom from the business.

And might have wanted the business without Aidan, whispered Grandpa Jack.

If Aidan had signed off on Herman and Colleen joining the Prosthetonics board, everything was probably fine.

But, Grandpa Jack asked, *might his business acumen have been warped by a gorgeous woman with a bundle of money?*

Chapter 29

All through breakfast Saturday morning my brain was processing what I'd learned from Jeff Gratrix about the new owners of Prosthetonics. I was just about to start my run with Cookie down Chesapeake Avenue when she began barking angrily. The translation of her savage shrieks: *Your castle is under attack.*

I headed to the door to head off the UPS assailant or whoever it was. Jason stepped onto my landing and rapped on the doorframe. Cookie's shrieks intensified.

"Down, killer!" I yelled so Jason could hear and opened the door.

Cookie sniffed him and began wagging her clipped tail stub. My detective friend had been the arresting officer of Cookie's former owner.

"To what do we owe the honor of a visit from Annapolis's finest?"

"News from the trenches."

"You still profiling Ferrari owners?" I asked.

"Funny you should mention that."

"Not funny ha-ha," I said. "Funny coincidental?" I motioned him to the kitchen and poured fresh coffee beans into the grinder at the same time adding water to the kettle.

"Exactly."

"I'm listening."

"We're combing Dr. Chen's Mercedes for clues to how the ambush went down."

"You find anything interesting?"

"What we've found, I think, will be of more than passing

A Sardonic Death

interest."

"I'm game."

"The forensics team concluded that the car was the target of two different shooters . . . at approximately the same time."

"And this was discovered *how?*"

"Shots were fired from two separate directions. For the sake of argument, we'll refer to the shooter waiting in the entry to the plant grower as 'the Ferrari.'"

"There you go again—"

"Penny. Hear me out. The *Ferrari* shooter's rounds, two to be exact, hit the left side of the vehicle without hitting either Chen or his passenger. The *second* shooter was directly in front of the car, probably waiting at the edge of the woods a couple hundred yards north where the road curves, with a view from dead ahead." He smirked audibly "Pun not intended. We think at least a half dozen rounds, maybe more, hit the car from that perspective: a headlight, both front tires, windshield, and the occupants. Dr. Chen lost control and flipped the car across the oncoming lane and into a power pole that broke. Heavy car and enough speed'll do that. When the first responders arrived, a power line was draped across the car that threatened the occupants with electrocution as they exited. Ms. Johnson was dead on arrival at the Medical Center and Chen was in surgery within the hour."

"The Ferrari shooter," I said, as I pressed the plunger on the carafe and poured our cups, "*didn't* cause the accident or Thalia Johnson's death?"

"Bingo."

"So it was the *dead-ahead* shooter that might have used a semi-automatic rifle."

"Double bingo. You've won the basket of fruit!"

"Jason?"

"What?"

"I met a guy you might want to talk to."

"Who and why?"

"This isn't much of a lead," I said, and then told him about 'Weems' with no last name and his restored black Falcon whose wife was a patient of Dr. Chen.

"Didja get his tag?"

"Sorry."

"What can I say?" He chuckled. "One demerit. But thanks for the tip."

I scrubbed my morning run and took Cookie for a demure circuit of the neighborhood. Called Mom. She sounded sleepy.

"Yesterday I asked about borrowing your gun. And I did have weapon safety training in the Navy. So may I come over and pick it up?"

"What on earth for?"

"I need to ask Jason to check it for recent firing."

For a few moments, she said nothing. I heard her coffee-machine hiss and click off. Finally, she spoke slowly, "I didn't mean for that woman to die. Just Chen."

Holy *Christ*opher! Mom had just admitted that she fired at Chen after telling me she was home all that night. For a nanosecond, I flashed on the second gift basket I'd won. "Mom, I have news for you. You didn't kill her."

Silence.

"I said you *didn't* kill her."

"I didn't mean to."

"Mom, Jason is not going to arrest you. At least not for manslaughter."

"He's not? How do you know?"

"I talked with him a few minutes ago. A couple of your

A Sardonic Death

bullets hit the car, but the shots that hit Chen and killed Thalia Johnson came from in *front* of the car."

I heard a sob.

"Mom. I need you to fill in the blanks. Tell me about your gun."

"It's a tiny one . . ."

"Go on."

"Aidan bought it for me when we moved into this big place. He wanted me to be able to protect myself if an intruder showed up when he was out of town. He said it was a 'Lady Smith' so it would be perfect for me."

"Did he teach you how to use it?"

"Of course. You just twist the thingie and put a bullet in each hole. Then every time you pull the trigger, you send a bullet to your target."

"Okay. I understand. But when did you decide to shoot at Dr. Chen?"

"He decided for me."

"How do you mean?"

I could almost hear a snarl as latent anger growled into her voice: "When we docked at his pier, it was obvious that he didn't love me. I've never taken kindly to people who don't keep their promises. It took a while but I finally decided how to deal with the scum."

"I'm curious how you knew where to ambush him."

"Simple. I knew his habits. *Our* Sunday habits. It was the second time I'd waited for him on a Sunday evening. Him and his precious Mercedes. He deserved to die."

Clearly, she had *tried* to kill Dr. Chen. Had she thought she was justified after the humiliation he had dumped on her? I empathized with her violent response even if I couldn't imagine attempting that kind of retribution myself. Now my

184

dilemma was whether I should tell Jason that Mom had admitted shooting at the red Mercedes. It didn't take long for me to come down on the side of letting nature (or the wheels of justice) take its course.

I had no proof that she'd made Water Celery soup for Aidan. Or put a slice of "Devil's Parsnip" in his veggie pizza. She must have considered it, though, in the fullness of her affair with Dr. Chen. But even if she hadn't dispatched Aidan in preparation for a "happily ever after," Chen's behavior had certainly rocked her sanity. I've never understood the adage that love and hate are close cousins, but her attempt to kill Chen seemed to be a case in point.

Another question immediately raised its ugly head. Since she'd admitted the attempt to kill her unfaithful fiancé, did I dare work the logic backward and assume that she dispatched her husband and now one more death was simply the price one had to pay to rectify the wrongs that had been done to her?

However you sliced it, poor Mom had lost her second husband *and* the man she'd wanted to escape with. Twenty-some years before, she'd escaped from her first marriage without, as far as I knew, even thinking of killing Dad. Nor, probably, ever considered how much she had sabotaged Spencer's and my childhood.

I never thought I'd even think it but I said, "Poor Mom," aloud before I clicked my phone off.

I didn't know if Mom was having a martini morning, but I could gamble with decent odds that after our conversation, she would. Like a character at the end of a classical tragedy, she'd been left bereft of everything she'd wanted. I actually realized that I was sorry for her. I didn't need an invitation from my Master Gardener friend Steph to know *I* needed a hit.

After a tumbler of chardonnay and increasingly tumbled

A Sardonic Death

thoughts about Mom and Aidan and Chen, I gave my four-legged housemates, Cookie and Thaïs, their belated breakfasts and went for a run.

Aside from Mom and Chen, Tanya and maybe other Prosthetonics people were now my only suspects in Aidan's death. They would have heard about the Water Celery from Mom and, as co-owner of Prosthetonics, with Aidan out of the picture, Tanya and her father would be free to profit quite handsomely if the neurothetics technology could be incorporated into marketable prosthetics. As much as I wanted to clear my brain and plot a course into the several puzzles I faced, I first had to pursue the possibility that Tanya Novak had launched Aidan's trip across the River Styx.

I needed to interview her.

Kalea, I remembered, would attend the police department's Junior Police Academy the week after next. Between now and then she could help me talk with Tanya.

At my three-mile turnaround, the sky turned overcast and began to drizzle. By the time I returned to my condo I was soaked. A warm shower went to the top of my agenda.

I called McGonagle's Upholstery after lunch to confirm that the couch cushions Cookie had ripped while I was in North Carolina had been repaired. Gus charged me less than I'd expected for the repairs, so I wore a smile as I lugged the first one from my van to Kalea's house.

"Aunt Penny!" Kalea screeched when she opened the door. I handed her the mended cushion. "Can you help me bring in the rest of them?" Gus had bagged the cushions in plastic so the light rain wasn't a problem.

"Shy-mom's at work today," Kalea said.

"Working on a tough case?"

"Probably with her *in*tern."

I wasn't ready to go down that rabbit-hole again. "And Madison?"

"Her doctor's removed her fixator, but she's still using a cane. She's out clothes shopping. End of the season specials, she said."

My landscape design professor was not a fussy dresser. Like me, she was more of a jeans, tee-shirt, and denim jacket with dancing bears kind of gal, so I was curious about what kinds of seasonal clothing she might be looking for.

"You all set for the Junior Police Academy?"

"Actually, I hope I get a chance to show off what I learned in North Carolina."

"How would you like an undercover assignment?"

Her face blossomed. "Where?"

"Here. It's something we could do together."

"When?"

"I'm thinking next week."

"Who would I be impersonating?"

I laughed. "Your*self*." I explained my idea in which she would have a summer assignment to write a research paper on the subject of advances in prosthetics that would be due on the first day of school.

"They've never assigned anything like that."

"The people at Prosthetonics don't know that."

"That's your *mom's* business."

"Partly hers now. They've never met me so I can pretend to be your aunt."

"Awesome."

Chapter 30

Saturday afternoon, Dylan Brody called. I recognized his number and touched the green dot. "Penny for your thoughts," I said, trying to be nonchalant.

"I knew I liked your style," Dylan said.

"Mr. Brody. Have you found a location for your flagship BoatWorks?"

"That's not why I'm calling."

"I'm all ears," I said.

"I'm planning to sail the *Elizabeth* across the Bay tomorrow and hoping you and your mom could help crew her."

"You've keelhauled your regular crew for insubordination?"

He chuckled. "Actually, I needed their bunks to make space for tomorrow's crew."

Double entendre? whispered Grandpa Jack.

"How many do you need? I have a few friends at the Naval Academy who'd love a Sunday sail."

"Along with the few who survived the keelhauling, your boss Tony, and his wife Sandy have already volunteered."

"Then Mom and I, if she's available, should be well chaperoned."

"Bring your harpoon. I understand the Kraken has been spotted in the Chesapeake."

"It's probably Chessie. She's a relative of the Nessie in Scotland. Been around for decades."

"But the Kraken makes for a better story. It swallows an entire ship and crew in a single mouthful."

"Now you're worrying me."

"Not to worry. Karim will serve us champagne and shrimp salad sandwiches."

"Oh, well," I said, "In that case, damn the Kraken. Full speed ahead."

"Hear, hear."

"What time, then, is morning muster?"

"Craig will be at the pier at eight bells. Don't be AWOL."

"Now it's called 'missing movement.'"

"Whatever." He laughed. "So don't do that either."

"Thank you, Captain. I'll give Mom a call."

"Oh ish you again." It *had* been a martini morning.

"Yep," I said, "with an offer you won't want to refuse."

"You're old enough to know that, as your Grandpa Jack used to say if an offer is too good to be true, it *is*."

"This one's true *and* good. You remember meeting Tony and our client Dylan Brody at Reynolds Tavern?"

"S'pose I do." At least it wasn't a question.

"Captain Brody has invited us for a day sail tomorrow. Across the Bay and back."

"Would I have to pull on the ropes or sheets?"

"Not unless you'd like to."

"Would I get seasick, you know, when it's keeling over?"

"Mom, Brody's yacht is the biggest sailboat you've ever been on. Not exactly as stable as an aircraft carrier, but it's large enough that it doesn't bounce around like Matthew's sailboat. Plus, you'll have a champagne lunch."

"Well then, I suppose I could be coerced."

"Drag out your boat shoes, and I'll pick you up at seven."

"Seven in the morning?" she squeaked. "I don't do anything before 8:30."

"Make it quarter after seven, then. We have to be at the

A Sardonic Death

City Dock at eight."

"Breakfast on board?"

"Mom. No breakfast on board. You have a lovely coffee machine. Use it. And make me a regular. I'll bring cinnamon buns and we'll eat them on the way to the dock."

"You drive a hard bargain, young lady."

"I think you'll enjoy the day. That means no martinis after dinner. And no 'hair-of-the-dog' in the morning. The *Elizabeth* is a sumptuous boat. I made its acquaintance the day Tony and I presented our ideas to Dylan. A gentleman of the old school."

"I remember he said '*À bien tôt*' after gushing about you. I guess that makes him 'old school.'"

"Tony says he's a world-traveler."

"Well, la-de-*da*."

☙

Sunday I was up early, dressed in a tee-shirt from Barcelona, shorts, boat shoes, Naval Academy ballcap and jacket. Fed the critters and walked Cookie around the block. Sunglasses and sunblock in my pockets. After a quick stop at Chick & Ruth's for a pair of still warm cinnamon buns, I was off to Ravenscroft. Mom's shirt read WELL-BEHAVED WOMEN RARELY MAKE HISTORY and she had a raucous red rose in her hair that matched her lipstick. She jumped in the passenger seat with a pair of travel mugs full of gourmet coffee ready for our expedition.

Back in town, I parked in the Hillman Garage behind Chick & Ruth's. We finished our continental breakfasts in my van and still managed to meet Tony and Sandy at the City Dock where Alex Haley's slave ancestor Kunta Kinte landed in 1767. Today, bronze sculptures of the storyteller and his enthralled young listeners could have overheard my introductions to Sandy, a buxom brunette probably in her late forties.

"Hi. I'm Penny. I work for your husband." I extended my hand while she exhibited a small frown and shook mine limply. "And this is my mom, Ophelia Reid."

"Now that's a name you don't hear often anymore," she said. "I once knew an Ophelia who'd been part of the Haight-Ashbury scene."

Mom smiled. "That's where I took the name. Didn't want to be a Joan forever when there were really great names for the taking."

Morning sun sparkled from the beautifully varnished tender as it came puttering down the inlet. As it neared, I realized Dylan himself had come to ferry us out to the *Elizabeth*. I grabbed the line he tossed and snugged the tender alongside the dock while the others climbed in. When they were seated, I coiled the line and made the leap as he bumped the Lizzie's motor into reverse.

"Thank you, Penny," he said, as I settled at the bow. Then, "Thank you all for coming out this morning. I've had a word with the wind goddesses and they've promised us a fine sailing day." The morning breeze veered as Dylan shifted into forward and goosed the motor. Its racket made further chit-chat difficult until, after we passed the Naval Academy's practice fields, the *Elizabeth* emerged, larger than anything moored in the harbor.

"Are you sure, Captain Brody," Sandy called out, "that you aren't kidnapping us for a voyage to the Indies?"

"Why? Where did you think we were going today?"

"Tony thought maybe Oxford," she said.

"Once we get across to London," Dylan joked. "Two weeks, maybe three." His sandy hair blew away from his tanned face, revealing a broad grin. "Fifteen men on a dead man's chest, Yo ho ho and a bottle of rum—" he sang.

Leaning closer, over the outboard's noise and Dylan

starting the next verse, Mom whispered, "You weren't kidding about the size of his yacht."

The outboard subsided to a gentle purr as Dylan allowed the tender to drift to the *Elizabeth's* landing stage. As the gunwale kissed the fenders, I stepped across with the line and made a figure eight around a cleat while Dylan did the same aft. With the tender safely snugged to the landing, he jumped up to provide a steady arm to assist the others across to the stage. "All aboard who's goin' aboard," he called. "My first mate Craig will welcome you at the top of the ladder."

Mom winked at me and beamed at Dylan as she took his arm, stepped onto the stage and started up the ladder. Tony and his wife hopped to the stage as if they were experienced crew. I followed and behind me, Dylan gave me a possessive squeeze on the shoulder as we started up to the *Elizabeth's* quarterdeck. "How's your mom holding up?"

I briefly flashed on the crazy notion that he might be thinking of asking Mom for my hand in marriage. Just as quickly, I dropped the thought. Outside of L&G business, we'd never had a date. On the other hand, he was not your average guy. "You raised her mood," I said, "with your invitation to sail today."

Arriving at the *Elizabeth's* quarterdeck, Dylan whispered that I was in for a surprise. A gentleman, yes, but an unconventional one.

"Welcome aboard, Penelope," Craig said as I stepped off the ladder onto the woven rope mat and checked myself before requesting permission to come aboard. He wore a broad smile as if he knew about the surprise Mr. Brody had in store.

Behind me, Captain Brody spoke to his first mate. "Craig. Let's get her majesty underway."

"Right sir." Craig rushed down the ladder and spoke into

his lapel radio. The first task was to motor the Lizzie around to the stern and get her hoisted to the davits. Almost at the same time, other crewmen arrived on deck and made their way aft. Within minutes, the Lizzie, with Craig on board, was lashed safely under the davits and Craig, with the crewmen, were back at the quarterdeck raising the accommodation ladder and platform up to the rail. I couldn't help but admire the quiet coordination with which all this was accomplished, knowing that the whole process would be reversed when we returned this evening.

"Can we help?" Tony asked.

"You can make yourselves comfortable in the cockpit," Dylan said, "and watch us get her majesty's sails up." He handed me a zippered canvas bag. "No peeking," he said, flashing an enigmatic smile. Craig made his way forward to release the mooring line.

Dylan accompanied us to the expansive cockpit where Tony and I had broached our ideas for his BoatWorks. At the control pedestal, he engaged the rumbling engine into reverse to back away from the mooring buoy. Soon we were clear of the Severn and out into the Chesapeake Bay proper. I estimated the north breeze at about fifteen knots. Perfect sailing weather—a reminder of the many times I'd sailed these waters as a midshipman.

"Main, mizzen, jibs, and topsails," Dylan yelled. With all that canvas drawing, it would be like putting the pedal to the metal.

Again, the crew cranked up the sails one by one. As a gaff-rigged ketch, the two largest sails had two halyards, one for the throat and one for the peak. The sailors at each mast had obviously done this many times. The gaff rose nearly horizontally until the throat was "chock-a-block." The peak

A Sardonic Death

continued into the sky until the gaff was at a jaunty angle, the sail in place and ready to be sheeted in. When both the main and the mizzen were drawing, the topsails were raised and the big sailboat began to heel, slipping into a comfortable broad reach as it leaned into its task of carrying us southeastward across the Bay toward Kent Island. Dylan adjusted the helm so the big *Elizabeth* would slip just enough to take us to the southern tip of Kent Island.

He turned from gauging the set of the jibs. "Penny, there's a small halyard at the mizzen mast. I'd like you to find it and raise the burgee in the bag." Curious Georgette went on alert.

"Yessir," I said, and unzipped the bag. Whatever was rolled up in there was the same color as the BoatWorks logo design he'd decided to use. "Holy—" I called back. I immediately understood Craig's smile when he'd welcomed me aboard. The burgee was too large to unroll in the cockpit, so I clambered to the mizzen mast and on a cleat found a small nylon halyard fitted with bronze snap shackles. I snapped the top one into the first grommet and snapped the second shackle into the other. I couldn't stop my grin. I held the bag and began hauling on the halyard. Momentarily, the entire assembly broke out in laughter. The burgee read BRODY'S BOATWORKS, but it was *upside down*. My euphoria plummeted into mortified embarrassment. It took only a minute to reverse the snap shackles and begin raising the burgee again. Even the logo image of the sailboat on the railway had been embroidered in bright yellow. As the burgee began climbing the mizzen mast, my efforts were rewarded with applause. Once it was fully aloft and flying proudly, I secured the halyard and gave my audience a theatrical curtsy.

"Would you like a trick at the helm?" Dylan asked. "Tony tells me you sailed at the Naval Academy."

He didn't need to ask twice. Craig relinquished the wheel and I found myself once again feeling the lovely balance between the tug of the wind and the insistence of the keel and rudder. John Masefield's line popped into my head: . . . *And all I ask is a tall ship and a star to steer her by* . . . Like riding a bicycle, it's a sensation that's old but always new. I gripped the decorative ropework on the wheel as if I were an "old hand." Nothing ahead except a distant freighter plowing north toward Baltimore. We'd be across the shipping channel long before it closed in. A glance at the main and its topsail as they began to luff, and a nod to Craig had the desired effect: a crewman cranked in the main sheet just enough to reduce the luffing.

Dylan punched a call button and Karim appeared balancing a tray with flutes of champagne and an array of small sandwiches. The *Elizabeth* was a perfect lady. She held her angle of heel and climbed slowly through the surges that rolled from the north. On land, I don't drink and drive, but I accepted one of the flutes. Exhilarating!

"Here's to Brody's BoatWorks," Tony said, raising his flute.

"Hear, hear!" Mom said, and we all raised our flutes. "To Brody's BoatWorks."

"Bloody Point lighthouse dead ahead," Dylan called out. In the distance almost directly ahead was the huge rusted cylinder with a flashing light at its top. We would leave it to port to avoid the shallows at the tip of Kent Island. Soon we rounded the end of the island and headed into the bight behind the Point. The luffing sails were lowered as we bobbed closer to the beach.

"Drop anchor," Dylan called to a crewman on the foredeck. The chain rattled out for less than a minute before the anchor

A Sardonic Death

hit bottom. Another few seconds and the anchor winch was braked. *Elizabeth* drifted a moment until the chain was taut and everything stopped. We all shrugged forward like you lift slightly in an elevator when it stops at a floor. A couple of small sailboats, moored close to the shore with their barbecue grills already aflame, gave off a fragrance that jump-started my hunger pangs.

The companionway from the main cabin and, obviously, the galley, slid open and Karim stepped into the cockpit with the first course, Satay Chicken Tenders. Behind him, one of the crew carried a tray of tumblers and several bottles. "Whiskey, sir?" he asked Tony. "And ice?"

Without being asked, he poured a Jameson for Dylan and approached Mom. "For you, miss?"

I shivered at the thought that she might need to be carried off the *Elizabeth* when we returned to Annapolis but, dutiful daughter that I am, kept my mouth shut.

"A white wine, if you please," she said. *Hallelujah!*

Sandy and I followed suit and settled in with the chicken tenders.

"How's your search for a BoatWorks location going?" Tony asked Dylan. For Sandy's benefit, he explained, "Dylan has asked us to help him launch a boat supplies franchise."

"There aren't enough already?" Sandy said.

"Not like what Dylan has in mind," I said.

"Commercial real estate," Dylan began, "close to the waterfront, is sky-high. And away from the waterfront is not where a boating supplies store will be very successful."

"But you're not looking at adding another store," I said as I discreetly licked a dab of peanut sauce from a finger. "Yours will be a *mega*-store, with discounts that'll entice boat owners from all over the Chesapeake Bay."

"I like the way you think, Penelope," Dylan said.

"Could you have free limos to and from Annapolis harbor?" Mom suggested, popping a chicken tender.

Dylan glanced at Mom with an appreciative smile. And back to me: "I see where you inherited your brains."

I actually smiled. "Thanks, Mom."

"I've started looking at out of town commercial real estate," Dylan said, with a glance at Tony. "In Severna Park, I saw a building that I thought might work for us. I was hoping you two would visit. When Raymond contacted the listing agent, he learned that just the day before a pair of women had put down ten thousand in earnest money. Seems they own some kind of company that makes medical devices and need room to expand."

"What kind of devices?" Mom asked. We were thinking the same thing.

"Something like tonics."

Mom and I looked at each other. "Did Tanya or Jeff mention expansion to you?"

"Nothing," said Mom.

"Guess we're going to have another chat with Mr. Gratrix," I said.

Dylan and Tony were clearly confused. "Does that business have anything to do with you?" Tony asked.

I briefly explained the business that Aidan had left to Tanya and Mom without revealing what we knew of the newest technology that Tanya and her father hoped would revolutionize the prosthetics industry.

"Crazy small world," Dylan said.

Sandy announced that, as a nurse practitioner with an orthopedics practice in Baltimore, she'd heard rumors about a Novak Research Corporation that was on the cutting edge of prosthetics innovation. "Tony and I looked into investing in it, but it turns out it's privately owned. The owner's name is Herman. Herman Novak."

Mom and I stared wide-eyed at each other.

Karim reappeared with plates of lobster with space for our choice of German potato salad or grilled vegetables that a second crewman offered. A waiter collected our appetizer plates while Dylan refilled our wine.

By the time the cherry cheesecake and coffees were served, First Mate Craig had the engine started and the anchor up. A family of mallards swam past the stern as the *Elizabeth* began moving gracefully back around Kent Point to head almost directly north toward Annapolis. The wind had nearly died as the evening settled around us, so Dylan instructed Craig to switch on the running lights and motor us home. Atop the mizzen mast, the new BoatWorks burgee snapped proudly. Crossing the shipping channel, Craig changed course briefly to pass a freighter southbound from Baltimore port-to-port. She was high in the water so we could see her props chopping the water as she passed.

At the City Dock, Dylan gave Mom a hug as he assisted her from the tender to the dock. We thanked him profusely for the perfect day and joked with Tony and Sandy that we should do this more often. But before bidding us *À bien tôt*, as if by magic, Dylan pulled three cymbidium orchids from a pocket, one for each of his female crew.

"Oh!" "Thank you, Captain," and "How sweet!" we echoed as he saluted us smartly and maneuvered the tender back out to the *Elizabeth*.

Mom and I walked back to where I had parked while I wondered what had changed between Dylan and me. Finally, I concluded that what had changed was that I refused to be a sucker for a handsome world traveler with a huge yacht. And then it hit me. Any thought of hitching my life to Dylan Brody and his beautiful oceangoing yacht would be a crazy echo of Mom's escape with Aidan when she was about the same age as I was now. Little Josh's death had precipitated that escape while apparently Aidan's lack of loving had led to her plan to wed Dr. Chen. I wondered if I had too easily given up on Aaron in order to open the door to richer possibilities. Maybe Mom and I had more in common than I thought. Scary.

En route to Ravenscroft, I explained to Mom my idea for Kalea and me to visit the Prosthetonics office to learn what Tanya and Colleen might be hatching.

"Good idea, Penny. While you and Kalea work that angle, I'll have another meeting with Jeff."

Chapter 31

Monday morning I phoned Kalea. I said, "Penny for your thoughts" when she picked up.

"Aunt Penny!" she shouted.

"Punkin."

"Grrrr. If you don't start using my real name," she barked, "I'll roll a curse on you."

"I didn't realize you minded your pet name."

"It was okay at first, but I've grown out of it."

"Okay, I'll try to grow out of using it.

Anyone who called Kalea "cute" or "adorable" was sentenced to be jinxed by taffy-rolling her arms and two index fingers aimed at their heart. So far, I hadn't been caught by her curse. But I had survived childhood with only one pet name other than Penny-lope: "Curious Georgette." And I never objected to it. I've worn it as a kind of badge of honor and still think of my curiosity as central to my growing reputation as an amateur sleuth, not that I've done anything more than been in the right place at the right time. Which is why I'd decided to go out on the proverbial limb to find who put the proverbial overalls in Mrs. Murphy's chowder.

Someone had poisoned Aidan with *Oenanthe crocata* aka Water Celery. Lately, I'd come to the conclusion that although Mom may have harbored murderous thoughts, she hadn't been the cook who added the poison to the stew. After Dr. Chen, my next suspect was a beautiful young woman with a prosthetic arm she'd won in the Afghanistan sweepstakes. I'd never met her but, with Kalea's assistance, I intended to.

"Last week, I mentioned an undercover job—"

"Thought you'd forgotten," Kalea said.

"We'll do it this week if you're not too busy with your forensics book."

"I can squeeze in one more assignment," she said, "if the disguise isn't too complex."

I laughed. "You'll only need to be a sixth-grade investigative reporter."

"And how do you plan on disguising yourself as my aunt? Adopted kids don't have aunts."

"I'll just let you call me 'Aunt Penny' a couple of times. The people at Prosthetonics will never know."

A few minutes before ten the next morning, I found a parking spot a couple of blocks from the Medical Arts Building on Riva Road where the Prosthetonics office was located. I didn't want any of their spies connecting my Summers Breeze Gardening business emblazoned on both sides of the van with the name I had used in making the appointment.

"Don't be surprised," I said, "when I pretend I know nothing at all about Aidan or the company. And you should ask about anything you think should be in your story."

Kalea rolled her eyes. "Duhhh."

We approached the building catty-corner through the parking lot. In the back row was a car that caught Kalea's attention. "They haven't made those since before I was born."

I'd never been keen on automotive history. "What is it?"

Then I noticed the driver's side door where it clearly said "El Camino SS."

"An El Camino," she announced. "A guy in my class has a scrapbook of old cars."

"Thanks, Sherlock," I said. It looked like it had just come from a showroom. "I doubt if it's the original color, though." It

A Sardonic Death

was lipstick pink.

On the other side of the El Camino was a car I *did* recognize - a dark blue BMW sedan suitable for royalty. Its front tag read "Tanya" in silver script.

❧

A moment after Kalea knocked on the door, it was opened. "You must be Penny Braithwaite," the woman said, "and Kalea. Come right in."

Kalea opened her new reporter's notebook, already in character. "May I make a note of your name?"

"Sorry. I'm Colleen Clemmons. The owner's assistant. Let's go through to our conference room."

The conference room was carpeted, boasted a contemporary table and six chairs, and on the walls framed photos of worldwide tourist destinations that I assumed Aidan had taken. At one end of the room was an enlarged photo of Aidan, caught mid-paddle in the canoe on his man-made pond. A smaller version, a favorite of Mom's, was on the mantel at Ravenscroft. "That's our founder," Colleen said, as she buzzed an intercom for Tanya to join us. "Aidan Reid, God rest his soul."

Whose death led to this subterfuge, whispered Grandpa Jack.

"What happened to Mr. Reid?" I asked.

"He died recently and we're still in shock but we're trying to maintain the fortitude he demonstrated by following his business motto: 'Helping those who have lost limbs protecting our freedoms.'" I guessed Aidan himself had written it.

"How long did you know him?" Kalea asked.

"I joined Aidan and Tanya in February, so it's been about four months. A nicer gentleman you could never meet."

"Aidan Reid was also a fine businessman," Tanya said as

she entered the room. She was more beautiful than I had imagined, and her right arm prosthesis was as futuristic as any Hollywood cyborg designer might have created. I could understand why Mom assumed Aidan was in love with her. "I'll never forget his faith in me allowing me to join the company," she said. Her admiration for the man was clear.

For a fraction of a second, Colleen scowled. Had Kalea caught it? Probably. She was developing a keen eye for discord, watching the dynamics between her moms. Perhaps, I thought, Colleen didn't share Tanya's admiration for Aidan, or she could have thought Tanya's regard for Aidan threatened *their* relationship.

Tanya extended her prosthetic hand to Kalea who, with only a nanosecond's hesitation, engaged in a handshake. "It's a pleasure to meet you, Ms. Novak," Kalea said. "I really appreciate your seeing me on short notice." She sounded unrehearsed and sincere. She was good.

"Thank *you*," Tanya said, "for giving us an opportunity to acquaint more people with our work."

"We noticed your gorgeous BMW," Kalea said.

Tanya laughed. "I applaud your powers of observation. You'll be a fine reporter."

As Tanya sat, she hugged Colleen. Colleen brightened. I had the distinct impression that these two women were far more to each other than simply business associates.

"Did you notice the old car beside it?" Colleen asked.

"The El Camino?" Kalea said. "Of course. It's stunning."

"She belonged to my dad," Colleen said. "I had her restored and repainted last year. She's the same color as Elvis's Caddy."

"She's beautiful," I said.

"Okay," Tanya said. "Let's talk about your article, Kalea. Do you have a theme for your essay?"

A Sardonic Death

"It'll be like an article that I'll submit to a middle-school feature-writing competition. About how prosthetic devices have evolved since the days of wooden legs."

Colleen chuckled. "That could fill an entire book," she said.

"By the time you worked your way up to today's technology," Tanya said with a smile, "it will have already moved on. You might never catch up."

"Aunt Penny," Kalea said, faking a worried expression, "d'you think I should concentrate on a smaller part of the subject?"

"I think once you start writing, you'll find yourself automatically finding your limits. You remember why Snoopy decided to write a short story instead of a novel?"

"Yeah." She rolled her eyes. "Only one sheet of paper."

Colleen and Tanya laughed. "If you want to primarily focus on the newest research," Tanya said, "you could quickly cover the birth of prosthetic design after the Civil War, when the government promised every amputee a replacement leg or arm to help reduce feelings of inferiority, and improvements during the world wars, and then jump to our latest designs and the research that's laying the foundation for our newest devices."

"Okay," Kalea said. "I'll research past history online. But I think what our readers will be most interested in is the latest advances and research." She must have role-played this with one of her moms. She opened her notebook, turned a page, wrote a headline, and assumed a reporter's pose, anxious for information.

Tanya and Colleen shared a look before Tanya said, "Here's a first line for you: 'A local company is making medical history developing prosthetic devices controlled by a patient's thoughts.'"

Kalea wrote it in her notebook and looked up at me.

"You don't have to use it verbatim," I said, "but it can be your theme."

Kalea nodded and turned back to Tanya and Colleen. "That sounds very fut . . . futuristic. How would that work?"

"We're hoping to fit a patient who's lost an arm . . . like me, a soldier who was wounded in Afghanistan, with a prosthesis that responds to the patient's—"

"How soon?" said Kalea.

"We hope to be ready before the end of the year," Tanya said.

Colleen picked up the thread. "At the same time, we're continuing to fit veterans with traditional technology."

"What we're working on," Tanya said, "is revolutionary. Our new patients will have tiny electrodes implanted under their scalps that will communicate wirelessly with electronic controllers in a prosthetic limb. That's the part that's brand new in our industry."

"*Wow!*" Kalea's enthusiasm bubbled over.

"You have no idea how many wounded vets we could help with this technology," Colleen said.

"Thousands," said Tanya.

"So," I interjected, "you're on track to become a national center for this kind of therapy. Sounds to me like there's a bundle of money to be made."

Tanya didn't blink. "You're absolutely right, Ms. Braithwaite."

"But the most important thing," Colleen said, "is that we can help so many amputees lead more normal lives."

"A wonderful legacy for Mr. Reid's family," I said, "not that anything could soften the devastation of the owner's death. Good point for your article, Kalea."

"Frankly," Tanya said, "they're no longer involved. Mr.

A Sardonic Death

Reid had no children and his wife's pretty much out of the picture. Colleen and I are the owners. We plan to change the name of the company to Prosthetonics International. Sounds impressive, don't you think, Kalea? Naturally, we'll need to expand our production area and hire a number of highly trained staff, but we're anticipating rapid growth."

Red flags waved maddeningly from every corner of my brain.

"Is there anything else you'd like to ask us, Kalea?" Tanya asked.

"How did the discovery of using brain waves or whatever to control electronic arms or legs get made?"

"My dad is spearheading that part of our work," Tanya said. "He's now on our board of directors. Really crucial to our success. For your article, his name is Herman."

"Neurothetics is in a research park in Frederick County," Colleen added. "That's where the links between neurological impulses and tiny prosthetic motors are being developed. They've found, for instance, that the number of impulses required to control hands and fingers is far more complex than those needed to control legs and feet in spite of the fact that body balance is critical in our feet and legs."

Kalea was making notes as quickly as possible. "Could we visit the lab?"

"Of course," Tanya said. "I'll give my dad a heads-up so you can give his office a call when you're ready." She handed Kalea a card with the Frederick office information.

"Thanks," she said.

"Our first Neurotech prosthetic," Tanya said, "will probably go to a vet who has lost a leg. We're talking with orthopedists at Walter Reed Hospital in Bethesda to identify our first recipient."

"Could I come back and meet him when he's ready to begin using the new pro-thesis?"

"It's *pross*-thesis," Tanya said. Kalea crossed out the word in her notebook and corrected it. "I can't see why not. We'll keep in touch."

Colleen gave Kalea a small stack of prosthetics and orthotics magazines. "You may find some of these articles helpful in your research." The cover photo on the top one was of Tanya serving a volleyball with her prosthetic arm.

"Call us if you have any other questions when you write your article," Colleen said.

"Thank you both," Kalea said as we prepared to leave. "I'm fascinated by your project and hope you'll let me know when I can meet the first patient with the new technology."

"You can count on it," said Tanya.

Colleen and Tanya gave me their cards. "We'll look forward to meeting your dad, Tanya," I said. "We'll stay in touch."

On our way to her house, I asked Kalea for her impression of the two women.

"They're into each other," Kalea said. "Like my moms used to be." She was quiet for a moment and added, "I also think Colleen is jealous of Tanya since she's so much prettier."

"I had the same impression." I was certain Tanya and Colleen were, as I'd read somewhere, two of the women the Greeks named that island after. "They're certainly serious about the business and excited about their new technology."

"I would really like, actually," Kalea said, "to see how it works out. It would be really awesome to see their first patient walking on his new leg!"

"Now tell me," I said, "about the competition you said you'd enter your article in."

A Sardonic Death

"I made that part up."

"Good job, Punkin."

"Haven't we spoken about that?" she said.

I apologized for using her pet name and begged her to give me another chance before rolling her curse on me. After a hug, I dropped her at her house. Then headed straight to Ravenscroft.

Chapter 32

I didn't recognize the car parked behind Mom's Ferrari. The vanity tag read BRENNAN. I pulled in behind it and rushed to the door, eager to share what Kalea and I had learned from Tanya and Colleen. I made a mental note that one of the sentinel Tropicana lily blooms had outlived its beauty. Mom would have to learn to deadhead these lilies or hire someone to do it. They were her babies now, not mine.

I knocked perfunctorily and swung the unlocked door open to hear her call, "We're in the living room."

I walked in and it took only a pair of nano-seconds to connect the man with his tag. "Dr. Brennan, I presume?"

He was somewhere in his sixties, wire-rimmed oval glasses, and a bow tie that was a collage of historic American flags. "Brilliant deduction, Penelope."

Once again, I was branded: *Smartass*.

"Doc and I've been talking about you—after a fashion," Mom said, and sipped her mystery martini.

"What kind of fashion would that be?"

"I asked Owen if he could stop in to answer the questions you asked about the day Aidan died."

"Oh. Great," I said, meaning it, and turned to Dr. Brennan. "How far'd you gotten?"

He smiled. "Actually I just got here." He took a sip of whatever Mom had plied him with in the thick-bottomed tumbler and set it down.

"So I'll start at the beginning. I got here that evening as soon as I could after your mom called—about six. She explained that she'd tried to take Aidan a celebratory Irish

A Sardonic Death

whiskey after a business meeting and then a mug of soup he usually loved—"

"Doctor Brennan, what was your impression of Aidan when you first got here?"

"Your stepdad was exhausted from the meeting, but otherwise okay. I wasn't worried about his appetite. That's a common reaction to the antibiotics he was taking."

"Mom tells me she had quite a gang here that afternoon. Some of them brought food."

"A couple of women from his office brought—" He turned to Mom. "Soup, wasn't it?"

"And my chiropractor brought a thermos of his veggie recipe," she added.

"So," I said, "he had three to choose from. Do you see why that could be important in understanding how he died?"

Dr. Brennan stared. "I haven't a clue what you're suggesting. He died from acute pneumonia."

Mom started to explain. "Penny has a theory that some part of a plant I brought back from Sardinia combined with the pneumonia—"

"Not in combination with anything," I said. "He would have probably survived the pneumonia. I'm certain he died from eating, probably either in soup or in a veggie pizza, part of a root that looked like a parsnip."

"I was called," Brennan said, "because he wouldn't eat anything."

"As far as you know," I said. "There were several others in the house that evening. Someone fed him a piece of the Devil's Parsnip."

"How can you be sure?" Brennan asked.

"Because the undertaker confirmed that he wore a sardonic smile. You might not have noticed—"

"What kind of smile?"

Once again, I explained the rictus that appears on victims of Water Celery poisoning.

"You know," he began, "I'd heard of the condition called *risus sardonicus*, but I never understood how it happened or to whom."

I then explained how the plant was used by the ancient Sardinians.

"Well, that's one for the books," Brennan said. "But I didn't notice anything inconsistent with pneumonia as the cause of death."

"So after you checked on him, as I understand it, Mom ordered pizzas and you all ate down here."

"Precisely."

"Mom, did anyone check on him before Tanya and Colleen found him . . . dead?"

She shook her head. "I don't remember." Slugged more of her martini.

"We were all concerned," Brennan said, "that he didn't feel well enough to join us. We went through several bottles of Chianti so my memory won't be perfect. But as the evening progressed, we all probably went up to him."

"I remember Jeff and Tanya," Mom said, "seeming delighted with their impromptu board meeting. For some reason, Colleen was more subdued."

"And Dr. Chen?" I asked.

Mom finished her martini and headed to the bar to pour another. "I remember," Brennan continued, "that he brought the soup that Aidan had apparently refused earlier. But I don't recall if Chen took him any while I was here."

"Do you remember if Mr. Gratrix or either of the Prosthetonics women took anything up to him?"

A Sardonic Death

"I suppose they did," Brennan said, "but if you're trying to nail down the chronology of who saw him when, and who might have given him a piece of your poison parsley, I can't help you there."

I laughed. "It would be more help if either you or Mom could be certain if someone *didn't* go up to the guest bedroom that evening."

"Then I've been absolutely no help at all," Brennan said, smiling adroitly.

"I don't think the Chinese lizard ever went up to him," Mom said.

Someone, Grandpa Jack insisted, *fed Aidan the Devil's Parsnip.*

"Mom, one more question. When Tanya and Colleen and the others from Prosthetonics arrived for their meeting with Aidan, did they have time for a walk around the garden?"

She held her refreshed martini that was already half gone. "I remember serving drinks," she said. "Stan whatsisname and Brad Wentworth. Jeff wasn't expected for another half hour and they couldn't convene the board meeting without him. Colleen and Tanya, as I recall, said they were detoxing that week and that was their day to have a walk between meals so they said they'd get some fresh air. I figured they needed time to coordinate their strategy before the meeting."

"Do you think they could have detoured to the big pond and pulled out a clump of Water Celery?"

Mom and Doc Brennan exchanged a glance. Mom finally said, "I can't believe you're thinking that Aidan's new partner might have wanted to kill him."

"All's fair in love and war, they say, and I'd think manipulating a business partnership might fall under either heading."

"What about it, Ophelia?" said Brennan.

"The day after his funeral, I remember walking around here trying to figure out what life was going to be like without him. On the path through the trees toward the pond, I remember seeing a handful of weeds that someone had yanked out and been too lazy to take to the compost. It bothered me that someone had been so thoughtless as to leave it for my maintenance crew to compost. But now that you mention it, those weeds could have been Water Celery."

"Did you take them to the compost?"

We rose at the same time. "Let's have a look," we said almost in unison. Mom, a bit wobbly, led us past the swimming pool to the path that led behind the tennis court to a garden shed. Beside the shed, inside a low fence, was the moldering compost. I leaned over it and began pulling off mats of smelly cuttings from a recent visit of her lawn maintenance crew. Under them were the weeds Mom had flung there. I picked up the wilted bundle and held them out to her like a child's offering.

"That looks like what I picked out of the pachysandra," Mom said. "What is it?"

I held a couple of floppy flower heads that resembled Queen Anne's Lace, a bunch of celery-lookalike branched leaves, one parsnip-like root, and evidence of where lacy-flowered stems had been snipped from a root. "Whoever tossed these," I said, "saved a root to send Aidan into the next world with a smile on his face."

Mom's face crumpled into disbelief. "*Who?*" she asked.

"If those were tossed in the woods the day of the board meeting," I said, "I'd guess either Colleen or Tanya."

"I tried to tell him he shouldn't trust them," Mom said, "in spite of her father's money and the technology. I knew it would

A Sardonic Death

go all wrong." She began to cry. "There was always something not quite right with Tanya and her friend. At the funeral, Herman was like a mask of sad condolences. Never met the man behind that mask."

Grandpa Jack whispered, *Aidan's funeral might have been the final step in the Novaks' plan for fame and fortune.*

"I've let you both down, Ophelia," said Brennan. "I'm so sorry."

Mom put her arm around him. "It's not your fault, Doc. Aidan wouldn't listen to me. Said the business had to keep up with technological advances. And Tanya was his best opportunity."

I also bet Doc that he'd never again miss a case of *risus sardonicus*.

Chapter 33

The next day after work, I returned to my condo, received my usual enthusiastic canine welcome, poured myself a glass of chardonnay, and phoned Jeffery Gratrix.

Before I could begin telling him what Kalea and I had learned during our visit to Prosthetonics, he began, "What a nice surprise."

"How so?"

"I've wanted to continue our conversation about the Prosthetonics situation."

"Anything new I should know about?"

"That's an *under*statement. First things first: Miss Tanya Novak was found dead this morning."

I wasn't in front of a mirror to see, but my mouth was undoubtedly wide open. For a moment I couldn't speak.

"*What . . .?* What about her father? What about Colleen?"

"As I understand it, when she didn't show up at the office this morning, Colleen went to check on her and found her in bed. She called the police and Mr. Novak at his lab in Frederick—he called me and then headed to the office. I'm guessing that she'll be autopsied. I have no idea if her apartment has been searched but there again, I would assume that it either has or will be."

"Where are Colleen and Mr. Novak now?"

"I left them at the Prosthetonics office about an hour ago."

"Does Mom know?"

"I haven't called her since so much is unknown and you know how she can get under stress."

A Sardonic Death

"What about provisions for the ownership of the company?"

"Legally it reverts to the two remaining members of the board, Colleen and Mr. Novak. Well . . . and your mom. Her predicament will have to be sorted out."

For a moment I silently digested this major turnabout.

"Mr. Gratrix, you said 'First things first.' Is there a second something?"

There was a pause. "If it's not too late for you, could you pop over to my office? I think we should continue this in privacy."

The suggestion was more than enough for Curious Georgette. "Twenty minutes?"

"I'll be here."

I'd scoped the Malakoff and Gratrix law office out on Forest Drive so I knew where Cheyenne worked. Fifteen minutes later, I lifted a brass door knocker and let it fall as I opened the peacock green door into the law firm's foyer. I knew I was in the right place when I saw an elegantly framed photograph of the Brantleigh Manor estate that Shy had taken in North Carolina. Seated under the photograph, the receptionist glanced up and asked if she might assist me.

"I'm Penelope Summers and . . . uh, Mr. Gratrix asked me to come in."

"Oh yes. He's expecting you, Ms. Summers. Come with me please." She extended her hand to the stairs. I followed to the second floor and to Mr. Gratrix's spacious office. A trio of windows at his back overlooked the tranquility of Forest Drive. Jeffery rose from behind his broad desk and pulled one of his client chairs close.

"Penny, I hope I haven't inconvenienced you by suggesting you come in this afternoon."

"You had me hooked when you implied there was a second topic you wanted to brief me on."

He laughed and cleared his throat. "I didn't intend to make it seem mysterious, but, in light of Tanya's death, I felt you'd want to know."

"Mr. Gratrix—"

"Please, just Jeffery."

"Then, Jeffery, I'm sure you're right. I *would* want to know."

"Right, then. It was last Friday morning after our regular board meeting. After the meeting, which was nothing more than bringing us all up to date on the business details, workflow, Mr. Novak's newest lab results, et cetera, Tanya walked me back to my car and asked me to call her that evening. Said she wanted to talk privately. When I called, she first confirmed that she was alone. Colleen had gone to pick up their vegan dinner—from someplace that doesn't deliver." He cleared his throat. "You know they're pretty close. They have separate homes, but they spend most evenings together . . ."

I said that I knew of their close relationship.

Jeffery's secretary knocked gently on the door frame and entered with two cups of tea. "Do you like Earl Grey?" Jeffery asked. "I usually have a cup about this time of day."

I nodded, accepted a cup, and took a sip as Jeffery thanked her and continued. "Well, the point of this is that Tanya told me she'd been getting strange vibes from Colleen lately and, in fact, had felt some hostility from her. I didn't mention this to you last Friday, but in light of her death, I thought it might be relevant."

"Did she have a reason or some new emotional reaction for the vibes?"

"I asked her essentially the same question. Her answer

seemed to hinge on an imagined jealousy that Colleen had of her, thinking that since Tanya was grieving over Aidan's death, Colleen may have imagined she'd been in love with him—"

"Jeffery, that mirrors Mom's impression that Aidan had been in love with Tanya. She apparently never had any kind of proof but said Aidan had been less attentive to her since about the time that Tanya became a co-owner. She was, of course, strikingly beautiful and that may have stoked Mom's imagination."

"It was clear to me," Jeffery said, "that Tanya was actually, if not quite *fearful*, at least apprehensive of Colleen. She was unsure what to do, how she might bring up her feelings and clear the proverbial air." He chuckled. "I reminded her that I'm a lawyer, not a counselor, or even a mediator. Tanya then said that Colleen was the type who was quick to anger if she feels wronged and had admitted in the past that she'd been labeled a hothead."

"I can tell you from experience," I said, "that it's hard to watch someone you thought you loved fall in love with someone else. Your own sense of worth goes down the drain. Lesbians certainly aren't unique in that respect."

"So," Jeffery continued, "I know nothing of the details of Tanya's death or what the police are thinking, but, as I said, I thought you'd like to know."

"Have you spoken to a detective?"

He humphed. "What I heard is totally hearsay. There could be a dozen ways Tanya might have died, so my reporting her reaction last Friday might only be worth a big fat zero. But I wanted to share Tanya's concerns and I knew I could trust you."

Grandpa Jack whispered, *Tidbits and hearsay sometimes suggest a pattern that could lead to a theory.*

"Then thanks for the information and your confidence."

Jeffery went on. "Cheyenne mentioned that you and Kalea met with Tanya and Colleen yesterday."

I explained our "undercover" visit to Prosthetonics and Kalea's impression that Colleen was jealous of Tanya, since Tanya was, as Kalea noticed, much prettier. "Kalea pretended to be researching an article on prosthetics for a summer writing assignment. She role-played the interview beautifully. Asked good questions and evoked real interest in the business."

"She's a bright young lady."

That's an understatement, Grandpa Jack whispered.

"But we didn't learn much beyond what I'd already heard from you about their strategy to squeeze Mom out of the profit-sharing."

"I'll make sure that doesn't happen."

"I can't imagine how Kalea will respond to the news of Tanya's death."

He was thoughtful for a moment, then said, "Cheyenne went home this morning to be with her as soon as we learned about it."

I walked to my van, started the engine, slipped it into gear, and punched up Mom on speed dial.

I heard, "What's up Penelope?" and the clink of ice cubes.

I told her what little I knew of Tanya's death. Jeffery's hearsay I kept to myself.

After several seconds of silence and an amplified sound of swallowing, Mom asked, "Where does that leave *me*?"

"That's something I suppose you and Jeffery will work out."

On my way back to Eastport, I couldn't help but ponder if Colleen's jealousy could somehow have led her to kill Tanya, and if so, might she also have been responsible for Aidan's demise? His death certainly removed what Colleen may have perceived as the "odd man out."

So it wasn't your mother, Grandpa Jack finally agreed, *who poisoned Aidan.*

Grandpa Jack's was the third vote against my one to clear Mom from suspicion. Although I still occasionally ruminated on my threat of mixing cat kibble into her granola for abandoning us all these years ago.

Once again, I needed expert guidance. What sort of woman would kill her lesbian lover believing that lover was agonizing over the lost love of a man? I left a message for Aaron to ask if he could arrange another meeting with Astrid, the Naval Academy's psychologist. Then I phoned Jason to learn if anything about Tanya's death would be in tomorrow's paper.

"If I had any juicy information for my favorite amateur sleuth, believe me, I'd pass it along," he said. "A couple of forensic investigators have been at her apartment today, but, unless I get a booster injection of ESP, there's nothing more I can tell you."

I was on my way to see Kalea when my phone alerted me to a reply from Aaron. Not, "How ya doing?" or any other social nicety. "What's happened that you want to chat with Astrid?"

I told him of Tanya's death and the possibility of its being the revenge of a jealous lover, silently hoping he'd be supremely grateful that *I* wasn't the vengeful sort.

"You know, of course, that Astrid will soliloquize on the subject, and, in the end, be noncommittal."

"I wouldn't expect her to identify the killer but at least I'll have the advantage of the soliloquy. Which is a whole lot more than I have now."

Aaron was silent for a moment. "I'd like to listen in on that one," he said. "Sounds interesting. I have to get back to Georgia next weekend so I'll try for Thursday evening. I'll give Elana a call. If I can wheedle Astrid's phone number from her, I'll give you a buzz. Actually . . . I'll get back to you either way."

Kalea must have been near a window because she was on the front porch almost before I'd shifted into PARK and switched off. Her sober countenance telegraphed her mood. "Did our visit sentence her to death?" she asked.

Once again, here I was in the role of counselor with zero training or experience. As a division officer on the USS Enterprise, I had counseled younger sailors in my public affairs division on their Navy careers and, more than once, about appropriate behavior on liberty ashore. But I'd never dealt with someone whose fear of karma had led them to question their behavior. I knelt on the stone landing and embraced my young friend. "Absolutely not."

"Then why did she die?"

"Kalea, you're old enough to understand that that's a question people have asked, probably since forever." I was still asking it about my little brother Josh.

"Can I still write the article?"

"Of course. You can dedicate it to Tanya and submit it to one of the orthotics and prosthetics magazines she gave you. Colleen can probably help us select one. If you can describe Tanya's enthusiasm and commitment to her work, I'll bet one of them will accept your article. Might even pay you. Ask your English teacher for some guidance."

We walked beneath overhanging maples around a couple of blocks in the quiet neighborhood, pondering the mysteries of life and death.

A Sardonic Death

"Tanya's life was worth living," Kalea finally reasoned, "if her new technology can improve the lives of more veterans."

"That's a great thread to weave into your article."

"Let's hope it actually works," she said. "Wouldn't it be great to have their first amputee using their prosthesis at the end of the article?"

"Or," I said, "at the beginning of the article."

"When can we go to Frederick?"

"It'll have to be this week if you don't want to miss any of the Police Academy."

"Friday?"

Kalea's enthusiastic hug made the afternoon worthwhile.

Chapter 34

Halfway to my condo, my phone began prancing out Chopin's "Heroic Polonaise," my new ringtone for Mom.

"I have a surprise for you," she announced.

I had no use for any more surprises. Enough already.

"If you haven't eaten yet, come, please."

A different car was parked behind Mom's Ferrari.

Her front door, as usual, was unlocked. I opened it and there was–Aidan?

He stuck his hand out, looked me up and down and called to Mom. "What a lovely lass." The Irish accent was stronger than Aidan's. "Ofee, you never told me you and himself had a gorgeous daughter."

Ofee, short for Ophelia? Give me a break!

Then he turned back to me. "You must be Penelope."

Grandpa Jack quickly reminded me that the dead very seldom come back to life. This man was a slightly younger version of my client. Same paunch, same hair, same affable manner, and a very similar voice.

"And who may I tell myself I'm speaking to?"

"I'm Brendan himself, brother to our departed Aidan, but just as saintly."

He carried a faceted tumbler of whiskey in one hand and, with a swig, motioned me to join him and Mom in the living room.

"Isn't he a spittin' image?" Mom said.

"If we were in Ireland, you'd call me a fetch," he said.

A Sardonic Death

"Sometimes they appear before a death." He chuckled. "But in this case, I arrived after."

Suspicions loomed, amorphous premonitions, probably just a primal fear of the unknown.

"After Aidan died," Mom said, "I sent a note to Mrs. Reid in Ireland."

"And I, poor sod, have been in New York, rehearsing a grievous mistake of a play that will undoubtedly have no more than a two-day run on Broadway." He chortled again. "An adaptation of *Borstal Boy*."

I'd read some of Brendan Behan's work in a modern poetry course at the Naval Academy, but the only quotes that came to mind were *"I am a drinker with writing problems,"* and *"There's no such thing as bad publicity except your own obituary."* I could easily imagine this Brendan as the poet on a Broadway stage.

"You can call me Uncle," he said. "Uncles are similar to dads, but more *craic*."

"Do I have a *craic* aunt, too?" I asked. Mom gave me a silent head-shake.

"Actually, you have another uncle, lass. My husband's a hottie on the soaps."

"I'll look forward to meeting him. So, Uncle Brendan, did you just hear about Aidan's death?"

"A telegram came from me mum in Ireland, but I couldn't get away until yesterday. The business side of the company is raising money to produce *Borstal Boy*. I'm out on the streets and free to get into trouble for a week or two."

I glanced at Mom. "Had you met Brendan before?"

"She's not sure she wants to remember." Brendan chuckled. "We met fifteen years ago when she and himself were in California. My brother and I were both after wanting her affections. Aidan won out and I went back to New York to seek fame and fortune." He belly-laughed. "Haven't found either one, but I couldn't stay away and let Ofee here think she was the only one in the world missing his saintliness."

"His mum named both her sons for Irish saints," Mom explained.

"My sister, Deirdre's also a saint. Didn't start out as one, though. Had her first kid while she was in the Sixth Form. But she kept the child and she's at the bar now. Helping youngsters like her keep their kids."

"Tell Penny what you've decided," Mom prompted him.

"I've decided to help you get at the truth of how Aidan died." In his delightful accent, it sounded like a pronouncement from a muezzin in a minaret promising heavenly intervention. "From what Ofee's told me, you've got a number of lads and lasses on your list of suspects. I can strum me golden harp to keep your brain focused while you perform your Sherlockian magic."

"I . . . uhhh . . ."

"It's the least I could do. Unfortunately, I don't have a harp of any kind, and never been musically inclined, so I'll have to fall back on me gift o' gab."

Now what? Grandpa Jack whispered.

Now what, indeed, I whispered back. I was up to my tramp stamp in competing allegiances: my day job and Dylan's signs for Brody's BoatWorks wherever it might take shape, my mostly non-existent romantic life, my professional relationship with our primary client, and being an "aunt" to Kalea. Not to mention getting Mom detangled from suspicions that she had helped Aidan into the next world to enable her to live happily ever after with Dr. Chen. And, of course, Summers Breeze's management of Chen's new entry garden.

A Sardonic Death

"Has Mom told you how he died?"

Brendan frowned at Mom. "What am I going to do for grins if you already know?"

Grins, Grandpa Jack whispered. *Interesting he should choose that word.*

"Penny decided he was poisoned with Water Celery root from Sardinia."

"Well . . ." He turned his frown to me. "That seems like a long shot."

"Not when it's growing in Mom's pond."

"And why would you think that?"

I explained the sardonic grin caused by the Water Celery poison, and how it was used in ancient Sardinia.

He tossed down the last half-finger of whiskey and set the tumbler on the coffee table. "And, surely, 'twas the headless Dullahan who brought it?"

"It was I, myself," Mom said.

"And the customs officers thought it was a jolly good plan for you to grow this poison in your pond?"

Mom started to explain what a fine-looking plant it was until I interrupted: "Apparently it was so well hidden the customs guys never saw it."

Brendan fumbled in a jacket pocket for a bent-stem pipe and tobacco pouch. His face wrinkled in several directions as he punched down the earthy tobacco and rustled in his pocket for a long wooden match. It flared over the bowl until he drew down the flame. After a deep toke and considerate exhalations of sweet smoke, he found the words he'd sought. "All we have to do, then, is eliminate anyone who helped himself to a piece of this root and didn't share it with my brother."

"Or . . . helped *her*self," I added. Mom laughed self-consciously.

The tradesman alert at the gate sounded. Mom glanced out front and pressed a knob that sent the gates rolling open. "Dinner is nearly served," she announced and called over her shoulder for me to open a couple of bottles of wine while she went to the door to meet the pizza delivery.

Brendan offered the blessing: "Good land, good harvest, good roof above, Good friends, good gab, Good helping of love, Good hearts in good prayer to the good Lord above . . . For this we give thanks. Saints be praised."

Mom poured a helping of wine, sipped it, and laughed. "That's far more of a blessing than a pizza has ever had in this house."

After a slurp, Brendan raised an eyebrow at me. "You said it might be a *her*self who pinched the Water Celery root. I can't believe my brother ever incurred the displeasure of a woman."

"One of the people who might have helped herself to a bit of the plant," I said, "was a woman he'd brought in a year ago as a co-owner. Tanya Novak."

"Then our plot has thickened," Brendan said.

"Doubly so," I said, "since this lady had the misfortune to die yesterday."

"Are you making this up?"

"Sorry, no. It's true."

"Had she a smile on her face?"

"Only her forensic pathologist knows for sure," I said, "and he, or she, hasn't yet announced anything."

"I'm onto thinking I should research the prosthetic options for a friend of mine in New York who's recovering from a horrendous motorcycle mishap."

"I'm sorry to hear that, Brendan," Mom said.

"You needn't be. He's fictional."

Mom and I both heaved a sigh of relief from the burden of

A Sardonic Death

condolence. But, to view the flip side of that coin, I wondered if we could accept at face value anything this consummate actor might reveal.

"Your point of contact at Prosthetonics now is the assistant to the co-owner who died. Herself now the sole owner. Colleen Clemmons was Tanya's partner—in every sense of the word. And we can't rule out the possibility that *she* was involved in Aidan's death. So, you might want to be a little careful in your questioning. The only other person you might meet is Tanya's father, Herman. He heads up the research and design lab."

From memory, I gave Brendan the address on Riva Road where Kalea and I had tried our hand at working undercover. "We heard through the grapevine," I said, "that Tanya and Colleen were planning a move to a larger place where the sales, research, and production facilities could all be under one roof."

"Then the company's positioning for an expansion . . ." he said and whispered, "Big *bucks!*"

Chapter 35

Thursday morning, I was at the City Dock when Dylan's tender arrived. He hopped ashore and saluted his first mate back to the *Elizabeth*. We walked up Main Street for a Chick & Ruth's breakfast and then picked up his Saab for a drive to the building he'd chosen for his flagship Brody's BoatWorks. His realtor had called the day before. The prosthetics company had changed its mind and forfeited the earnest money.

A half-hour later, we were north of Annapolis on Route 2 toward Glen Burnie. Our banter had been friendly and professional but I was beginning to wonder if there was something wrong with me. I no longer felt an ounce of electricity for this handsome man sitting inches away. My romantic track record was becoming less and less impressive.

"It's huge," I said as what had been a mega-organic-grocery came into view beyond the expanse of parking he had entered. "The 'Mister Carrot' sign will have to go."

He laughed and continued to the entrance.

"Tell me," I said when we were stopped, "what *you* imagine."

Dylan looked up and down the highway. "Port and starboard buoys at the entrance."

"You could park a thirty or forty-foot ketch out front," I said. "On calm days, instead of raising her sails, fly a BoatWorks burgee like you have on the *Elizabeth*."

"That's brilliant, Penny."

"But," I said, "this'll be a bit too far from the boat shows to bring customers in converted golf carts."

"Then we'll have limousines leave the harbor every hour on the hour, and offer promotional gifts for being our guest," he said. "In addition to boat show specials."

Dylan had keys to the main door so we entered and paced the vacant interior. I asked for a scaled floor plan to begin working with our interior design team. I snapped a few shots that could jumpstart Steve's perspectives.

On the way back to Annapolis, I called Herman Novak's Neurothetics lab in Frederick. He'd heard from Tanya about Kalea's article and, of course, from Colleen, and agreed that Kalea and I could visit the lab tomorrow. He would expect us at 2:00 P.M.

By the time we returned to Annapolis, Dylan and I were sharing visions of boat owners from all over the mid-Atlantic flocking to Brody's BoatWorks, the newest and largest yacht supplies emporium on the East Coast. Inwardly, I was happy that I hadn't heard any more about working for him. My life had more than enough complications, thank you *verrry* much.

Kalea picked up on the first ring. "Hey Punk . . . oops, Kalea, would you be up for a visit to Mr. Novak's lab tomorrow?"

We agreed that as soon as I could get Steve started on the concepts for Brody's BoatWorks in the morning, I'd pick her up.

"I hope we can see Aaron before he goes back to Georgia," Kalea said.

I hadn't had the heart to tell her Aaron and I were no longer engaged.

"I'll check in with him," I said, "and see what his daybook looks like."

Aaron returned my call during Cookie's postprandial walk. "I'm outta here Saturday morning. How about tomorrow if Astrid's available?"

"Not too early. Kalea and I will be in Frederick."

Friday morning, I fed my four-legged housemates and walked the canine half of my menagerie, checked in briefly with Steve, and picked up Kalea about ten. An hour and a half later, we were lunching at Firestone's on Frederick's Market Street.

Kalea was growing up fast. My C.S.I. assistant already had enough on her plate wondering if one or both of her moms might be losing interest in her family. When I was her age, my childhood was ripped apart. I couldn't bear to think that hers might be similarly destroyed. Although, if her family did fall apart, I knew in my heart that I would be there for her.

"I hope you can learn things today to use in your article," I said.

"For sure."

I leaned closer and spoke softly. "Before we go to the lab, I want to tell you a couple of things. I hope you can understand, but I don't want you to freak out and think I'm being morbid."

"Okay."

A waitress materialized and set down glasses of water and menus. It took us only a minute to order crab cake sandwich platters and iced tea. "Be right back," she said.

"First off, you know I'm trying to learn how Aidan died. I haven't told you, but it wasn't natural. He was murdered."

"You sure?" She kept her voice low but almost upset her iced tea.

"Very."

"Are you going to be a cop? And pull*eese,* can I help?"

I laughed. "The police don't know what I know. Aidan was fed a piece of a poisonous plant that my mom brought back from Sardinia last year."

She gasped. "Your *mom* killed him?"

"I thought so, but now I doubt it."

"Then what makes you think he was murdered?"

"Because I'm certain he was poisoned."

"Who's your suspect now?"

"I'd been thinking that if Tanya wanted to become the sole owner of Prosthetonics that could happen if Aidan were dead."

"Tanya? Really? Could you prove that?"

"I don't think anyone could, and now I don't think it matters."

"Aunt Penny, you don't really think it doesn't matter who killed Aidan?"

"I meant just whether Tanya killed him."

"But with Tanya dead, what are we supposed to do?"

"I'd like to know how *she* died."

"She definitely didn't look sick or anything," Kalea whispered.

I wondered if I should share my suspicion of Colleen but decided not to. Kalea needed years to grow before she'd be able to handle the kinds of issues that might be involved. Issues that even I would probably never fully comprehend.

Our crab cake sandwich plates arrived loaded with French fries. Kalea dug in like a champ.

It didn't take long to find the research park adjacent to the old Army base where biological warfare agents had been researched during the Cold War. Herman Novak met us in his Neurothetics lab's lobby. "It's a pleasure to meet you, Miss Kalea. We've heard about your interest in our work here.

And," he said, glancing at me, "pleased to meet you, too, Miss Braithwaite."

"Thank you," Kalea gushed, "for allowing us to visit your lab, Mr. Novak."

I guessed he was in his late fifties, casually dressed in khakis and an open-collar gray shirt. His voice had a bit of accent, somewhere from Eastern Europe. Again, a guess.

We followed him down a hall to his office where we paused to admire models of tiny electrically-driven levers and pistons on a workbench. "There's a boy in my class who built something like these for a science fair last year," said Kalea.

"We're always looking for new talent," Herman said, smiling.

"He said he wants to be an astrophysicist like Sheldon."

"Aha," he said, "the Big Bang Theory. Does your classmate use a big white board to diagram his formulae?"

"I think so, but I like Leonard better," said Kalea. "At least he's not weird."

Herman picked up one of the little machines. "Well . . . these are a few of our early efforts at engineering the devices in our new prosthetics. We're continually researching ways to reduce their size and electrical requirements. And improve their reliability. Micro-circuitry is the name of our game here."

Stacks of reports and research protocols were piled on his desk. Herman picked up a prosthetic arm with a jointed wrist and hand with fingers that looked similar to Tanya's. He seemed about to explain its intricacies.

"Please accept our sincere condolences on the death of your daughter," I said.

Herman looked up, his eyes welling with tears. "Thank you."

"Have they figured out what happened?" Kalea said. "She

A Sardonic Death

seemed so full of life last week."

"She was a wonderful daughter and the brain behind our new technology. Unfortunately, we don't yet know how she died. The police aren't saying anything and the medical examiner thinks she was suffocated."

Suffocation? said Grandpa Jack.

"What does Colleen think?" I asked.

"Poor darling. She just breaks into tears when she thinks about Tanya."

Grandpa Jack added, *You never know what bedroom games couples will play.*

"So she's running the business alone now?" I said.

"We get together almost every evening," Herman said. "I'm a bit worried that she's having some psychological reactions to first losing Aidan and then Tanya."

Curious Georgette couldn't leave it at that. "What kind of reaction?"

"In a word," Herman said, "*melancholy*. Since I've known her she's always been an upbeat sort of woman. Now she seems less able to live with her grief."

That was something I could ask my pediatric neurosurgeon brother about.

Novak took a deep breath. "But we're here to talk about your article, Kalea. Any questions?"

"Are you still hoping to fit your first veteran with a neurothetic prosthesis this year?" Kalea asked. "Because I'd like to see it work. It'd be the highlight of my story."

"We hope so, but we may have to delay a few months," he admitted. "But not too long. Perhaps you could write a follow-up article."

Herman shepherded us through room after room of technicians at work on segmented flesh-colored models of prosthetic arms and hands, knees and legs, ankles and feet. "Some of these," he explained, "use Bluetooth technology, and we're also exploring other kinds of wireless energy transfers. In some cases, for instance, we can fit a mini-motor in the hollow of an arm, and run simulacrous microprocessors to the fingers. These are exciting times for this kind of research."

More than once, Kalea asked Mr. Novak to spell the names of the devices and mechanics he described. Most of his narrative sounded like so much voodoo to me. But at least she'd have her spelling correct.

"We understood that some of your research involved neurothetic testing on volunteers with missing limbs," I asked. "Are any of those tests ongoing?"

"Unfortunately, not at this time," Herman said.

So we never witnessed what should have been the most relevant research for the new generation of prosthetic devices. If Gratrix's spies had given Neurothetics a high score, though, their expectations were undoubtedly legit, but I was more than a little dubious about the hype Aidan had swallowed that had led first to Tanya, then to Colleen and Herman Novak taking over Prosthetonics.

Chapter 36

Astrid, Elana, and Aaron waved to get our attention as Kalea and I walked into the Paradiso Pizza a few minutes after seven. Aaron rose to welcome us. To Kalea, he said, "I was hoping you hadn't forgotten about me," then shed a wary smile in my direction.

Kalea jumped up and planted a kiss on his cheek, then turned from Aaron to me and back to Aaron and asked, "What happened to kissy-kissy?"

Elana smiled self-consciously, realizing *she* was what had happened to the Penny and Aaron show.

"Punkin," I said, as she scowled at my use of her pet name, "Aaron and I have decided to be ordinary friends for now."

Kalea frowned, not quite understanding, then concentrated on the menu. We ordered her favorite, a mushroom and sausage pizza to share.

Elana glanced in my direction. "Have the police solved the death of your . . . your stepfather?

"Nothing new, I'm afraid."

"How's your *mom* doing?" asked Astrid.

I lowered my voice to a whisper. "She attempted to kill her ex-fiancé. So, her new fear is that she'll be arrested for attempted murder. She doesn't seem concerned about being blamed for Aidan's death."

"That's not paraphrenia, then. That's real."

"Except the police only have circumstantial evidence that a car like Mom's was seen near where her ex's car was attacked." There was no reason to share Mom's admission. The wheels of justice, if there were to be any, would grind slowly.

Kalea, who was taking in every word, piped up, "What's *paraphrenia*, Aunt Penny?"

I said I'd fill her in later because our pizzas had materialized.

"Was that when the woman passenger was killed?" asked Elana.

I nodded.

"Read about that."

"Damn shame," said Astrid.

"She was killed and he was wounded," I said, "by bullets fired from directly ahead, not from where the car like my mom's was."

I cut wedges from our pizza and slipped them onto our plates. Kalea's root beer was delivered with a flourish just as my wine and our hosts' second brews were delivered.

I slugged my wine and bit off the tender point of my pizza wedge. "Astrid," I said, "thanks for making time again for my weird questions."

"No problem." She handed me a card. "By the way, I offer a discount after our second consultation." Elana and Aaron laughed.

"Okay then. If you had a client who had inherited a company after the mysterious deaths of the owner and co-owner, how would you counsel her to finish grieving for the original owner and for the co-owner who'd been her partner?"

Aaron piped up. "I'd counsel her to sell that cursed company as soon as possible before the Grim Reaper comes for *her*." Our laughs were the reactions he'd hoped for.

"There's really no time limit for grief," Astrid said.

"Is there any connection," Elana asked, "between the two deaths?"

"Only that the survivor sang both their praises. And, of

A Sardonic Death

course, stands to benefit."

"So she's the common denominator."

Why didn't I think of that? whispered Grandpa Jack.

"Is our hypothetical client," Astrid asked, *"hypothetically* capable of causing the two deaths?"

"You mean Col*leen?*" Kalea said.

I had to agree that she could be. I hadn't considered *her* for Aidan's death even after learning that either she or Tanya had harvested Water Celery roots the day Aidan died. That was when I suspected Tanya. But now?

While Kalea and our hosts mulled over the mysterious deaths, I tuned out the conversation when I recalled Grandpa Jack's suggestion that aberrant sex might have been involved in Tanya's suffocation. Unconventional sex gone wrong, or *planned* to go wrong? Once again, P.D. James' Chief Inspector Dalgleish's mantra came to mind that the motive for murder can always be traced to one of the four L's: love, lust, loathing or lucre. Which was it in Aidan's case? And which in Tanya's?

And Herman Novak had said he thought Colleen was under psychological strain. I thought, cynically, yes, killing two people could definitely cause the perpetrator to be under *strain.* Particularly if the perpetrator had a conscience—which I wasn't sure Colleen had.

There was a lot to consider here, but I wasn't comfortable discussing it in front of Kalea, no matter how eager she'd be to help investigate.

I remember finishing another slice of pizza and a second glass of wine, plunking a couple of twenties on the table, thanking Astrid again for this second meeting, giving Aaron a sisterly hug along with best wishes for a safe trip back to King's Bay, and shepherding Kalea back to my van.

"I think we need to talk to Colleen again," Kalea said as we left the Paradiso.

After a couple of beats, wondering how Kalea had come to the same conclusion as I had, I wondered aloud. "Why?"

"I'd like another chance to psych her out." She twined her fingers and turned her hands inside out with a tiny click. "Both my moms, you know, say I'm psychic." She snickered. "Not really, you know, but sometimes I'm pretty good at knowing what they're thinking."

Kalea and I are alike in many ways. I, too, had experience in tuning in to others' hopes and fears. As a kid, when Dad and Mom got into what they called a "discussion," I understood what they were going to say before they spoke, and, in the wardroom of my aircraft carrier, I often knew what the pilots and squadron officers were discussing even if I couldn't hear their words. When I would interview a crew member for a story in *The Shuttle*, the ship's newspaper, I'd often only need to ask questions to confirm what I already had picked up by osmosis.

Finally, I said, "That's a splendid idea. But what about your Police Academy next week?"

"Psyching out Colleen is more important. Find out if she can see us and let me know."

In the back of my mind, Grandpa Jack was pondering whether it would be a great idea for either of us to be close to a woman who may have killed both Aidan and Tanya.

Back at my condo, I fed and walked my critters and poured my thoughts of the day into my diary with Grandpa Jack's old Mont Blanc fountain pen, still giving yeoman service seventy-five years after he'd brought it to Annapolis as a freshman at St. John's College.

With my entry complete, I poured two fingers of Laphroaig as a nightcap. But neither finger helped me to sleep.

A Sardonic Death

While Thaïs snoozed soundly on the pillow next to mine, I lay awake. It had been a month since I'd returned from North Carolina. I'd weathered the shock of my life when I found that my client's wife was my long-lost mom. Now I was caught between imagining her as a murderer, knowing that she'd also attempted to kill her faithless fiancé, and Mom as the hapless part-owner of a prosthetics company that planned to cheat her when it was on the brink of a major surge in its fortunes. Or not.

Chapter 37

Saturday morning, I was pleased to see the Tropicana lilies at the Ravenscroft front door had been deadheaded. A couple of stalks had buds that looked like they'd be ready to bloom again in a few days.

Inside, I heard a piano recital. At first, I thought it was a recording, but it stopped when I opened the door. It was Mom, polishing a mazurka that I remembered her working on when I was knee-high to a grasshopper, as Grandpa Jack used to say.

"Go on," I said on my way to the kitchen. "I can operate the coffee machinery." She backed up a few bars and the mazurka's zest began anew.

A few moments later, I carried my cappuccino to the living room and waited for her to take a break.

The tune was the same one I'd downloaded for my cellphone ringtone. I'd never realized it had banged around in my brain since childhood. But there it was. Just like twenty-five years ago.

"Penny-lope. You remember that tune?"

Caught up in my interwoven brainwaves, I said nothing. It took a minute or so after the final chord for me to realize the music had ended.

Back to the present. "Where's Uncle Brendan?"

"Couldn't tell you. I haven't heard from him since he went to Prosthetonics yesterday." She paused. Then asked, "What's on *your* agenda?"

"Kalea and her Aunt Braithwaite have decided to visit Colleen again."

"Why on earth? She's nothing but bad news."

A Sardonic Death

Motion through a window drew my attention to Brendan's car coming to a stop behind my van. With mock indignation, when he came inside, Mom confronted him. "Where have you been, young man?"

He glanced from Mom to me. "You should have been there."

"I'm sure you're about to explain it," Mom said.

He heaved a mighty guffaw and settled into an overstuffed chair. "You want the whole truth, nothing but the truth, or the capsule version?"

I said, "I doubt that any Irishman ever shortened a story—"

"I must resemble me brother rather closely," he interrupted in his native brogue. "Colleen actually fainted right in front of me."

Mom frowned. "And this is the woman who's now running our company?"

"By the time the emergency techs arrived, she'd partly recovered. And then she was just scarlet. She stumbled over her explanation, but in essence, she thought a dead man had come back to haunt her."

Specially if she'd been responsible for that dead man's death, whispered Grandpa Jack.

"I agree," I said. "We should have been there."

"The EMTs checked her vitals and assured her that I was nae ghost. I was very much alive and truly hadn't intended to frighten the bejayzus out of her."

"Like when I first saw you here Wednesday," I said. "I couldn't believe my eyes. So . . . did you and Colleen hit it off?"

Brendan instantly morphed into Mona Lisa—at least the lower half of his face mimicked her smile. "It's been donkey's years since I've spent as much time with a woman. But she'd had a terrible shock and I was responsible. When she closed up the office, we went to Galway Bay for a lash and chinwag. Sorry—that's drinks and a chat. Not enough to get ossified, though. After a couple of pints, we went for dinner and more banter. It's beyond my ken, of course, but I think she really liked Aidan. Were they an item?"

Mom's eyes widened. After a beat, "What on earth makes you think that?"

"She spoke rather reverently about his kindness and thoughtfulness."

"Since he brought Tanya in as a co-owner," Mom said, "I had the feeling that she became his mistress as well as a co-owner. So, no, it never occurred to me that Aidan took a special interest in Colleen. Or vice versa."

"What did she have to say about their expansion plans?" I asked.

"We never got to that. Our chats were more about our personal stories and her reactions to Aidan's death and, of course, Tanya's. Oh, and she mentioned that a student named Kalea is writing an article about the business for a school project."

I said, "Hold that thought," and returned to the coffee machine to replenish my caffeine. While the cappuccino hissed into the cup, I pondered how much to say.

Back in the living room, I said, "Breaking news." And then explained Kalea's and my "undercover" visit to Prosthetonics.

"And what, pray, did you learn?" Brendan asked.

"As the business flourished with their new technology, Tanya and Colleen planned to exclude Mom from the equation. And that ties in with what we'd heard about a potential reorganization."

"We're going out again this evening," Brendan said. "I'll

A Sardonic Death

try to sniff out anything that supports your theory. I've always been a bloke to live a bit dangerously. Plus, I find the lass intriguing."

"Mom," I said, "Have you told Brendan that Tanya and Colleen were lovers?"

"That's only our supposition, dear."

"Colleen said she met Tanya at an LGBT bookstore event," Brendan said, "so it's entirely possible."

"Believe me," I said, "it's much more than a supposition."

"So I'm treading on hazardous ground," Brendan said.

"When you see her tonight, don't mention Kalea or her Aunt Penny," I said. "We plan to see her again and she doesn't know Mom and I are related."

"You can't be thinking she'll admit her relationship with Aidan was anything other than respectful of him as a generous employer?"

"I couldn't say, but I've been thinking it's also possible that she could be responsible for Tanya's death, if not Aidan's as well. I have no idea what would have been her motive, but the police don't seem to have any better idea."

Brendan groaned.

"Look," I said, "including Aidan, they were a triangle. Suppose both Tanya and Colleen had feelings for him stronger than what they may have had for each other."

"Wait a second," said Mom. "If that were true, how could that translate into either one of them wanting Aidan dead?"

"Jealousy?" Brendan suggested.

Chapter 38

At Prosthetonics Saturday morning, Colleen arrived to find Herman Novak ready for their weekly conference. He set his City Dock coffee mug on the conference table and rose to embrace her. Neither was looking forward to Tanya's funeral.

Colleen began to cry. Through her sobs, she said, "I miss her so much."

"I do too," he said and sat down again. "It's not going to be easy if we're going to see this through. The setbacks we've had at the lab are going to take a while to turn around. It's going to take time . . . and money. By the way, is our financial guy going to get a refund of any of the Severna Park earnest money?"

"Brad's working on that. He thinks we may get a break."

Colleen changed the subject. "Last week, Tanya was upset—and she wouldn't tell me why. I've been trying to figure it out, and now I'm getting panicky that she's not around to be our public face. Which reminds me, how did you handle that kid's visit to the lab? I'm sniffing a spy. She and her Aunt Penny seem too curious about the future of the business."

"Let's just say that I told them more than I showed them. They want to be on hand when we have our first patient from Walter Reed."

"Speaking of visitors, I had a shock yesterday."

"What kind of shock?"

"I thought Aidan had come back from the other side. But it was his brother. Brendan."

"What did *he* want?"

"He's hoping to figure out how his brother died. Seems to be close to Aidan's widow. She must have told him where to find us."

"Another spy?"

"If he is, he's an awfully nice one. He's an actor. On Broadway."

"You like him?"

"Well, yeah, but not romantically. We're going out again tonight. Maybe take in a play at the Summer Garden Theater."

"Colleen, tell me honestly . . . are you going to be able to guide this business without Tanya . . . or Aidan?"

"I've always gotten what I've wanted, Herman. I was born into the university of hard knocks so learning on-the-job is my M.O. What I'm dealing with right now is our lawyer. Jeff Gratrix isn't happy with our ideas to reorganize. He seems to be locked into our arrangement with Mrs. Reid's monthly payments."

"Probably because he'd been Aidan's lawyer for a long time before Tanya joined the company."

"Do you think we should find another law firm that would look more favorably toward a reorganization? If we have to continue payments to Mrs. Reid based on our present formula, Brad says we might have trouble borrowing for our expansion."

"Ms. Braithwaite. Miss Kalea. Thanks for coming." At St. Anne's Church, Herman Novak greeted us.

Behind us, Colleen, on Brendan's arm, held her head high as she introduced him to Herman. I dawdled until they caught us up and then panicked, hoping Brendan wouldn't betray our subterfuge to Colleen.

"Kalea, Penny, how sweet of you to come," Colleen said

and turned to Brendan. "This is Brendan, a brother of Prosthetics' founder." And to Brendan, "Kalea is going to write a magazine article about our company."

I needn't have worried. Brendan and Kalea were both troupers—born actors.

"Would you care to dine with us," Colleen said, "after the funeral?"

I glanced at Kalea. "I'm afraid our afternoon is booked. But thank you."

Brendan and I exchanged sly winks.

Kalea and I found an empty pew near the back. Kalea whispered, "What do we have booked?"

"It'll be a surprise."

At the end of the service, an honor guard from Tanya's Army Reserve Unit carried her casket from the church to the hearse after which it would meet it at the gravesite where a bugler would honor her with "Taps."

While Colleen and Brendan went off to lunch, Kalea and I found our way to the Liberty Tree Townehomes development where Tanya had lived. We parked in a spot adjacent to her building and were immediately accosted by a middle-aged woman with a pair of pampered show dogs. Their tails swept the sidewalk as they approached. Kalea kneeled down to tousle the dogs. Beady inquisitive eyes smiled up at her.

"One of my friends," I said, "Tanya Novak, always boasted about her community."

The woman looked us over. "You're thinking of moving here?"

"I'm considering it."

"Poor Tanya," the woman said. "I'm afraid there aren't any units available at the moment. Hers is the only condo that'll be

A Sardonic Death

on the market—once the legalities have been taken care of."

Kalea patted both dogs and stood.

The woman smiled. "I'm Mel. And these are Jodie and Julie, Cavalier King Charles spaniels."

"Nice to meet you. I'm Penny." The two dogs wagged their tails, apparently giving me their approval.

"And I'm Kalea." She reached to shake Mel's hand while her other hand was treated to spaniel slobber.

"Did you know Tanya?" I asked.

"She lived next door. So yes, rather well."

I wondered how "rather well" would compare with "really well."

"Did you meet any of her other friends?"

"She had only one regular visitor, but we weren't ever introduced. She drives a bright pink car."

"I think I know who you mean," I said. "She worked in Tanya's office."

"She spent a lot of nights here. Most mornings they'd leave at the same time. I had the distinct impression they were lovers but Tanya never told me."

"Some people are private about things like that."

"But one night last week . . ." She paused. "Jodie's tummy was upset and I'd brought them both out for a middle-of-the-night walk. It was about two-thirty when the pink car drove off. Tanya's BMW was still in its spot."

"Maybe Tanya was sick and her friend took her to an emergency room."

"I don't think that was it. The pink car returned in the morning a bit after nine. There was a scream that came right through the wall then the door slammed and the car roared away. Next thing I knew, a couple of police cars showed up. The cops were inside only a short time before an ambulance with no siren pulled up. That's when I knew there'd been trouble. The next day her death was on the news. No mention of the cause."

"Could that have been Tuesday?" I asked.

"It *was* Tuesday because I'd taken Jodie to the vet that morning. Her new pills hadn't agreed with her."

"She seems better now," Kalea said.

"Mel," I said, "if I don't take Tanya's condo, I hope your new neighbors are nice."

She laughed. "They'll have to get Jodie and Julie's approval."

Back in my van, Kalea took a deep breath and said, "Wow."

"If I had known . . ." I said.

"What?"

"I wouldn't have brought you out here if I thought we'd learn . . . you do understand what Mel said. Right?"

"That Tanya was already dead in the middle of the night or whatever time Colleen left."

I thought for a minute or two while I found my way back to Route 50 toward Annapolis.

"Kalea, of course you can't forget what you heard, but you mustn't tell a soul. If Colleen had any inkling of what we know, we'd be in danger."

"You can count on me, you know. All in a day's work. And never fear. Julie and Jodie are cute pooches, but I like Cookie better."

Chapter 39

There I was again on that wacko merry-go-round where Jimi Hendrix screeched the Star Spangled Banner. We had just learned that Tanya had been smothered, undoubtedly by Colleen, but what could I do with the information?

Brendan was on the town with a murderer. And Kalea and I alone knew it. There was only one person with whom I could safely share it: Jason. And he'd categorize it as hearsay. But Brendan was my first priority. Kalea and I drove to Ravenscroft, buzzed the gate, and watched the elegant halves roll silently apart.

Mom met us at the door. "Is Brendan in?" I asked.

"No. And who's this," Mom asked. "Your detective friend?"

"Kalea, I'd like you to meet my mom."

"It's my pleasure to meet *you*," she replied.

"Kalea was a big help in North Carolina. Her mom's Madison, my landscape design professor. Her other mom is a lawyer with Jeff Gratrix's office."

"I'm happy to meet such a talented young lady," Mom said. "And I'm worried that Brendan hasn't returned." She looked down at one of the blue pots. "I think he and Colleen went to Tanya's funeral. You should know that she and Brendan aren't suited for each other."

"Colleen prefers women, Ms. Reid," Kalea said. "But maybe she likes men too."

Out of the mouths of children, whispered Grandpa Jack.

"If you ask me," Kalea said, "I think your Uncle Brendan

250

kind of likes Colleen too."

"After the funeral," I told Mom, "Brendan and Colleen went somewhere for lunch. He should be back soon."

"Well, I won't worry then." Mom adjusted the red rose in her hair. "So, what have you and Kalea been up to?"

"We talked to a lady where Tanya lived," Kalea said. "She told us about how the police and an ambulance came to Tanya's house, but she didn't know what had happened until she saw the news on TV." Kalea looked at me questioningly. I gave her a confirming smile.

"Mom, can you ask Brendan to buzz me when he returns or if you hear from him? Nothing urgent."

"Nothing urgent?" Kalea said in disbelief when we'd left. "What could be more urgent than to warn him about Colleen?"

"I couldn't tip off Mom to what we'd learned. And I didn't want to take a chance that Colleen would learn that you and I had visited Prosthetonics under false pretenses. Don't forget. We only talked to a woman who saw police cars and an ambulance."

I dropped Kalea at her home with a promise that we'd see Colleen again next week. Only later I realized it wouldn't be just Kalea and her Aunt Penny . . . .

On my way to my condo, I left a message for Jason. A few minutes later when my phone began the Chopin minuet, I assumed it would be either Brendan or Jason. As it turned out, it was my oldest friend, Gina. "It's been almost a month," she said. "Where've you been keeping yourself?"

She was waiting for me at Harry Browne's. I climbed to the second floor, caught my breath and joined her. She'd ordered two Dark and Stormies that Bart was setting down beside a bowl of cashews. Popped one and took a tentative sip.

"What's new?" Her standard opening.

I had no idea where to start, but I had an idea where it

A Sardonic Death

would end and decided to jump in that direction. "I'm going to need some additional protection, Gina."

"What on earth are you talking about?"

"This afternoon I learned how a murder happened. I have to keep that knowledge under wraps, at least until I can talk with my detective friend."

"So, there's no point in my asking."

"None at all."

She glanced at my neck. "You're still wearing the labradorite."

"Won't I need something stronger now?"

"Trust me. That stone's doing you a bundle of good, whether or not you're aware of it."

All hogwash as far as I was concerned but I've never doubted Gina's good intentions. "You sure?"

She smiled enigmatically. "I know it sounds like some kind of weird voodoo, but it'll help with your sleuthing. Now tell me what else Miss Sherlock has been up to."

"Surprise! Aidan had a brother . . . an actor."

"And you learned this how?"

"Uncle Brendan showed up at Mom's, wanting to help me find his brother's murderer."

"Is he helping?"

"I hope so. Today he's with one of my suspects, the new owner of the company."

"Tanya . . . somebody, right?"

"Tanya *was* . . . but today was her funeral. As of last Wednesday, Tanya's so-called *assistant*, Colleen, is running the company."

"First, your step-dad client. Then his what? Understudy? Do either of these women know anything about the prosthetics business?"

"Tanya certainly did, but I'm not so sure about this Colleen Clemmons."

"Where did she come from?"

"Turns out she's Tanya's partner."

"Nothing like a little nepotism," Gina said, "as long as you keep it in the family."

"A primary reason Aidan took on Tanya as a co-owner is her wealthy dad. Herman has a research firm working toward a revolution in the prosthetics industry." I explained that Kalea and I had visited there and filled her in on the neurothetics idea as well as I could. "What I can't be sure of is if there's fraud involved. Kalea and I didn't see any honest-to-God evidence that the technology would work as advertised."

"How's your mom dealing with that?"

"She's hoping Colleen can keep the company turning a profit with traditional prosthetics so she can get her share of the profits."

My phone began Chopin again. "Give me a minute," and then, to the phone, "Penny for your thoughts."

It was Brendan. He'd survived lunch with Colleen and was about to go back to his car at the Hillman garage.

"You know Harry Browne's on State Circle?"

"That's where Colleen and I had lunch."

"I'm in the bar on the second floor with someone I'd like you to meet."

A few minutes later, he clomped up the stairs. I waved to get his attention.

"I'd like you to meet my friend Gina McBee, entrepreneur extraordinaire. We've been friends since our dear old school days. Brendan . . . Gina."

He shook Gina's hand and said something that sounded like *deeah gwit*. "Sorry, that just means 'Hi.'"

Gina smiled. "Hi, yourself."

A Sardonic Death

He went on: "Brendan *iss anim-dum.*"

"I think he's trying to tell you his name in Irish," I said.

He turned to Bart. "A pint of Gat if you please, sir. And if you're not up on your Irish, that means a Guinness." Back to Gina. "So tell me about your entrepreneuring."

While Bart polished a pint glass and held it under the Guinness tap at the end of the row, Gina began to explain. "My shop's the Flights of Fancy. Gems and minerals for your health and welfare." She gazed into his eyes. "I can sense that you could use some help for your love life."

"Sure, and you must be part Irish," said Brendan. "The blarney slips so easily off your tongue." Gina and I laughed.

I displayed my labradorite pendant. "Gina says this keeps me aligned with my planets or something." Which earned me a derisive scowl from my friend just as Brendan's Guinness was set down.

He took a sip. "I can assure you my love life needs no help. I just wouldn't want my New York husband to know of my latest conquest." He took another. "Of course, she hasn't been conquered in a physical way. She's just a kindred creature."

"Paying for her lunch today," I said, "must be a New Yorker's definition of conquest."

Brendan smiled knowingly as he set the Guinness back down. "Well, I'm not . . . that's, as I might say, I don't think . . ."

I never expected to hear Brendan stammering, but that's exactly what it sounded like.

"Ted, on the other hand," he said, "I've known for a goodly while. And all I can say is that he would be considering divorce or murder if he learned I hadn't completely sworn off the attraction of the female of the species."

"That's exactly the kind of dilemma where one of our gems

could be helpful," Gina said.

Brendan gave her a playfully skeptical smile.

Time to change the subject. My curiosity was getting the better of me. "Was Colleen any help in our pursuit of Aidan's killer?"

"God rest his soul . . ." Brendan said. "According to Colleen, it seems my brother was rather keenly liked by everyone. She couldn't say enough nice things about him. Of course, she's emotionally fragile now that Tanya's gone too, but she told me she sometimes calls on Aidan's spirit to help her sort some of the decisions she has to make at the business."

Armed with my new information about Tanya's death, I couldn't evaluate Brendan's report of Colleen's reliance on Aidan's ghost.

That's when I had one of those rare *aha* moments or, if you prefer, a whisper from Grandpa Jack: *If I were to engineer a meeting of Gina with Colleen, might Gina's supposed telepathic abilities assist us?*

"So she keeps one ear in the spirit world," Gina said. "That's a good sign. But what I don't understand—"

"Whoa," I interrupted. "There's something you both need to know." I lowered my voice to a backstage whisper. "But I need to swear you both to secrecy."

"My, my," Brendan whispered gleefully, "the plot is becoming more intriguing by the minute."

"Gina?"

"Of course. I've still never told anyone some of the things you told me when we were in high school."

I endured an inquisitive grin from Brendan.

"Uncle B?"

"For sure."

"Okay." To Gina: "This is why I figured I'd need something stronger than the labradorite for protection." Back to

A Sardonic Death

a whisper. "So here it is: Kalea and I met a woman this afternoon in Tanya's development. Actually, Tanya's next-door neighbor. The night Tanya died, Colleen apparently spent part of it with her. The woman said the pink El Camino left between two and three A.M. when she was walking her pooches in the middle of the night. Don't ask. Anyway, Colleen's El Camino came back in the morning. This neighbor heard Colleen scream in what we assume was fake surprise. Next thing the woman knew, police cars and an ambulance surrounded their condo and the El Camino left. She didn't learn what had happened until the TV news the next day."

"You think she was telling the truth?"

"No reason to think she wasn't."

"How do you explain what she reported?"

"Since the M.E. reported that Tanya had suffocated, I'm thinking it was some kind of sexual adventure that caused her death. And my guess would be that it *wasn't* accidental. I suspect Colleen *planned* it since, with Tanya gone, she would have control of the company."

"Lord love a duck!" Brendan exclaimed. "So I've been consorting with a *murderer?*"

"Hang with me for a moment," I said, "Since Colleen seems receptive to spirit messaging, "I'm thinking we might benefit from a séance where you could contact your brother. Your voice, apparently, is very similar to his. If you could pretend to channel him, you might find that she would respond at a subconscious level, like under hypnosis."

Brilliant, whispered Grandpa Jack.

"I'm an actor. Not a hypnotist. Or even a psychologist."

"You're an *actor,*" I said. "And a good one, or you wouldn't have come to New York. And you understand, at some level, Aidan's desire to keep his company at the forefront

256

with the newest technology—what induced him to bring in Tanya and her father."

"I'm thinking that he recognized the new technology," Brendan said, "for the wealth it would represent if his company could be the first to bring it to the market."

"So you could slip easily into Aidan's persona," I said.

"Brendan," Gina began, "if I understood your description of Colleen's dependence on Aidan . . . or on his spirit . . . maybe adoration isn't the right word, but her regard for him certainly seems stronger than usual for a former boss. And if she said so many nice things about him," Gina said, "she might easily be encouraged to talk about him and his relationship to Tanya."

And maybe about her own *relationship to Tanya,* Grandpa Jack suggested.

"Gina, with your insight into all things psychic," I said, "I'm thinking you should be there. You might hear something that would go right over Brendan's or my head."

Grandpa Jack whispered, *You might also learn whether she had anything to do with Aidan's demise."*

"The mind of someone who would take her lover's life, for *any* reason, is hard to fathom," I said.

Brendan shuddered. "Indeed," he said.

"The more I think about her," I said, "the more I think she's somewhere on the sociopathic spectrum." I made a mental note to ask my psychiatrist brother who should know about such people.

Brendan's eyes widened. "So you want me to, overnight . . . become a medium in a séance *and* a forensic psychologist?"

"What could be easier?" Gina said. "You'd be your brother's alter ego."

"It might be my most challenging role ever. But fortunately, there won't be any critics' reviews the next day."

A Sardonic Death

"By the way, when you check in with Mom," I said, "she'll tell you I asked you to call. I told her it wasn't urgent, but the truth was that I needed to warn you about Colleen without letting Mom guess what Kalea and I had discovered."

"Speaking of Ophelia," Brendan said, "she tells me she has a swim party planned a week from Sunday. Assuming I can stick around, you think we could pull this off at Ravenscroft?"

"So you're willing?"

"Doesn't look like I have a choice."

Brilliant, whispered Grandpa Jack.

I would invite one other person who could help us. Astrid.

Chapter 40

As soon as I stepped out of my van, Cookie's barks in the distance propelled me into full alert mode. Evening shadows had begun to creep across the condo community and I knew she hadn't seen me or my van. Before I could cover the space between my parking spot to my condo, I knew well that her muffled yelps were nothing like her "welcome back" whiny-woofs. Cookie was doing what she'd been trained to do—alert any intruder who approached her former sailboat home that she would, indeed, tear them apart without mercy if they should attempt to board her master's boat. Once before I'd heard this vicious alert—the time Jason arrived unexpectedly.

I rounded a corner to approach my condo and recognized my prospective visitor. Tanya's nemesis stood at my door dragging on a cigarette.

Preferring to not come face to face with Killer Colleen, and fairly sure she hadn't spotted me, I did a brisk about-face and headed back toward my van as if I'd forgotten something. I kept walking, hoping she'd been there long enough for Cookie's full-throated shrieks to attract my neighbors' attention, perhaps to call the city's animal services or at least our condo security to sort out the noisy intrusion. There were even commiserating echoes from dogs in nearby condos. Yet Colleen was apparently unfazed.

Fearing her murderous tendencies, I didn't fancy approaching her but how long could I hide out in my own neighborhood hoping for police intervention? If I could wait her out, assuming she was smart enough to realize I wasn't at

A Sardonic Death

home and would disappear before the neighborhood nuisance vigilantes appeared, I could return to my condo, assure Cookie she'd done an amazing job of protecting our home, and await Colleen's next move. But *then* what?

My pulse ratcheted upward with each consideration of how the game might play out. All the while surrounded by nearby canine displeasure. If a police officer had been summoned, he or she might be en route. But how long might Colleen stand there creating hate and discontent which would ultimately be my responsibility for failing to rein in my Dobergirl? Cookie wasn't winning any popularity contests with my neighbors.

After another turn around a neighboring building, I walked back toward my minuscule porch. "Oh, hi," I shouted as if I'd just recognized my visitor.

She waited until I was close enough to talk amiably. "Miss Summers."

"Can I help you with something?"

"Herman and I are fed up with your snooping around Prosthetonics."

"Snooping?"

"Exactly."

Grandpa Jack released a sigh of relief. *Apparently, she hasn't learned of your chat with Tanya's neighbor.*

"I'm sorry to disappoint you," I said, "but my niece heard about your business and thought it would be fascinating to write an article about recent improvements in prosthetics technology. She's quite the brilliant student, as I'm sure you realize. Since we visited the Neurothetics lab, she's been writing it."

Cookie, hearing my voice, had quieted.

"Herman sniffed an ulterior motive in your visit to Frederick. Some of your questions, he said, seemed like they could have come from a competitor trolling for privileged information."

"I assure you . . ."

"Then how do you explain your using a false name?"

It took a second to think my way past that one. "It isn't. Braithwaite's my maiden name. The one my niece knows."

A tiny frown flitted across her face as she considered it. "When you left Herman's Neurothetics lab last Friday, he noticed the business name on your van and was immediately suspicious."

"I wouldn't have blamed him," I said with the ghost of a smile to acknowledge our "understanding."

"Herman's on edge since Tanya died," she said, "and I'm a bit nervous now with the responsibilities of the business on my shoulders."

"Would you care to come in for coffee?"

After a slight hesitation, I assumed wondering if she could accept a token of friendship from an erstwhile "spy," she accepted.

I unlocked and opened the door to Cookie who emerged to face Colleen with her hackle patch standing proud. "Cookie," I said, in a lighthearted tone, "this is Colleen." Cookie stood her ground and uttered a fearsome low growl suggesting she wasn't certain that allowing Colleen into the house was a good idea. I pulled Cookie back, commanded her to sit, ushered Colleen in, and asked if she would wait for my French press to do its thing. Again, she accepted and followed me to my minuscule kitchen where I started a fire under a kettle and poured beans into a grinder.

Until the water boiled, I fed Cookie and introduced Colleen to Thaïs. Instant bonding. Thaïs curled her plumed tail around Colleen's ankle, begging to be picked up. Which Colleen did at

A Sardonic Death

once. "My dad had a Maine Coon when I was little," she said. "Slept with me. Played with me . . . I never got over her when she died. And they wouldn't let me have another one."

"What happened?"

She hesitated, momentarily debating something within herself. "I'm ashamed to tell you. Kids aren't supposed to play with matches." She began to cry.

Grandpa Jack was quick: *Don't ask.*

"I'm so sorry," I said, and attempted to accept her grief. "Thaïs is actually a Weegie," I said, "a Norwegian Forest Cat. He's often mistaken for a Maine Coon."

I poured the hot water over the grindings. "His double coat is like a Maine Coon."

Colleen held Thaïs to her cheek but continued to sob. The lovely essence of coffee brewing enveloped us.

Grandpa Jack pondered, *Wasn't this evidence of a sociopathic personality?*

Killing a pet, even by accident, definitely raised red flags—certainly an indication of some kind of aberrant behavior.

As I pressed the plunger, I decided I didn't need Spencer to diagnose Colleen. I had all the evidence right in front of me.

I decanted the fragrant elixir into a pair of hand-made mugs from a local potter. While we sipped, my brain began wondering if I could actually entice Colleen to meet with Brendan and Gina for an amateur séance. If she actually talked with Aidan's ghost about the business, she might be responsive in the kind of fake séance we had planned.

"So I guess I shouldn't ask how's business?" I said, mocking myself.

Colleen chuckled self-consciously and set Thaïs in her lap. "You could, but I wouldn't answer."

"Suppose I ask about something we talked about last

week?"

"You can try me."

We were seated at the kitchen table and putting up with an occasional whine from Cookie who was hoping I'd take the hint that she wanted a walk around the block. But if Colleen was willing to chat, I needed to chat while the chatting was good. Allowing me to ask another question meant I'd need to keep poor Cookie waiting.

"Okay. Here goes. I remember you allowed that there was potentially a lot of money to be made with your new technology. But I also remember how much you admired the owner, Aidan Reid. Then I think Tanya said that with some reorganization his family probably wouldn't share in the new wealth. Is that still in the reorganization plan for Prosthetonics International? And how would you square that with your conscience?"

Again, she considered the question. Finally, "Do you know Aidan's family?"

"No," I lied. "Have you met them?"

"There's only the wife," she said, "and she seems to be well off."

"How do you mean?" I sipped my rapidly-cooling coffee.

"She's got this huge fancy house, swimming pool, tennis court, the whole nine yards. I can't believe she's hurting for money."

"What's she like?"

"Nice enough, but I didn't think there was much love lost between her and Aidan."

"You think Aidan was in love with Tanya?"

"I thought so. I think Mrs. Reid thought so too. It seemed like she resented Tanya. Not overtly but that was the vibe I got. Of course, I've been with the company for only a few months,

A Sardonic Death

so there was a lot of time for Aidan and Tanya to get cozy."

"You and Tanya were good friends . . ."

She put her mug down. "We were *more* than good friends."

I cruised closer to the questions I really wanted to ask. "Were there ever any problems with jealousy around the office?"

Colleen reddened. "If you must know, I was in love with Tanya, but we both admired Aidan in our own ways. Now, more to your point . . . a couple of months ago, soon after I started working for him, he mentioned that some cute woman was designing something for his house. Don't remember if he said what, or maybe I blocked it. To me, it sounded like he was hoping to acquire a mistress. And that worried me because I knew Tanya was beginning—at least I thought so at the time—to have mixed feelings about me, and probably Aidan."

Cookie's whine shifted to a more urgent tone.

"Cookie—*Shush.*"

"Look," Colleen said, "I've got to go."

"I'm sorry if I've seemed so nosy. But this kind of thing interests me. I don't get many opportunities to talk about feelings. Usually it's all about what kinds of flowers—"

Colleen cocked her head slightly. Her eyes popped wider. "*You!*" she screamed. "Okay! It was the *garden* he said was getting a new design. You're a garden designer. *You* were Aidan's mistress. You charmed him away from not just his wife, but spoiled Tanya's chance for happiness." She angrily shoved Thaïs off her lap and yelled, "I *loved* her. I wanted *her* happiness more than my own." Colleen slammed her mug down so hard it shattered, splashing coffee droplets across the table and onto the wall. Cookie's hackles went to full alert. Colleen stood, still screaming: "I should have *known*. Penny Braithwaite *indeed. You!*—I'm glad I—"

264

With Cookie there, I felt brave. "*What,* Colleen? *What* are you glad about?"

I began again. Almost a whisper: "Were you relieved when Aidan died? Did you think that if Tanya wasn't to have him, then no one could?"

"Yes . . . I mean no! I mean—"

"You're not sure?"

No response.

I whispered gently again. "Colleen, we know Aidan died from eating water celery root. Did you put any of that in Aidan's soup?"

Colleen crumpled back into her chair but said nothing for several minutes.

Finally, "I am so messed up."

Chapter 41

The next day was Sunday—a week before Mom's midsummer swim party. Brendan and I had arranged to meet over brunch at Mom's house. On my way, I picked up an assortment of breakfast pastries from Chick & Ruth's to complement Mom's egg and sausage casserole. And with a supply of caffeine from her machine, we would survive and, doubtless, be able to access a sufficient number of neurons to choreograph our game plan for the following Sunday.

I first explained to Brendan that Mom had agreed to our plan to engage Colleen in a sham séance. She'd said that, at the very least, we might learn more about Aidan's last day. Then I explained my encounter with Colleen yesterday and the white lies I'd told to assuage her ire at our perceived conspiracy to snoop. It took longer to clarify the pickle I'd got myself into when she deduced that I was the "cute" garden designer she thought Aidan was attracted to. I was appalled that she expressed her relief at his death based on her screwy idea that Aidan's death would keep him from having me as his mistress. I described as well as I could her confusion over Tanya's apparent attraction to Aidan and her willingness to renounce her own love of Tanya for Tanya's potential long-term happiness with Aidan. But with him dead at least the cute designer couldn't steal him away.

"I'm dreadfully sorry," Brendan said, "but that reasoning makes absolutely no sense to me."

"I never thought it would. She, herself, told me she was, quote, so messed up, unquote. So we can't expect logic or clear thinking to be her strong suit."

"Exactly the type of person you'd want managing the family business." He chortled.

Then I explained, as carefully as possible, that Colleen had come close to admitting she had added Water Celery root to Aidan's soup.

"She's crazier than a freakin' loon," Brendan said.

Thinking ahead for a change, I said, "Let's connive to get our questions answered at the party. I assume you're planning to bring Colleen? Or do you want Mom to invite her?"

"Wouldn't it blow her mind if she saw *you* again here?"

I considered that for a moment. "It might blow her mind to be a guest of her dead boss's wife."

"It wouldn't be her first time."

"But that was when Aidan was alive, for God's sake."

"Good point, lass," said Brendan.

"Colleen believes I'm actually Kalea's aunt, and was probably, briefly, Aidan's mistress, but she doesn't know I'm related to Ophelia."

"So," Brendan said, "I could tell her that I've invited Kalea and her 'aunt' to tag along with us to learn more about Prosthetonics at the party. I'm a fairly charming bloke when I try. I'll bet she'd be agreeable."

"And I'll put a bug in Mom's ear to invite Gina, which would be a nice surprise for her since she hasn't seen Gina since we were fourth-graders. That way Gina can be present at your *séance.*"

"She'd have to remember that you're Kalea's Aunt Penny Braithwaite. And no relation to Ophelia."

"Mom's swim party," I said, "could become a macabre reincarnation of Shakespeare's *Comedy of Errors*. Quite a few guests would have to pretend not to know me."

I pulled out my phone and tried Gina's number. "Let's get

A Sardonic Death

Gina here. She doesn't open her shop until one on Sundays." Then to my phone, "Oh hi. Brendan and I are scheming and hoped you could join us." I gave Gina directions to Ravenscroft and instruction to press the button on the stone pillar outside the gate.

"Save her the cranberry Danish," I said. "Her favorite. She's on her way."

"Where shall we conduct this comedy of errors?" Brendan asked, as Mom brought in the delicious-looking casserole and set it between us.

"Mom, is there a place in the basement we could use?"

"Our floral room? Take a look and see for yourself."

"Floral room?"

"It's opposite the utility room. It's where we arrange cut flowers into vases and arrangements. And when you come up, could you bring up a couple of bowls for the midsummer party. Please?"

I opened the door to the stairwell and Brendan started down the steps into the gloom. Without warning an overhead light switched itself on, illuminating the steps and the central area below. "We'll need to disable that sensor," I said. "That much light would spoil the effect."

"Could we switch out the bulbs for low-wattage flickering candle-effect bulbs?" Brendan asked.

Grandpa Jack agreed.

Another switch illuminated the floral room. "We'll use candles in here," I suggested. A faint odor of floral bouquets from the past permeated the room.

A sink with a water faucet centered on a wall was flanked by wooden worktops for cutting stems, pruning foliage, and arranging the containers. Shelving on the opposite wall held arrays of brass containers and a selection of china vases with

268

floral patterns in primary colors, mostly red, I noticed. Bolts of ribbons of various colors and widths were alongside a box of floral wire and green floral tape, useful when nature hadn't provided the necessary support for the blooms. There were also a trio of flower-arranging books for occasional inspiration. The room was quiet, apparently well insulated from the main floor above.

"We should keep it dark and shadowy so Gina can be here unseen," said Brendan.

"Dark and shadowy will create the right atmosphere," I said, "but I think Colleen and Gina should have a chance to get acquainted before the séance. She can reassure Colleen if she has any apprehension about joining the séance."

The door above opened and Mom called down. "Gina's here."

"Thanks, Mom. Please send her down."

A minute later, Gina joined us. "You never told me your mom has a mansion."

"Trust me," I said, "it's just a house."

"Yeah, sure," she said. *The double positive that means the opposite.*

"What d'you think of our séance space? We're going to unscrew the lights and bring in candles."

Gina's eyes scoured the room, then nodded. "Nice."

"Do you think," Brendan said, "that Colleen could be talked into leaving the swimming pool long enough to come down here for a cozy chat?"

"I'll introduce the idea gently . . . and hope she'd want to reconnect with her dead boss."

"Can you bring her a sacred stone?" I suggested. "Maybe let her think it will help her reconnect? I'd thought about having Thaïs here for her but now I think both Colleen and the

A Sardonic Death

cat might be spooked. A stone from your shop might be better."

"Great idea. I'll bring her the most powerful aventurine I have in the shop. It will definitely assist her connection with Aidan. She can also use it when she calls on his spirit for guidance."

"We want to probe her feelings about Aidan," I said.

"Brendan," Gina began, "I'd begin with her memories of Tanya. Happy ones. Then she may have something she wants to say to Tanya. And finally, you can suggest that with true concentration on the stone, she can learn if Tanya has any guidance for her. You'll have to play that by ear unless you can feel Tanya's presence and "hear" any advice she has for Colleen. If she can work through her feelings there, then step back further to Aidan. You can speak for him, of his adoration of women and particularly the two who toiled with him, his hope that they . . . no—just Colleen . . . will succeed in the life that's left to her. Finally, ask her if she has anything she wants Aidan to know about. Or any guidance for the future. If you get tongue-tied, I'll do my best to re-center the conversation."

"Do you really believe," I said, "that Colleen is sufficiently gullible to fall for this kind of voodoo?"

"My dear," Gina said patiently, "it's *not* voodoo. Colleen's susceptibility will depend on several factors, none of which we can foresee. With an appropriate introduction, which I intend to ensure, she will let Brendan's voice wash over and through her and we'll learn what her soul may have to tell us."

"Mimosas are ready!" Mom's voice echoed down the stairwell. *Perfect timing.*

Chapter 42

Krysta called me over as soon as I waltzed into L&G Monday morning. "Captain Brody called. He'd like to hear from you ASAP." She said it with a crisp voice that made me wonder what I might have done wrong or worse, what I hadn't done.

"G'morning Penny," Brody said. "Great news. The Mister Carrot sign will come down today. Brody's BoatWorks signed the lease on Saturday."

"Wonderful. I'll see if we can pick up your big sign this morning."

A half hour later, we met at Chick & Ruth's for coffees and their calorie-intense apple fritters. "How's your mom doing?" Brody said.

"She's good," I said. "And she wants me to invite you to her *famous*, according to her, Fourth of July pool party. Next Sunday."

"You can tell her that I'd be happy to come. What should I bring?"

"Your swim trunks, sunscreen, and an appetite. And a thirst."

"Will there be any wealthy investors in the crowd?"

"Who knows? S'not something she's ever mentioned. Why? Don't tell me you need investors for Brody's BoatWorks?"

"Maybe for a second store?"

On the Route 2 bridge over South River, to ease the

A Sardonic Death

uncomfortable silence between us, I told Dylan that the police had connected Mom, without proof, with the attack on my Feng Shui design client that killed his passenger.

"Is she going to be charged?"

"Apparently forensics discovered that the fatal shots came from a different direction, from a different weapon. Mom hasn't heard from the gendarmes."

"That's good news, then. Your poor mom has had enough bad news lately."

Fortunately, Dylan didn't know the extent of Mom's bad news, and since he seemed interested in her, I wouldn't spell them out.

"Which reminds me," I said, "I need to invite Mom's pond maintenance guy to the party. Jason will also be our onsite gendarme Sunday afternoon. His day job is detective."

"What kind of altercations is your mom expecting?"

I laughed. And then, in a serious tone, "Don't ask. If I spilled the beans, it'd spoil the fun."

"Maybe I should back out before I get in the line of fire," joked Dylan.

I turned into Phelan Hurst's sign-carving studio. Phelan's elegant entry sign was carved in a dark wood with a natural finish. "You picked the right man for our signs," Dylan said.

"I hope you like what he's done."

We went through into his workshop. Phelan wasn't there and there was no whine of woodworking tools. I explored further and soon was following the scent of paint thinner into a small space with large windows all open to the ambient air and the sound of a compressor. Phelan was maneuvering a small spray gun on a pair of signs for a counseling group. He glanced up, smiled in recognition, and gave me a two-minute sign with his free hand. Then I saw the big BRODY'S BOATWORKS sign hanging at the opposite end of the space. I got Brody's attention and pointed to it. A broad smile burst out on his face as he recognized the colors he'd chosen and the gold leaf he'd specified on the silhouette of the old sailboat.

We approached it, careful not to touch any other signs whose surfaces might not be completely dry. Up close, the artisan's genius was on full display. "I hope I can afford for him to make all the indoor signs we'll need," Brody said.

Phelan Hurst shut off the compressor and joined us, pleased to notice our delight in the finished sign. "I hope that's what y'all wanted," he said. "I'd never been asked for those two colors before, but I think it turned out right good."

"Beautiful," was all Brody could say.

"Mr. Hurst," I said, "this is Dylan Brody. He's the man we have to please."

Phelan Hurst stuck out his hand. "Pardon the paint," he said, "but I'm shore happy to meet y'all."

"You've done an outstanding job," I said, as he shook with Dylan.

Hurst began unsnapping the hooks that held the sign aloft. "I've got more of those two colors if you'll be needing any more."

"And more gold leaf?" Dylan asked.

"You betcha. You can't just buy a little of that stuff. You gotta buy an armload." He laughed, went to his desk, and pulled an invoice out from under a bronze boathook he used as a paperweight. "Here you go, sir. Just let me know what ones more you'll be needing, the sizes, and if they need to be double-sided. I'll get them done for you right smart."

Dylan handed Phelan his check, signed with a flourish. "Thank you, sir. I commend you for your beautiful work."

"Now don't you go gettin' my ego up, Mr. Brody. I do

A Sardonic Death

what I do, and I'm happy you're pleased. That's all the thanks I need. Well . . . that and an occasional check."

"We'll be back in touch with you as soon as we figure the other signs we'll need in the store," Dylan promised, with another handshake.

With Hurst's help, we maneuvered the big sign into the back of my van, cushioning it with a pair of movers' blankets.

"You have time to share a drink?" Dylan asked.

"Where'd you have in mind?" I asked.

"You know the Boatyard Bar and Grill? It's a couple of blocks across the bridge in Eastport."

"I jog past it almost every day," I said. "And been looking for an excuse to stop in."

We joined a lively gang of like-minded sailors and survived three rounds before we parted, as *friends*. The elephant that might have been in the room never trumpeted. "Looking forward to seeing your mom again," he said, before a quick cheek kiss.

In my van, headed home, I tried to recall John Greenleaf Whittier's verse that ends, "It *might have been*." But I couldn't.

Chapter 43

With a glass of chardonnay and a couple of pita chips in front of me, I phoned Jason. "If you'll be off duty next Sunday, Mom and I would like you to stop by in the afternoon. It's her annual midsummer bash. Swimming, tennis, and open bar. No sobriety tests."

Jason laughed. "Sounds like fun."

"Has Mom ever asked you to take the Water Celery out of the big pond?"

"Not yet. But I haven't come across any smiling corpses yet either."

"Then just bring your swim gear and your appetite. By the way, has Mom dodged the bullet in the Ferrari shooter investigation?"

"Meant to tell you thanks for the 'Weems' Taylor tip. We searched his house and found the 'borrowed' M-16 that fired the rounds that wrecked Dr. Chen's car and killed Ms. Johnson. We also found Mrs. Taylor and her half-Asian baby. Looks like Weems will get court-martialed out of the reserves in addition to whatever a civilian jury awards him for killing Ms. Johnson."

Tuesday, Tony called me to his office for a surprise—twice over. The first was a bonus check for outstanding work on the BoatWorks account. He handed me an L&G envelope and in Tony's typically droll fashion recommended that I not open it until I was sitting down and recommended that I "try to spend it all in one place." He dismissed my sincere thanks and surprised me a second time with a brief on my next assignment.

A Sardonic Death

For the State Office of Tourism Development, no less. I would be tasked to create a new initiative coordinating all of Maryland's counties' tourism promotion. I was not to mention the project to anyone until the kick-off announcement by the governor in his office the next Monday. "The governor thinks it's time to retire the 'America in Miniature' tag. You'll need to visit tourism offices in every county and probably other states to collect suggestions for the initiative. You'll be reporting directly to the governor. So your first meeting will be at a luncheon with the guv and several of his departmental secretaries right after the announcement ceremony."

"Sounds to me," I said, "like we're in the big leagues now."

"And you're the manager of the winning team. So take the day off and mum's the word."

Who'll be the manager of Summers Breeze Gardens, Grandpa Jack whispered, *while you hob-nob with muckety-mucks?*

"*I'll figure that out later,*" I replied silently.

"Tony," I said, "before I go happily hop-scotching home, Mom and I are hosting a midsummer swim party. Next Sunday afternoon. You and Sandy are cordially invited. You're to only bring your swimsuits and your appetites." I handed him a map to find Ravenscroft.

"You expect me to give up my golf for a swimming party?" Tony was only half-kidding. Golfing with potential clients for his public relations business was how he kept us in customers. Although how he'd picked up the governor as a client I had no idea, even though his office was right across the street from ours. It was probably better that I didn't know. "Now that you've twisted my arm to attend your party, I expect your powers of persuasion to be on display with the governor next week."

With my afternoon free, I called Dr. Chen to invite myself over to deliver the estimates for his new entry garden. Happily, he was at home and would welcome me. On my way to his house, I mused on the fact that the governor's office in the Old State House is, truly, in State Circle, the centerpiece of our city! If the governor ever wanted me to report to him directly, I could knock on his office door five minutes after the call. Or be across from him in his always-reserved front booth at Chick & Ruth's Delly. (Talk about a short commute!)

Dr. Chen offered me a left-handed shake when he answered my knock. "My right arm's still a little sore," he said.

"You can still write checks?"

He smiled. "Absolutely. How much is it this time?"

"Let's sit so I can explain the figures."

On his back deck I opened my portfolio and pulled out the itemized invoice. "Look this over and we can discuss anything that isn't clear." I watched his face as he looked over the estimates. "I hope you realize those figures are estimates and the final costs could be a little less or a little more."

He rose, saying he would brew tea to celebrate. "Give me a few minutes. You know we Chinese cannot rush making tea. None of your American bags." He pronounced it as if he were dropping one into the garbage.

I looked out across his herb garden, but my mind's eye was focused on his new entrance garden. Roy and I, with Jason's help with the bubbling boulder, would soon bring that design to life. It would be as stunning in its own way as Mom's new entry.

Chen returned with a steaming china pot and a pair of cups on a tray. "We will have oolong tea today in celebration of this

A Sardonic Death

auspicious beginning to my new garden. It also assists in maintaining a slender figure." He chuckled. "At least that's what the tea masters promise."

We both sipped the gently-flavored tea.

"I read that our police department has arrested the man who ruined my car and killed my friend."

"So it wasn't my mom as you initially thought," I said.

"Right. And that's a good thing. No one wants to live with the guilt of killing another person."

Grandpa Jack whispered that the conversation had taken a strange turn and suggested that my mentioning Mom might not have been the best idea.

Chen talked about gardening, his herb collection, and how he was happily contemplating his new entry garden.

I, of course, refrained from mentioning that I was the tattletale who tipped the police to "Weems."

At L&G the rest of the week, I researched all I could find about Maryland's tourism industry. Wednesday I visited the Annapolis Visitors Center to interview a sampling of the thousands of visitors to our fair city. I wanted to be able to mention a factoid or two to the governor. On Thursday I visited Fort McHenry for the same reason. And on Friday, to Baltimore's Inner Harbor where I joined a line of tourists to wander through a World War II submarine. I was glad to have served on an aircraft carrier rather than a submarine which probably wouldn't have had much use for a public affairs officer anyway. But my visit served to bolster my appreciation for Aaron's sub service.

Thinking of Aaron left a nostalgic twinge in the pit of my stomach. But then, these days, I had so many irons in the proverbial fire that I had no time for romance. Not with Aaron, nor a charming mega-yacht sailor, nor with anyone.

Chapter 44

Sunday, Mom's midsummer party day, dawned for me when Kalea called. "Aunt Penny, are you awake yet?"

I stifled a yawn. "*Now* I am."

"That's good, 'cause I have a problem. Shy-mom won't come to your mom's swim party. Says she needs to work." The annoyance in her voice was unmistakable. "Something about a case she and Christine are working on. She's prepping her intern to argue the case. Prep her for the bar exam is what she says."

"Will Madison come?"

"Yes, but it's not right for Shy-mom to pay more attention to her intern than to spend time with her own daughter."

"I would agree with you but, really, you know, Cheyenne gets to make her own decisions."

"I was afraid you'd say something like that."

"Don't forget that you'll probably have a chance to talk with Colleen about your prosthetics article. Have you written the opening?"

"Prosthetic limbs have been available to wounded veterans since the Civil War. But the era of 'iron men and wooden legs' is long past. The newest technology for controlling artificial arms, hands, and fingers, and legs and feet is being developed by Prosthetonics International, a small company in Annapolis, Maryland." Kalea had memorized it.

"Nice."

"You really think so?"

"Absolutely. Think of it as your launching pad. After that, you can lead into anything we've learned from Tanya, Colleen,

A Sardonic Death

or Herman. You could tell Colleen the opening this afternoon and let her bring you up to date with their plans to outfit their first amputee. Don't forget your reporter's notebook."

"'Kay. I hope she'll let me interview her again."

"You can make it seem like it's two friends having a chat. One of the friends is a writer and the other is anxious for the story of Prosthetonics to be publicized. Simple as that. You could tell her it was Brendan who suggested it. And don't worry. I'll stay with you when you're with her."

"Aunt Penny, you forget I don't scare easy." I could almost hear her lower jaw jut out.

I told her I'd see her there, then prepped breakfasts for my long-suffering critters. And for my own, I brewed French press coffee and enjoyed a left-over frosted pecan cinnamon roll. While Cookie and I ran down Chesapeake Street, I began to mentally check the party arrangements.

I was reminded of the process a visiting author described to my creative writing class at the Naval Academy. Essentially, the author said, she created a cast of characters with various strengths and weaknesses, aspirations and dreams, faults and foibles, and dropped them into a setting while asking herself "what if" and taking notes on their interactions. Usually, the first "what if" involved introducing an "out of the blue" unexpected event, like tipping over the first domino in a row, and keeping watch as that event affected a second character, then seeing how the others get involved in response. Or, she said, it was like watching expanding rings in a pond after tossing a pebble in. Each of her characters would follow the script ordained by the traits she'd given them. Eventually, she would discover who was in love with whom, who took offense too easily, and if one was found dead (her genre was romantic suspense), determine if the death was "natural" and if not, which characters would become suspects, and, eventually, which of the suspects was guilty. According to the author, there was nothing easier than simply letting her characters act out their parts on the stage she'd created for them and then taking notes as if she had plotted out the story. Occasionally, she admitted, one of her characters might do something uncharacteristic which would be a surprise for her as well as for the other characters. When that happened, she said, she would have a quiet heart-to-heart with her errant character.

That's exactly how I felt about Mom's pool party. The stage was set: the Ravenscroft estate—the house, the pool, the tennis court, the pond, and the pavilion over the pond. Lawns were mowed, flowers deadheaded, and beds mulched. The tennis court was cleaned, rackets and balls readied, and musicians hired. The characters had all been invited and provided with maps to find their way. Pool and patio umbrellas were erected, poolside tables and chairs arranged on the surrounding deck, balls and a volleyball net in the pool, and a couple of poolside chaise lounges were in place.

Pineapple and ham pizzas, Polynesian pork, Hawaiian fried rice and teriyaki chicken skewers had been ordered from Mom's favorite caterer, waiters and waitresses hired, and two Hawaiian-attired bartenders would serve from a poolside bar. Unbreakable margarita pitchers and drinks glasses had been rented, and sufficient spirits of the liquid variety would be delivered this morning.

The Paradise Partners Hawaiian Band with ukuleles and a couple of Hawaiian slide guitars would play all afternoon and evening. Everything was as ready as it could be. I planned to watch, fascinated, as the characters came on stage and interacted. The only part of the day that we had actually *planned* beforehand was the séance. Which I was

A Sardonic Death

beginning to think was a crazy idea.

Before leaving my condo, I explained to Thaïs and Cookie that they were not being abandoned. "Like General MacArthur," I said, "I shall return." Cookie cocked an ear, but whether they understood me or not, I couldn't be sure. Cookie was eyeing the couch.

It was mid-morning when I parked behind Mom's Ferrari on the circle. The new entry garden was blooming, the evergreens healthy, and the fountain trio shot skyward, ready for the photographer I would soon hire to take my portfolio photos. Brendan met me at the door where I suggested we move our wheels beyond the big pond to leave room for party visitors. After he got his rental's key, we drove out of the circle, past the pool and tennis court, past the turn-off for the pavilion and big pond, to the parking pad at the pier where Aidan's diesel yacht, the *Ophelia* was moored.

"Did Aidan know how to drive that thing?" Brendan said.

"Never took me for a spin," I said. "Not even in his canoe."

In the distance, Naval Academy chapel bells began calling the faithful. We started back to the house. A moment later St. Anne's echoed the invitation.

We were almost to the bend in the lane. "D'you think the Goddess will forgive us," I said, "for being hedonistic heathens today?"

"I suspect she'll grant us immunity," Brendan said, "for bringing so much happiness to so many."

I had to laugh. I love sarcasm.

I said I'd asked a psychologist friend to join our séance. "Astrid Bradley teaches at the Naval Academy and has helped me understand Mom's hallucinations. She said she'll try to get here by mid-afternoon."

"Why not ask *her* to hold the séance?"

"*You*, sir, are Aidan's spirit voice," I said. "You all set?"

"Shaking in my boots," he joked. "But a good actor is always on edge before a performance. Without a twinge of stage fright, the performance is never as good as it might be."

"Take your cues from Gina," I said. "She's into weird stuff, as she calls it, and will lasso Colleen when she senses the time is right."

A couple of hours later, gentle Hawaiian luau music wafted over the entire garden. A string of cars and Jason's tequila sunrise Harley were parked along the edge of the long driveway. Laughter and splashes filled the swimming pool. In a corner of the pool deck near the diving board, bartenders mixed summertime drinks, poured wine, and served beer from a keg.

On the tennis court, Dylan Brody and Tony's wife Sandy swung rackets at each other and chased missed balls good-naturedly. On the sideline, Tony and Mom, wearing a bright red orchid from Dylan in her hair, yelled advice and kept score. I'd briefed them all that they weren't to let on that "Mrs. Reid" was my mother.

Madison and Kalea arrived, hoping to find Colleen. Madison, bravely, wore a swim suit that revealed the surgeon's repairs on the leg that had been wounded at the Civil War reenactment in North Carolina. Kalea explained to Mom that her other mom begged to be forgiven for missing the party because she was "up to her neck" in work. The brave kid didn't let on how upset she was about it. When we noticed Colleen's pink El Camino cruising for a parking spot, Kalea and I headed to meet her. Herman jumped from the passenger seat and asked for Mrs. Reid. I pointed him to the tennis court while Kalea explained to Colleen that Brendan suggested she might have time to talk with her about prosthetics.

A Sardonic Death

Colleen smiled evasively. "We'll see," she said and headed for the house with her swimming togs rolled into a bright pink beach towel.

"She's not interested in my article," Kalea pouted.

"Hang in there," I said. She'll have time, I thought, after our séance.

Kalea peeled off a tee-shirt and her gym shorts down to her swim suit and cannonballed cheerfully into the pool.

Gina and Jeff Gratrix, sat side by side on a double chaise longue, sipping margaritas from colorful oversize glasses. In the pool, Brendan and Jason tossed a ball back and forth over Madison's head, who couldn't jump high enough to knock it down. As the morning waned, Jason excused himself to visit the big pond he maintained where Water Celery still flourished among the Arrow Arum and Arrowhead I'd planted last year.

My older friends Stephanie and Lionel had brought Lionel's widowed sister, Zena. The trio sipped peach daiquiris and laughed about *The Full Monty*, which they'd seen the night before at the Annapolis Summer Garden Theater.

I was finishing an exceptionally strong Mai Tai when I realized it was three o'clock and I hadn't seen Colleen since she'd arrived.

Gina and Brendan were relaxing with drinks after a strenuous bout of pool volleyball. "Have you seen Colleen?" I asked.

They looked around and shook their heads.

"The afternoon's going to get away from us if we don't get going," I said to Gina with a wink. "I'll head down to the floral room, unscrew the bulbs, and light the candles."

"Want some help?" Gina asked.

"Sure. Brendan can wait here and start channeling his brother."

"Pretend not to notice my stage fright," Brendan whispered.

"When my friend Astrid shows up, tell her to stay close so Gina can notify you both when the stage is set."

"And how, pray tell, will I recognize Miss Astrid?"

"Short curly black hair, round wire-frame glasses, and she's what you'd call willowy."

To Gina, "I shall await your trumpet."

We gave him meaningful smiles. And headed to the house.

I was thinking aloud, "I wonder where Colleen is."

If she went to the pond, Grandpa Jack whispered, *I hope it wasn't for a Devil's Parsnip.*

I didn't repeat that aloud for Gina's consideration but the possibility, as unlikely as it was, rattled me.

Tony and Mom had traded places with Sandy and Dylan on the court. Mom saw us headed for the house. "Don't snack too much," she called. "The caterers should be here soon."

"Have you all seen Colleen?"

All four shook their heads.

"Mom said Aidan had a shortcut to his canoe," I said.

"We'd better check it out."

Sure enough, Aidan's footpath was behind the garage and compost enclosure along the fence line. I was about to tell Gina what a crazy idea this séance thing probably was, when we saw Colleen headed toward us, picking her way carefully as if she'd had a few drinks, a mischievous smirk on her face.

Chapter 45

W ell, fancy meeting *you* here," I said.

Colleen adjusted her face to a smile. "I could say the same."

"Gina and I were hoping you could join us," I said, as we turned back toward the house.

"What's the occasion?"

"Do we need one?" I said.

Colleen seemed non-plussed.

"As a matter of fact," Gina said, "we *have* an occasion."

Colleen tensed. "What occasion?"

Neither Gina nor I answered, doing our best to appear mysterious.

By the time we'd arrived at the entry circle, Colleen's curiosity spilled over. "So, do I have to bribe you?"

I stepped between the pots of red lilies and opened the door. "Brendan told me that in Ireland he worked as a medium. So, we planned a kind of a séance," I said slowly, "for you to be in touch with Aidan."

"You *what*?"

"You're now the manager of the business."

Gina turned away to find Brendan and Astrid. I motioned with my head for her to bring them to the back door into the kitchen. She gave me a quick wink.

"You and Tanya," I said, "worked closely with Aidan before his death."

Colleen winced at the last word.

"You both admired his management style."

Reluctantly, Colleen nodded and followed me into the house

where I took her to the conservatory. "What are you drinking?"

"Gin and Tonic please."

"Coming up." Mom's conservatory bar, fortunately, was well stocked. I made the G and T a bit on the stiff side. "Make yourself at home," I said. "Just relax. I'll come back for you."

This was too easy.

I went to the kitchen, picked up the candles and incense and headed down to the floral room. I'd worked all this out a couple of days ago so it took me only a few minutes to unscrew the light bulbs and arrange the candles to maximize shadows. I then lit the two fat candles and set them close to the center of the little table where Gina would put the green aventurine. Several smoldering incense cones suffused the room with patchouli as I headed up to get Colleen.

Even in the shadowy dark I noticed her smile as she entered the séance chamber. "This might be fun," she said. "I've never been to a séance."

Gina and Brendan came down quietly and entered the room, Gina tilting her head toward the stairs to confirm that Astrid was seated out of sight.

Brendan fluttered both fat candles as he sat opposite Colleen. Gina and I sat opposite each other between them. In slow motion, Gina placed a green aventurine heart between the two fat candles. "Aventurine helps to balance emotions and reduce toxicity," Gina said. "If you're receptive to its energy, it may help us make contact with Aidan."

"And perhaps Tanya," I said. Colleen's eyes widened a bit but she settled into her chair.

Gina set the mood, leading off with a convincing prayer of summoning and protection that she must have found online.

Then, after a moment of silence, "Aidan, are you with us?"

Brendan, muting his brogue to imitate Aidan's accent, said

A Sardonic Death

in an eloquent tone, "I am here."

Colleen said nothing. I feigned astonishment for effect.

"To make contact, let us touch the heart," Gina said, slowly reaching to put two fingers on the aventurine. Brendan and I did the same. Colleen reached and put a gentle finger on the stone. "Aidan, who would you like to address first?"

"Colleen," Brendan ventured, "our new Prosthetonics manager." Colleen slowly nodded.

"Aidan needs to *hear* you," Gina said quietly.

"Okay," she agreed. "But . . . are you *really* . . ."

"Don't you remember me?" Brendan intoned. "You were one of my best, Colleen. Ambitious, creative, conscientious."

Brilliant, I thought. Appealing to her ego.

"Of course I remember."

"I remember you, too, but I don't know whether you liked me."

"I liked you, Aidan. You were an excellent manager."

"Did you ever *love* anyone, Colleen?"

"Once."

"Colleen, do you love your*self*?"

Angrily, "No!"

"Why is that, Colleen?"

"Because . . ."

"But you *did* love *some*one—"

Slowly, "I *did*."

"Who did you love, Colleen?"

Like she was fearful of saying her name, tantalizingly slowly, "Tanya."

"And did Tanya love someone?"

"I *thought* she loved *me* . . ." Colleen began to pull something from a pocket. "But she loved you, Aidan."

"*Why* did Tanya die?"

"Because she didn't love me enough."

"*How* did she die?"

Colleen lashed out in a scream and moved whatever it was toward her mouth. In an instant, I realized it was one of the Devil's Parsnips and smacked her hand. The "parsnip" flew across the room and landed somewhere in shadow.

"Jesus, Mary, and Joseph!" Brendan boomed. "Do *you* want to die?"

Meekly, "My friends died."

"Talk to me." Brendan was falling out of character, but Colleen, entranced, didn't notice. She picked up the stone heart and passed it back and forth from one hand to the other and back again.

"Colleen?"

"I used to work for a guy . . ." *Our séance was working!*

Brendan waited. "A *guy*?"

Colleen began to sob. "It's complicated."

"You can help me understand."

"My girlfriend . . . partner . . . whatever . . . began having feelings for him."

"Tell me about your partner."

"She died."

"I'm sorry."

Colleen whimpered.

"So both you and Tanya worked for this man?"

"That's what I said," Colleen said, with hostility, not realizing that she *hadn't* said so.

"And did he reciprocate her feelings?"

Colleen moved the green heart back and forth. Tears formed. "I loved Tanya, but if she wanted him I decided she should have him." She paused. "I told you it was complicated."

Brendan said nothing.

A Sardonic Death

Colleen's eyes drifted toward a candle beyond Brendan's shoulder and her face crumpled slowly into a fearsome mask. "There was only one way to deal with it," she shrieked. Her hand slammed the table. "They had to go."

At that, Astrid slipped into the room to stand silently in shadow—her first view of the subject of our chat over pizzas.

"Go where?" Brendan asked gently.

Now in a screeching howl, "*To die!*"

I had *known* she'd done it, but her confession *stunned* me.

Suddenly creepily calm, Colleen went on, "Tanya's dead. I'm going to join her. I'm *not* going to jail." She jumped from her chair and scrambled toward the white root, searching the floor with her hands. Brendan rose and caught her up in a bear hug. "Eating poison won't solve anything, my dear."

"Gina," I whispered, "please get Jason. Gray ponytail. He's a policeman."

A few minutes later, Jason came down the steps with Kalea in tow.

Kalea looked from Colleen, still the captive of burly Brendan, and back to me. With a straight face, she said, "I guess this wouldn't be such a great time for us to talk about prosthetics."

Brendan laughed so hard he nearly lost his hold on Colleen. Gina cackled like a goose galloping the sky to rejoin its formation.

Astrid briefed Jason succinctly on Colleen's breakdown, at which he quickly morphed into his police persona. "Sir," he said to Brendan, "Can you hold her a coupla more minutes till I can get to my bike?"

"Oh aye. We're quite comfortable here." Colleen was no longer struggling, resigned to Brendan's bearhug. His stage presence was impressive.

Chapter 46

Jason returned with a pair of purple plastic handcuffs which he slipped over Colleen's hands and tightened around her wrists. "If you relax, Miss Clemmons, these won't hurt."

Then, "I need to get this woman to a hospital, and I'd rather not attempt it on my Harley. Would one of you be willing to volunteer a vehicle?"

"If you don't mind using a landscaping van," I said, "my old Chevy's available. But, of course, you know I don't speed."

"There's a first time for everything," Kalea whispered.

Colleen's eyes shot jagged daggers at me but she said nothing as Jason ushered her out. She gave Gina a devious smile that I guessed meant she considered the whole concept of energy from a carved green stone to be hogwash, but nevertheless held the shimmering aventurine heart tightly and nodded thanks as Jason shepherded her up the stairs.

"Goodbye, lass," Brendan called after her. Then to us, "I could never have imagined what hearing 'Aidan's' voice would awaken in her."

"You now have another performance for your résumé," I said and left Gina and Kalea to snuff the candles and replace the light bulbs. Gina smiled and, glancing at my labradorite pendant, said, "It's all good."

Jason opened the passenger door of my van and helped Colleen into the seat. He then went to the doors in the back and hopped in, and, using my upside-down wheelbarrow as a seat, snugged it as closely as possible to the front.

"Seat belts," I ordered, latched mine, and turned the ignition.

A Sardonic Death

Jason helped Colleen, who was still manacled, maneuver her belt into its latch.

"No siren and no lights," I said. "Sorry."

"And a driver just sober enough to drive at a civilian speed." He chuckled but I didn't. Mom's remote opened the big gates.

"To where?"

"You know the Gund Memorial Hospital?"

"Sorry."

"It's on Crownsville Road, across from the fairgrounds. Our go-to Emergency Room for this kind of situation."

"I know the place," Colleen said.

"The emergency room?" asked Jason.

Colleen nodded.

Curious Georgette asked, "Were you in an accident?"

"You could say that," she answered. Which set my imagination humming.

Jason found the Gund ER's number on his phone. "Nurse in charge, please." Then: "This is Detective Jason Keller. Inbound with a confessed murderer and suicide risk." He listened and added, "We're not in my unit. A friend's landscaping van." A chuckle. "ETA about fifteen, plus or minus. No siren."

"If you've been here before," Jason said to Colleen, "You know you'll get fine care."

She didn't respond, probably preferring not to recall her previous visit.

Twenty minutes later, Jason directed me to the POLICE ONLY space at the emergency entrance of the Stacey Gund Hospital. He came to Colleen's door, helped her down and steered her, still holding the green heart, to the entrance. Jason suggested I stay in the van since there was no need for my name to be on the inevitable police report. I was grateful, more than ready for this day to be finished.

While he coped with the check-in procedures, I scrolled through my phone messages. It was time for things to get back to normal. I wasn't sure what *normal* would look like, but it definitely wouldn't involve poisonous plants or crazed poisoners. Back at the party over margaritas Jason and I might discuss the bubbling stone fountain he would install in Dr. Chen's entry garden. So when he returned from signing Colleen into the ER, I asked if he'd heard from Roy.

"Don't recall a call from any Roy."

"I guess he'll get in touch when he gets the final plan. I mentioned it to you a couple of weeks ago and you said you'd probably need a diamond drill bit to create a bubbling boulder for Dr. Chen's new entry garden."

"Right. I remember. But he hasn't called yet."

"All in good time."

It felt good to talk about something pleasant and safe. I knew we'd debrief later, but for now, Jason and I were landscape design colleagues on our way back to a party.

Back at Ravenscroft, I found a spot on the entry circle. Even this early in the evening, I could appreciate the magic I'd created with the three colorful gushing fountains.

Distant Hawaiian harmonies drew us down the drive toward the pavilion and the tuneful ambiance of the party's last chapter. Circulating fans near the ceiling kept a gentle breeze for dancers swaying under strings of pineapple-shaped yellow lights. On the periphery, caterers' arrays of food in chafing dishes were adorned with bouquets of orchids and bougainvillea. I could have sworn a Bird of Paradise flower winked at me. It had been a long day.

Jason and I chose Hawaiian ham and pineapple pizza and Teriyaki Chicken Skewers and ready-made margaritas in colorful glasses.

A Sardonic Death

Opposite the musicians, we joined Mom at a table with Uncle Brendan, Dylan Brody, Gina, and Kalea. Brendan and Dylan were sharing a bottle of Jameson's. Mom and Gina sipped Mai Tais, and Kalea nursed a glass of Hawaiian Punch.

"Your party is ending on a high note," I said. "The caterers have outdone themselves. And the music's wonderful."

She didn't respond. Something on her mind. "Gina said there was a fracas in the floral room." She was staring right through me. "That's why you and Jason drove away with Colleen. What was going on, Penny-lope?"

I cringed, fearing Gina might try that pronunciation.

Kalea piped up. "Colleen tried to eat a poison parsnip. Jason said he had to get her to a hospital."

Brendan set down his whiskey to elaborate. "We'd had a chat and she as much as admitted she sent both Aidan and Tanya to the other side."

"She did *what*?"

"I was going to tell you, Mom. Colleen's in serious need of psychotherapy."

"I told you Tanya and Colleen were angels of death."

"I think I know, I said, "why Colleen had the Devil's Parsnip."

"I'd sure like to know," Mom said, "how she got it without anyone seeing her."

"Gina and I found her on Aidan's shortcut to his canoe," I said. "But we didn't know then that she'd yanked out any Water Celery."

"We found that out during the chat," Brendan said.

"Would you like to hear my theory of *why* she had it?" I asked.

Nobody spoke up so, after a sip of my margarita, I decided to tell them anyway. "Okay," I said, "after Tanya died, Colleen

294

and Herman were essentially the owners of Prosthetonics. There was only one bug in their plan to expand the business with the new technology. That bug was *your* percentage of the company's profits, Mom. I doubt if Jeffery would let them reorganize you out of the company. But you were in the way of their complete control. I think Colleen planned to poison you, and she wouldn't have cared if anyone else died too. I had her figured for a sociopath and I think this proved it."

Mom broke into tears.

"I believe Colleen planned to introduce the Water Celery into the vegetable salad. It would have been a danger to anyone who might have eaten it," Gina said.

"Especially to *me*," Mom said, stunned by her close call.

The Mai Tai pitcher on her table was empty.

"Life is short," she said as if she'd just realized it. "It's mirto time." She rose unsteadily and wended her post-party wobbly way to the bar. She returned with two bartenders in tow, one with a tray of liqueur glasses and a second with a bottle of chilled mirto. "They had to make sure I didn't shpill any."

They poured each one full and passed them around. "Pearl la vostry salute," Mom said in her brutally butchered Italian. "If you've been to Italy, you know that means 'To your Health.'"

Under the circumstances, an especially poignant sentiment. We raised our glasses. To the bartenders, Mom added, "Thanks, gennelmen."

I savored my mirto—just as delicious as it was the day I first met Ophelia.

Mom sipped hers, smiled at Dylan then turned to Jason. "You know," she said, "I've changed my mind."

What now? Grandpa Jack whispered.

"When you can make time for it," she said, "I'd like you to dig out all the Water Celery from the pond."

A Sardonic Death

"For heaven's sake," Jason said, "it's about time." He sounded as weary as I felt.

Echoes of July Fourth fireworks boomed and crashed across the night sky all the way from the opposite side of town when the musicians started a slow Hawaiian version of "Goodnight Ladies," the last tune of the evening. I wiped an errant tear as I thought about my self-imposed loneliness since Aaron returned to King's Bay. When the musicians finished the instrumental version and began to sing the last verse a cappella, Kalea snatched my hand and yanked me upright. "I promised Maddy-mom you'd take me home."

With an *À bien tôt* for Dylan, we bid the others goodnight. I held her hand and tucked my other arm around her, dancing her toward the doors as we sang together: Sweet dreams, ladies . . . sweet dreams, ladies, we're going to leave you now.

Echoes of the distant fireworks' final fusillade crashed again and again as we finished the chorus together and headed up the lane to my van.

"That's sad," Kalea said.

My arm was around her shoulder. "What d'you mean?"

"'We're going to leave you now.' That's not sad?"

"I suppose it might be."

"Shy-mom is probably going to leave."

I pulled her closer.

"But," she said, her face a fusion of anguish and trust, "you'll always be my Aunt . . . Penny-lope, *right?*"

I gave her a playful shove and hugged her closer. "Always, Punkin."

Other books by J. Marshall Gordon

Available from Taylor & Seale Publishing, LLC
Amazon, and Kindle

Malice at the Manor

Katelyn's Killer

Made in the USA
Columbia, SC
23 June 2019